THE COMPANY YOU KEEP

A Kendra Clayton Mystery

ANGELA HENRY

Cover Image by © Eka Panova/Shutterstock

Cover Designed by Scarlett Rugers Design
www.scarlettrugers.com

ISBN-13: 978-0692269909

PRAISE FOR THE KENDRA CLAYTON SERIES

The Company You Keep

"A tightly woven mystery..." —Ebony Magazine

"This debut mystery features an exciting new African-American heroine... Highly recommended."
—Library Journal

Tangled Roots

"Smart, witty, and fast-paced, this second Kendra Clayton novel is as likeable as the first."
—CrimeSpree Magazine

"...appealing characters...witty dialogue...an enjoyable read." 4 Stars
—Romantic Times Magazine

Diva's Last Curtain Call

"It's the perfect script for a great summer read." —
Broward Times

"...this series is made of inventive storytelling, crackling wit and that rarity of rarities in American publishing: an authentic, down-to-earth slice of Black life." —Insight New

PROLOGUE

Jordan Wallace parked in front of the brick ranch and turned off the ignition. He checked the visor mirror. With the exception of the slight receding of his hairline, he liked what he saw. "You still got it," he said to his reflection and silently thanked his mama's side of the family for his good looks. He pulled the note out of his shirt pocket and read it again.

"Maybe, my luck is changing," he whispered. He looked at the house and the red car in the driveway. *The bitch had better be home*, he thought and smiled with satisfaction. He knew she'd see it his way. He always got what he wanted—eventually. He also knew what this meeting could mean. If this worked out he, wouldn't have to kiss anybody's ass again—well at least not for a long time. He'd already had to butter Bernie up to let him use her car while his was in the shop. He had to agree he'd come to that damned recognition program that evening. He'd also had to make a promise that at that very moment he was breaking.

He'd have to be extra nice to Bernie that night. Maybe even move out of the guest room back into the master suite. After all, somebody had to pay for his car repairs because he was broke as a joke. He started to get angry all over again when he thought about the way his car had been keyed. He knew who'd done it and would deal with that later.

He got out of the car and looked around a moment before walking up the driveway. He rang the doorbell and waited a few minutes. There was no answer. He felt his anger rising.

"I don't have time for this bullshit!" he hissed after ringing the doorbell a second and third time. He cupped his hands and looked into one of the small windows that ran along both sides of the door. Was that movement he detected? It was so dark inside. Why didn't she have the curtains drawn? Jordan fumbled in his pants pocket for the key to the front door. Bernie would have a fit if she knew he still had his key. But if this meeting went well, he could kiss her, this town—and all the problems he'd had since he got here—good-bye soon. Still, it wouldn't be wise to burn any bridges just yet. He smiled at the thought and let himself into the dark house.

ONE

I, Kendra Clayton, am a very easygoing person. Mellow is my middle name. Actually, Janelle is my middle name. But you get the point. I've never been the type of person to let a whole lot bother me. But even someone as laid back as me has a limit. And after waiting for more than an hour in an empty parking lot in the middle of the night, I'd about reached it. Plus, my feet were killing me, and you know when your feet hurt, everything hurts. I looked over at my friend Bernie and saw that her bottom lip was poked out and her eyes were narrowed in an expression that was a cross between a pout and a scowl. Truth be told, it was not her most flattering look. And if I weren't so annoyed, I'd have told her never to make that face again. I'd finally reached a point where patience and common sense were fighting a hard battle. After telling me she wanted to wait ten more minutes, patience got its ass kicked as I felt the last of mine disappear into the night air.

"This is ridiculous," I sighed in exasperation. "I'm taking you home."

"But," she began before I held up my hand to shush her.

"Not in ten minutes or ten seconds, right now. It's getting late, and I'm tired. So get in the car!" As I've said, rarely am I this annoyed, but tiredness and foolishness, especially hand in hand, had a way of doing a number on my disposition.

"Well, all right then, if you're sure it's not too much out of your way," she said meekly as she opened my car door and got in.

It was out of my way. Bernie lived on the other side of town. But I wasn't about to let her keep waiting in the dark for her boyfriend to pick her up when it was obvious hours ago that the slimeball wasn't coming.

"I really appreciate this, Kendra. I just don't know what could have happened to Jordan tonight. He's got my car. His is in the shop," she added quickly, just in case I thought he had free run of her car, along with her house and her money, which I already knew he had.

"I called him several times, and he's not picking up. I just hope nothing's wrong." She sounded close to tears.

I had a pretty good idea where Jordan was: out

creepin'. But I wasn't about to voice my opinion to Bernie. Bernice Gibson has been a coworker of mine at the Clark Literacy Center for the past three years. I'm an instructor with the General Educational Development program, and Bernie is the center's tutor trainer and coordinator.

Tonight had been the literacy center's annual recognition program honoring all of this year's GED graduates and all the students who had worked so hard throughout the year. The ceremony had gone smoothly. It wasn't until the reception afterward that I noticed that something was bothering Bernie. First of all, she didn't eat, which definitely wasn't like her. Bernie and I have a shared love of food, especially sweets. Most of the time when we get together, it's at Estelle's, my uncle Alex's restaurant, or at one of our homes to try some new recipe.

"That last piece of carrot cake has your name all over it. You better go get it before it's gone," I had told her.

"Oh, I will," she said absently as she looked around the room.

"Who are you looking for?"

"Jordan said he'd come tonight. I thought he'd be here by now."

"I'm sure he wouldn't miss it for the world," I said. But I couldn't quite manage to keep the sarcasm out of my voice because Bernie gave me one of her 'don't start on Jordan' looks and walked away.

Bernie and I get along very well—except when it comes to Jordan. It's not that I'm jealous. It's just that I hate to see a woman as nice as Bernie being taken advantage of by a slicker than slick bastard like Jordan. Jordan Wallace blew into Willow, Ohio, a little more than a year ago. Bernie met him when he started renting the house that she owned and had lived in before she moved in with her sick mother.

Everything about him is a little too extreme for me. He's extremely fine—in a smarmy sort of way—extremely well dressed, extremely charming, and extremely phony. He also doesn't seem to have a job. Bernie says he's self-employed as a business consultant. I'm not buying that mess for a minute. From what I've seen, the only business Jordan seems to be involved in is using his good looks and charm to get what he wants out of women.

Bernie and I drove along in silence. I decided to avoid all mention of Jordan.

"I thought Regina gave a great speech tonight, didn't you?" I asked, trying to make conversation.

"She sure did." Bernie agreed. "I'm so proud of that girl," she said with the first real smile I'd seen all evening.

Regina's a student in the GED program. She could barely read when she first started coming to the literacy center when she was eighteen. Now, two years later, after a lot of hard work and help from Bernie, who's her tutor, she’s at a high school reading level and is about to take her GED exam. The speech she had given at this evening's program had been about how her self-esteem and self-worth had risen along with her reading level. It had been so moving that there was hardly a dry eye in the house.

I started to comment on the wonderful job the caterers had done on the reception, when suddenly a car pulled out from a side street and cut right in front of me, coming within inches of hitting my car. I slammed on my brakes. Bernie and I flew forward in our seats. I instinctively threw my arm across Bernie's chest. I don't know why people do this. It isn't like it would keep anyone from flying through the windshield if the impact were great enough. I looked up in time to see a carful of teenagers, rap music blaring, speed off down the street.

"I swear these damn kids are going to kill someone one day!" My heart was beating so fast I thought it might jump right out of my chest.

I looked over at Bernie. The smile that was just on her face was gone and had been replaced by a very tense look.

"Well, I'm about sick of this shit!" she said suddenly. I was shocked. I rarely heard Bernie curse.

"I know what you mean. These kids drive like damned fools."

"No, I' m not talking about that," she said with a

dismissive wave of her hand. "I'm talking about Jordan."

Now I was really shocked. As bad as Jordan treated Bernie sometimes, I'd never heard her say one negative thing about him.

"You know this isn't the first time he's done this to me, Kendra," she continued angrily.

I knew all too well how many times Jordan had disappointed Bernie and had stood her up. I decided to keep quiet and let her vent.

"And I know where he is too: with that little hussy renting my house!"

So she did know about Jordan and Vanessa Brumfield. I always wondered how she couldn't know when it seemed like everyone in town did. Vanessa Brumfield's a petite brunette who started renting Bernie's house after Jordan—at Bernie's insistence—moved in with her. Bernie's mother had left her the family home and a large sum of money when she died. Bernie never sold her house and used it as a rental property.

I remembered Vanessa from high school. She had been one of those disgustingly peppy chicks who had been involved in everything from drama club to cheerleading. I do remember hearing through the grapevine that Vanessa's father had disowned her when she married a black man. Vanessa is now separated from her husband, which is why she's renting Bernie's house.

"Kendra, will you do me a favor and take me past my old house?" Bernie asked.

I smelled trouble and was not about to get in the middle of it. I got a sudden mental image of two grown women rolling around fighting in the yard while Jordan stood there with that shark's tooth grin of his. It didn't seem normal for anyone to have that many teeth.

"Listen, Bernie, why don't you go home and cool off first before you go confronting anyone? He may not even be there." She looked at me as if I'd lost my mind.

"I'm not going to confront anyone! All I want is my car. She can have Jordan, and *she* can cart his sorry ass around until his car is out of the shop!"

I couldn't help wondering what brought on this sudden change of heart. Had almost flying through the windshield a second ago made her see the light? Somehow I doubted it.

"Where's all this coming from? First you're about to cry because he didn't show up, now you're ready to kick him to the curb, and all in the space of a half hour." I glanced over at Bernie. She was twisting the leather strap of her purse in both hands as if she were trying to wring a good answer to my question out of it.

"I'm just tired of feeling like a fool, that's all. Ever since he moved in, things have been going downhill between us. He borrows money from me left and right, he won't lift a finger to clean up after himself, and he expects me to wait on him hand and foot!"

I was bursting to say "I told you so." But I could see how miserable she was and didn't want to kick her when she was down, so I kept my mouth shut.

"I know how much you hate Jordan, and I didn't feel like hearing 'I told you so', she said as if reading my mind. "I kept hoping things would get better but they haven't. I found out about two weeks ago that he's been messing around with the girl who's been renting my house. I should have known something was up when he started volunteering to go over there and pick up the rent. The first time I asked him to do it he acted all put out and told me he'd only do it once because he wasn't a damned errand boy. After that, he was always over there any time she had any little problem with anything, which was all the time. Now I know what's really been going on!"

"I think it's all for the best, Bernie," I told her. "I'm just surprised you put up with him this long. I'd have sent him packing a long time ago." I wouldn't have gotten involved with him in the first place. But I felt it best to keep that to myself.

Bernie's head whipped around so fast I half expected it to snap right off her neck.

"Well when you get to be my age and you're trying to hold something together because you're tired of being alone, we'll see how much you're willing to put up with!" She glared at me.

Now it was my turn to look at her like she was crazy. It never ceased to amaze me how the fear of loneliness will cause perfectly sane women to put up with situations they'd never tolerate in any other aspect of their lives. Bernie was older than me, and I've always looked up to her as the older, wiser sister I never had. I knew that the death of her mother three years ago and the sudden death of her brother, Ben, last year had devastated her. But I had no idea how vulnerable she'd become.

"Bernie, I'm sorry. I didn't mean to offend you. It's just that I've always thought you deserved better than Jordan," I said, trying to ease the tension that had suddenly developed between us.

"No, I'm the one who's sorry. I shouldn't have bit your head off like that," she said, giving me a smile. I breathed a sigh of relief.

"Just take me over there. I know he's there with her. I have an extra set of keys. I'm just going to get my car and go home. Believe me, this is the last straw, and I have nothing left to say to the man. If he's not there, you can just take me home."

"All right, but only if you're sure you'll be okay."

"I'll be fine."

I made a right turn at the corner and headed toward Archer Street where Bernie used to live. I was relieved not to have to drive all the way to the north side of town and back. I suddenly remembered how tired I was.

Archer Street was a quiet, tree-lined, lower-middle-class neighborhood with a mixture of well-kept one-and two-story homes that were built back in the forties. Bernie's house was a small, brick ranch toward the end of the block.

As we approached the house, I could see Bernie's blue Lexus parked in front. A red Mustang convertible, that I assumed to be Vanessa's, was parked in the driveway. I couldn't see any lights on in front of the house. I figured they must be somewhere in the back, like the bedroom. I pulled up alongside Bernie's car. I could tell that despite what she'd said, Bernie was very upset to find her car here.

"I knew he'd be here," she said in a voice trembling with tears.

"I wonder how long it'll be before he notices the car is gone?" I asked.

"Oh, I'm sure it won't be for a while. I imagine they're very busy at the moment," she said bitterly.

"You should report your car stolen. That would teach him a lesson," I said, half joking, trying to lighten the mood.

"Yes, wouldn't it be something to see his arrogant behind in jail. He's not even worth the effort." She got out of the car, keys in hand. "Thanks, Kendra. I'll call you this weekend, and maybe we can have dinner or something."

"Call me later if you want to talk."

A light rain had started to fall, giving the street a glossy look under the streetlights. As I drove off, I looked in my rearview mirror and saw Bernie standing by her car and staring at the house. "Bernie, just get in the car and go home," I whispered aloud. Maybe it would help her deal with Jordan's betrayal better if she confronted him. All I knew was that I was ready to go home. I was tired and visions of a hot bath and some wine took over my thoughts as I turned the corner.

My mind should have been less on home and more on the road because I had to brake to avoid hitting a kid on a bicycle who came pedaling out of the alley that ran between Archer Street and River Avenue. I caught a glimpse of a black baseball cap and a fluorescent orange rain poncho. I couldn't see his face because he was hunched low over the handlebars of the bike. I watched as the kid shot across the street and back into the alley on the other side. Probably in a hurry to get home where he belonged. Two near misses in one night were more than enough for me. It was time I got home.

I live about five blocks from Archer in a duplex on Dorset. Sometimes it amazes me that I'm still living in this town. When I was growing up, I was so sure that I'd have some exciting life in a major city far away from Willow, population sixty thousand. It doesn't appear to be in the cards. Ten years out of high school and I'm still here. The only time I lived anywhere other than Willow was when I was away at Ohio State getting my degree in English. After graduation, I moved back home with high hopes and started sending out resumes. However, teaching jobs were few and far between. I started working as a hostess at my uncle Alex's restaurant. After many months—too many to mention—I finally landed a position teaching English at one of the local high schools. The job was less than rewarding. I spent more time disciplining smart-assed teenagers who thought they knew everything than I did teaching. After a year, I lost my job due to budget cuts. So, it was back to hostessing, which I actually enjoyed more.

Bernie was a regular at my uncle's restaurant. I always made a point of speaking to her every time she came in. That's how I found out that the literacy center where she worked had an opening for an instructor in its GED program. I got the job and have been there ever since. I've found that dealing with adults is very rewarding. It's nice teaching people who want to learn and who come to class, in most cases, because they want to be there and not because they have to.

That's not to say we don't get our share of special cases. For instance, there was a woman who would only do her work with a Magic Marker because she was convinced that using a pencil would give her lead poisoning, or the man who wrote everything down in secret code so no one could copy off him. My time at the literacy center has been an eye-opening experience.

Regretfully, the job is not full time. I supplement my income by continuing to hostess at my uncle's restaurant.

I pulled in front of the duplex and noticed that Mrs. Carson, the woman I rent from, was sitting on the porch as was her habit every evening. Mrs. Carson is a friend of my grandmother, which has its perks, one of them being a good deal on the rent. Of course, the downside is that my grandmother, thanks to Mrs. Carson, always seems to know my business—whether it be what time I get up in the morning, what came for me in the mail, or who spent the night, which hasn't happened in a very long time. My grandmother usually knows it all and doesn't hesitate to comment. Not that she comes right out and says what she knows. She usually let's it slip during casual conversation. Of course, I could never question her as to how she knows so much about my life. I know it's just her way of watching over me for my parents, who moved to Florida after my father took early retirement from his job two years ago.

I was hoping to get up the steps to my apartment with just a simple hello before Mrs. Carson could stop me and tell me all about her latest set of ailments, imaginary or otherwise.

"Evenin', Kendra."

"Hi, Mrs. Carson. How are you this evening?"

"Oh, I can't complain too much, 'cept my arthritis been actin' up with the rain and all," she said, rubbing her knee. "My blood pressure's up too. You know a stroke's what took my mother years ago. I'll probably go the same way." She was dressed in her usual striped housedress and faded slippers. Her thick gray hair was braided into a crown on top of her head. Even in her seventies, her smooth chocolate skin was unlined.

"I'm sorry to hear that," I said as I eased my way up the steps that led to my part of the house. You'd think I'd learn to stop asking. She's a sweet woman, and sometimes I do sit out on the porch and talk for a while. But not tonight. Between my normal workday, Bernie's melodrama, and the recognition program, I was worn out.

"How was your program?"

"It went just fine." I eased my way up a few more steps.

"Gettin' in kind of late, ain't you? It's almost ten o'clock."

"I gave a friend a ride home." I was resenting the fact that I was explaining myself but could see no polite way around it.

"You young girls need to be careful runnin' these streets at night. All kinds of crazy fools around nowadays."

Running the streets? I was not about to argue with her. I was too tired, and besides, I'd never win. Instead I just smiled and nodded in agreement. "Good night, Mrs. Carson," I called over my shoulder as I climbed the remaining steps to my front door. I heard her mumbling about not being safe in your own home anymore. My phone started ringing as I stood at the door fumbling for my keys. By the time I got through the door, the ringing had stopped. I was relieved because I wasn't in the mood for conversation. I kicked off my pumps and headed straight to the kitchen.

After pouring myself a glass of wine, I sank down onto the couch and propped my feet up on the trunk that served as my coffee table. I looked around my apartment and mentally patted myself on the back for managing to make it look nice with so little money. The Oriental rug that covered the center portion of my living room had been purchased at a tag sale. The worn places on the rug were strategically covered by my cream leather couch, my only extravagance and bought on sale at that. I used a large tan trunk with brass trim that I rescued from the Salvation Army and cleaned up as a coffee table. An overstuffed recliner and a wicker rocking chair, both bought at garage sales, as well as various plants, lamps, and a couple of end tables rounded out my living room furnishings. I liked to think that I have a good eye for a bargain. A lot of people just think I'm cheap.

The phone started ringing again. I reluctantly answered it.

"Well don't sound so excited," said the familiar voice of my best friend, Lynette Martin-Gaines.

"It's hard to feel excited when you're dead tired. But I guess you wouldn't know about that since your butt's still on vacation," I teased.

"I'd hardly call taking care of a houseful of sick people a vacation. Ma, Monty, and India all have colds. Even the dog's looking pitiful. I can't wait to get out of this house tomorrow night. Have you decided what you're going to wear yet?"

"So, when do you have to rejoin the workforce?" I asked, purposefully ignoring her question.

"Don't you dare try and change the subject, Kendra Clayton. You said you'd come, and you're gonna come if I have to drag you by that little bit of hair on your head!"

"Calm down. There's no need for violence." I ran my hand through my short curly hair. "And can you really blame me for being skeptical? The last two blind dates I went on made me want to join a convent."

“Quit exaggerating, Kendra,” said Lynnette with a sigh. I knew she was probably rolling her eyes.

“I’m not! Remember Antonio? The man laughed like an asthmatic donkey and had on so much foundation and eyeliner he looked like raccoon in drag. And then there was Marcus, the personal trainer.”

“And what was wrong with *him*, Miss Picky?”

“He told me the calorie count of everything I had for dinner. The man actually glared at me when I ordered hot fudge cake for dessert, then tried to sign me up for a gym membership. You know I don’t do sweat, Lynette, and I’m not giving up cake for nobody.”

“Is that all?”

“Uh, that was plenty. Plus, he wore his cologne so strong my nose hair ignited!" I didn’t care what she thought. I’d had my fill of craptastic dates and didn’t want to add another one to my already long list.

"Well, I don't know who hooked you up with those two fools," she said, laughing, "but this time will be different. Drew’s cool, Kendra. And if you don't go out with him, I can think of plenty of other women who would gladly snap him up."

Damn! I couldn't see a way out of this.

"Okay, I said I'd come, didn't I? But if this man starts laughing like a donkey, I'm outta there."

"Don't worry. Greg and I will be there. It'll be fun. What else have you got to do?" Leave it to Lynette to point out the inadequacies of my social life as if I weren't already aware of them.

After she gave me a few more details about my much-dreaded upcoming double date, Lynette and I said good night. I felt the relaxing effect of the wine coming over me. That, combined with the soft tap of rain against my window, made me drowsy. *Maybe I'll skip the bath,* I thought as I sank back farther into the cushions of my couch.

I don't know how long I'd been asleep on the couch when the phone rang again. It was long enough for me to be disoriented and unaware of my surroundings for a few seconds before I reached for the phone.

"Hello," I said groggily, not recognizing my own voice.

"Kendra," said a breathless female voice. "Oh, thank God you're there," the woman said, sobbing.

"Who is this?" I asked, struggling to come fully awake.

"He's dead. Oh, God, he's dead!"

I sat bolt upright. I was wide-awake now.

"Who's dead? Who is this?" I asked again. Suddenly I was scared. A cold knot of fear formed in the pit of my stomach. Who's dead? Please God, not Daddy or Alex, I prayed, remembering two years ago when I'd gotten a similar call from my mother when my grandfather died.

"Jordan," said the now-familiar voice of Bernie. "He's dead, Kendra. I don't know what to do!"

"Bernie? Where are you?" Was she serious?

"I'm still at my house on Archer Street. I'm on my cell phone."

"Bernie, calm down and tell me what happened." I heard her heavy breathing begin to slow down a little.

"I wanted to end things with Jordan once and for all," she began, sounding as if she could barely get the words out. "I was going to tell him not to bother coming home and that his things would be in the garage for him to pick up tomorrow. I knocked on the door. I could hear someone moving around inside but no one would answer. That just made me even madder. I could just imagine the two of them in there laughing at me. I used my extra set of keys to let myself into the house. It was dark in there, and I couldn't see a thing. I was fumbling around for the light switch when I heard someone go out the back door. I started walking toward the back when I tripped over something and fell. When I got up and finally got the lights turned on, I saw what I tripped over. It was Jordan!"

"Are you sure he's dead? Did you check his pulse?"

"No! I didn't want to touch him. His... his head was all smashed and bloody! It was horrible, Kendra! I felt like I was going to be sick. I ran out the back door and got on the phone to you!" I could hear the hysteria creeping back into her voice.

"Bernie, listen, I'm on my way. You need to call nine-one-one as soon as we hang up!"

Without thinking, I jumped off the couch, stuffed my feet into an old pair of tennis shoes, and was out the door.

TWO

I drove back to Archer Street. My mind was racing. Could Jordan really be dead? Then it dawned on me: Bernie hadn't said anything about Vanessa. Was she dead as well?

By now the rain had stopped and the streets were enveloped in fog. I turned onto Archer Street. Was the fog heavier on this street than any of the others I'd driven down? Given the circumstances, I was probably just being paranoid. I mentally kicked myself for watching so many scary movies. I made my way slowly down the street. When I came upon Bernie's car, I pulled up alongside and looked in. Bernie was sitting behind the wheel with her head in her hands. Her head jerked up when I honked my horn. I parked in front of her and got out.

"Thank God!" she said as she jumped out of her car

and ran up to me. We both stood staring at the house for what seemed like a long time.

"Did you call nine-one-one?" I asked finally.

"Yes. They should be here any minute now."

"Bernie, did you see Vanessa in the house?"

She looked for a second like she didn't know who I was talking about. Then the realization of what I'd just asked hit her.

"Oh, my God! I forgot all about her! She could be in there too!"

"That is her car in the driveway, isn't it?" I asked, pointing to the red Mustang.

"Yes," she said, looking confused. "That's her car. But I don't know if she's in there, Kendra. I didn't see her!"

"It's okay. Try and relax. I'm going inside to check and see if she's in there."

Bernie's look of horror wasn't lost on me. I wished I felt as confident as I had just sounded about walking into what could quite possibly be a murder scene.

"Vanessa could be in there hurt or unconscious. I have to go check to make sure." I wondered who I was trying harder to convince, Bernie or myself.

"Kendra, this is a job for the police. If she's in there, a few more minutes aren't going to make much difference."

"If she is in there and she's hurt, I'm not going to have it on my conscience if she dies when there was something we could have been doing until help arrived," I said impatiently.

Bernie gave me a look that told me I was on my own and went back to sit in her car. I walked around to the back of the house. I figured the door must still be open. I noticed how neglected the backyard looked. The grass was overgrown. The high wooden fence that surrounded the backyard and separated it from the alley was in need of painting, and the wood was warped in places. I also noticed that the gate that led out to the alley was open. Bernie said she had heard someone going out the door. The alley would be the quickest way to get away from the house.

I stood at the back step and looked at the door. It was slightly ajar, and I could see that the kitchen light was on. Maybe Bernie was right. I certainly wasn't feeling very heroic at the moment. If a crime had been committed, I'm sure the police wouldn't want me traipsing through the house and messing up evidence. On the other hand, if I were Vanessa, I wouldn't want to be alone in the dark with only a dead body to keep me company. My mind was made up. I nudged the door open with my elbow, carefully avoiding touching any part of it. As I stepped inside, I was immediately struck by a foul smell. "Good Lord," I said aloud and put my hand over my nose. I tried hard not to think about the probable source of that odor.

The kitchen looked much the same as the last and

only other time I'd been in the house, which was a few months ago. I'd helped Bernie get the place ready for Vanessa to move in. The walls in the kitchen were painted a bright gaudy yellow. The cabinets were white with the center panel painted in the same yellow. White lace curtains hung in the window over the kitchen sink.

I could see that Vanessa had added her own personal touches to the kitchen. Plants lined the windowsills of the two windows that faced the backyard. The front of the refrigerator was covered in magnets that look like mini pieces of fruit and held a dozen or so snapshots in place. A few of the pictures were of children of various ages. The rest were of Vanessa with different people. In one picture she was with a group of women dressed in hospital scrubs and white uniforms. Vanessa was blowing out the candles on a birthday cake as everyone looked on. It must have been taken at work. Bernie had told me once that Vanessa was a nurse.

I walked through the kitchen to the small dining room and stopped dead in my tracks. Lying halfway between the dining room and the living room was Jordan. He was lying on his stomach facing the wall with one arm flung over his head and the other by his side. Bernie hadn't exaggerated. The back of his head was a mass of blood, bone, hair, and what I assumed to be brain. Dried blood stained the carpet underneath his head, as well as the back of his neck and white shirt.

Thankfully, I couldn't see his face, as it was turned toward the wall, which was also splattered with blood. The smell that had greeted me when I came in was much stronger here. Jordan must have released his bowels at the moment of his death. I swallowed hard to keep from throwing up as I hurried away from the sight in front of me. I backed right into a metal serving cart that was against the wall. The sharp corner of the cart caught me right in the back, sending a jolt of pain through me.

At that moment, all of my Good Samaritan intentions left me. I fled the house. I sank down on the step and breathed in great gulps of fresh air that smelled of rain-soaked dirt and somebody's recently cut grass. Did I really think that I could walk into this house and step over a dead body for any reason? Lord only knew what I would have found if I'd looked through the rest of the house. Who the hell did I think I was, Christy Love, or maybe one of Charlie's Angels? Or more likely a female Barney Fife, only this wasn't funny. Bernie was right. This was a matter for the police.

Almost as if on cue, I heard the sound of approaching sirens. I got up to walk around to the front of the house when I caught a glimpse of something white lying in the grass between the step and the overgrown shrubbery. I stooped to pick it up. It was a soggy wet envelope. Before I could look at it more closely, I heard the sound of voices. Without thinking, I stuffed the envelope in the pocket of my blazer.

The voices were coming from inside the house. Bernie had let the police in the front door. I walked around to see what was going on. I didn't care if I ever saw the inside of that house again.

Bernie and I gave our statements to a rumpled-looking detective named Charles Mercer who looked more like a department store Santa Claus than a police detective. I guessed his large stomach and ruddy complexion must be indications of a fondness for rich foods and alcohol, with an emphasis on the latter. But, despite the lateness of the hour and the fact that he'd been roused from a sound sleep, he was very kind and patient with us. Especially with Bernie who, upon seeing Jordan's body being wheeled out in a body bag and taken away by the coroner's wagon, became hysterical.

As for Vanessa, I needn't have bothered. She wasn't in the house or anywhere to be found for that matter. The police searched the house from top to bottom with no luck. Vanessa had disappeared, leaving an unspoken question on everyone's mind as to her role in all of this. Was she a victim, too, or the killer?

The night air had become very cool, and I pulled my blazer around me. By this time, many of the neighbors had come outside to watch from across the street. I watched them whispering among themselves and shaking their heads in disgust. Some were already turning to return to their houses. No doubt they were horrified that the violence that they saw daily on television and read about in the papers had now come to their neighborhood.

I looked around for Bernie and saw her standing by her car talking to Detective Mercer's partner, Trish Harmon. I could tell from where I was standing that the conversation was not a friendly one. Bernie kept looking from her car to Detective Harmon and back again. If looks could kill, there would have been another homicide on Archer Street. I started to walk over to see what was going on when a hand touched my shoulder. It was Detective Mercer.

"I'm sorry, Miss Clayton, but I'll have to ask that you and Ms. Gibson stick around just a little longer until our forensic tech arrives. You'll both need to be fingerprinted." He noticed my shocked expression and continued before I could raise an objection.

"It's just a routine procedure so we can identify and eliminate any fingerprints we find in the house." I remembered how careful I'd been about not touching anything when I entered the house. But in my haste to get out, who knows what I'd touched. I imagined that Bernie's prints would be all over the place.

"Do you know how much longer it'll be?" I asked. "I'd like to get home, and I know my friend would too. It was horrible for her finding Jordan the way she did." I looked over and saw that Bernie was still talking to

Detective Harmon and was still looking pissed. What were they talking about?

"Miss Clayton, do you know of any reason why Mr. Wallace would have been at this house?"

Why was he asking me? I wondered. Bernie and I had given our statements separately, and I assumed she'd have told him about Jordan and Vanessa.

"I couldn't say, Detective Mercer," I began and hoped I didn't look and sound as untruthful as I was about to be. "I remember Bernie mentioning that Jordan had done some repairs for Mrs. Brumfield, but other than that, I don't know," I said innocently. Technically speaking, he did ask me if I knew of any reason. I gave him a reason, just not the right one.

"Do you know Vanessa Brumfield?" he asked.

"We were in the same graduating class in high school but we weren't friends." That was putting it mildly. Vanessa Cox, as she'd been in high school, and I hadn't exactly hung with the same crowd. She'd been homecoming queen. I'd been in the library club.

"And you dropped Ms. Gibson off here at the house so she could get her car, is that correct?"

"Yes, that's right." I was feeling uneasy. What had Bernie told him?

"Did you think it was strange that Ms. Gibson called you before she called the police?" The thought had crossed my mind, but who's to say what I'd have done in her shoes.

"I guess she just panicked and didn't know what else to do. It's not every day you find a dead body."

He gave me an odd look and started to ask another question when a uniformed officer came over and whispered something in his ear.

"Thanks," he said to the officer and then turned his attention back to me. "Well, Miss Clayton, our forensic tech just arrived. It shouldn't take too long and then you and Ms. Gibson will be free to go home."

"And then what happens?" I asked, knowing that this couldn't be all there was to it.

"I'll need for you and Ms. Gibson to come to the station sometime tomorrow and go over your statements and sign them."

Great! I'm scheduled to work tomorrow morning at the restaurant, and now I'd have to find someone to cover for me for who knew how long.

"Now, if you'll just follow Officer Howard, he'll take you on over." Detective Mercer gave me a curt nod and headed back toward the house.

I followed the stocky blond officer over to the curb where a white van was parked. Inside sat a very angry Bernie, who was having her fingertips cleaned with a cotton ball by a tired-looking bald man with glasses and a wrinkled shirt. Detective Mercer wasn't the only one who'd been dragged out of bed.

"I was told we could go home after this, Bernie."

"I'll have to trouble you for a ride home again. That

detective's little sidekick told me they're impounding my car for evidence! Said she could have a police car run me home. Now that's all I need is for my neighbors to see me brought home in a police car!"

Bernie's mother, Althea Gibson, had been the first black realtor in Willow. When she couldn't get a job with the white-owned real estate companies in town, she'd started her own company, Gibson Realty, and had been very successful. She had also been the first black person to build a house in the affluent, all-white area of Willow known as Pine Knoll. Bernie had never felt completely comfortable living in Pine Knoll and was always worried about what the neighbors thought.

"Of course I'll give you a ride home," I assured her. But my assurance didn't wipe the anger from her face, and I knew from experience that I was about to get another earful.

"It isn't their keeping my car that pisses me off," she started and then glanced at the bald man in front of her, thought better of it, and didn't say any more. Instead she lapsed into a stony silence.

I knew I'd be getting the lowdown in the car on the way home, so I didn't press her for any more details.

Once again I found myself driving Bernie home. It was well after midnight and, except for an occasional person here and there, the streets were deserted. Bernie was rattling on about her encounter with Detective Harmon, which was good because her voice was the only thing keeping me awake.

"I just don't like the way she talked to me," Bernie said again. I didn't miss my cue and dutifully asked what Detective Harmon had said.

"It's not just what she said, it's what she implied. When I asked why they had to keep my car, she acted like I was hiding something. Then she started asking me questions about Jordan's family. When I told her I didn't know anything about them, she acted like she didn't believe me. Said she thought it was strange that we'd been living together for almost a year and I didn't know anything about his family."

I thought it was strange myself but didn't comment. "I thought you said he was from Columbus."

"He is... I mean was," she said sadly as if she had momentarily forgotten Jordan was dead.

The neighborhoods were becoming more expensive and the houses bigger with each passing street. Pine Knoll is located on what used to be—you guessed it—a pine forest. The streets have names like Pine Cone Drive and Pine Forest Lane. Bernie lives on Conifer Circle. In the twenty-odd years since the Gibsons had moved to Pine Knoll, there were only three other black families living there now, one of whom is Bernie's late brother Ben's family who lives three blocks away on Blue Spruce Trail.

"You know she killed him, don't you?" Bernie asked as matter-of-factly as if she'd said, "you know it's raining, don't you?"

"Who, Detective Harmon?"

"No, I mean Vanessa," she said slowly through gritted teeth as if she were speaking to an idiot. "She'd probably just done it when I let myself into the house. She must have panicked and ran out the back door!"

I couldn't help but wonder if Bernie was right. But the timing was wrong. "When was the last time you saw Jordan?"

"Around eight o'clock this morning, why?"

"Because his blood was dried, meaning he had to have been dead a while. He couldn't have been killed right before you walked in."

"Well, then she killed him in the morning and is probably long gone by now!" she said irritably, which told me she didn't like me poking holes in her theory.

"If you feel this way, then why didn't you tell Detective Mercer about what was going on between Jordan and Vanessa? He asked me if I knew why Jordan would have been at the house."

"And what did you say?" she said in a shrill voice that set my teeth on edge. I could hear her panic, and it bothered me a lot.

"Don't worry," I said, glancing over at her. She was so tense she looked like she would shoot right through the roof of my car if anyone said *boo* to her. "I told him I didn't know. I figure it's your place to tell him."

"Like hell it is! If I told him, it would point

everything right back to me. He would automatically think I did it because I was jealous. You can forget it, Kendra. I'm not saying a damn thing!"

"Bernie, it's not like they aren't going to find out." I may as well have been talking to a wall. Bernie had turned away from me and was staring out the window.

I pulled into the circular driveway in front of Bernie's house. The house never ceased to amaze me every time I came here. It's an exact replica of the antebellum home where Bernie's mother's relatives had been slaves down South. I'd heard that Althea Gibson had loved to tell anyone who'd listen how she'd painstakingly traced her family tree. She'd been led all the way back to a plantation in Louisiana where her great-great-great-grandmother had been born and had died a slave. She'd had a smaller replica of the house built when she'd been able to afford it. It had given her great pleasure to be able to say that she was the master of this house.

In the process, many people in the black community resented Althea for building a house in Pine Knoll—or the Knoll, as it's known throughout town. They felt she had made her money off her community and then had taken it to the white side of town. But in true Althea fashion, she had said to hell with her critics and went on about her business. Bernie had told me that no one would ever know how hurt her mother had been when people she'd known for years had stopped speaking to her.

I turned off the ignition and looked over at her. "Are you going to be all right?" She turned toward me, and I could see that she'd been crying.

"Kendra, please stay with me tonight. I don't want to be here alone."

She looked so utterly lost and upset that I couldn't say no. And I really wasn't up for the drive back home. I followed Bernie up the wide front steps and stood there waiting for her to get her keys out. Her fingers shook as she nervously hunted through her big leather purse. "Damn it," she muttered and walked over to one of the wicker chairs on the porch and dumped the contents of her purse out. I heard the jingle of keys and saw the relief on her face as she picked them out of the clutter of gum wrappers, used tissues, and wadded-up paper along with the normal contents of a woman's purse. It's a wonder she could find anything in that mess. When she saw me watching her, she hurriedly stuffed everything back inside and quickly unlocked the door. Once in the house, she promptly reset the security code on the panel of buttons by the door.

"The guest bedroom is at the top of the stairs," Bernie said, gesturing toward the staircase. "You can go on up while I get you something to sleep in."

The inside of the house was very ornate and in sync with the exterior Greek revival architecture with its columns and veranda. The house was decorated in shades of cream and gold. The cream marble on the floor of the large foyer had swirls of gold in it. The railings that ran along either side of the marble staircase were gold and richly ornamented with cherubs and grape leaves entwined between the rails. Although the house was worthy of the cover of any *House Beautiful* magazine, it lacked warmth. It was all that cold marble that was everywhere, and it must have cost a small fortune.

I wearily made my way up the steps and walked straight into the first room at the top. I switched on the lights. The room was a mess. The bed was unmade and clothes were piled high on a chair next to it. A man's robe was lying on the floor, as were a pair of boxer shorts and a bath towel. The room had the musty smell of stale cologne and unwashed clothes.

I turned to leave and almost jumped out of my skin. Bernie was standing behind me holding a nightgown in her hand. Her expression was unreadable.

"Well I guess I can finally clean this room now," she said in a flat voice. She handed me the gown and opened the door to the room across the hall. "Jordan had been sleeping in there for the past couple of weeks. He'd get furious whenever I tried to go in there. Can you believe that, Kendra? He was living in *my* house, not paying a dime, and was telling me I couldn't go in that room. And I put up with it because I was afraid he'd leave me."

I didn't know what to say to her. She shook her head and walked back downstairs to her bedroom suite on the first floor. I went inside the room and shut the door, flipped on the lights, and hurriedly changed into the gown. It fit but was a little too short. I turned off the lights, slid between the cool sheets of the queen-size bed, and lay there looking at the ceiling. I shut my eyes but kept seeing visions of Jordan's smashed and bloodied head. In all the activity of the previous hours, I hadn't stopped to think about one simple question—why?

Who hated Jordan enough to kill him? I'd be the first to admit I disliked the man intensely. I'd even go so far as to guess that I wasn't the only one who felt that way. But murder? What had he done that had made murdering him the only option? Where the hell was Vanessa? If she had killed him, leaving his body in the house and taking off on foot wasn't the smartest thing she could have done. And if she had killed him, why? I thought of Bernie's troubled face as we sat in the car and she begged me to stay with her. It suddenly occurred to me that she was scared to death. I guess in her shoes I'd feel the same way. But surely whoever killed Jordan wouldn't come after Bernie.

THREE

I woke to sunlight peeking through the slats of the window blinds and casting striped shadows across the bed. The events of the previous night came rushing back to me and had the same effect as someone splashing cold water in my face. I sat up and looked at the clock on the nightstand. It was eight fifteen in the morning. I got up and was immediately hit with a throbbing pain in the small of my back. I remembered bumping into the serving cart after seeing Jordan's body. I slowly made my way over to the window and looked out.

To the rest of the world it was a typical Saturday morning, and the people I saw were engaged in typical Saturday-morning activities. There was an elderly couple out for a morning walk. A teenage boy was cutting grass in the yard across the street. A woman was walking her dog—or rather the dog was walking her. I watched her trying without success to slow the dog down as it dragged her up the street.

I went into the bathroom adjoining the bedroom and looked at myself in the mirror. I looked whipped. My face was greasy and my hair was sticking up in curly tufts all over my head. My eyes had that puffy look I always get when I haven't had enough sleep, plus I had sheet wrinkles all over my body. "It's a good thing you don't have a man," I said to my reflection. Mornings are not my thing. Had this been a normal Saturday morning, I'd be rolling out of bed closer to the noon hour, much to the dismay of my grandmother, who thinks it's a sin not to be up at dawn.

I found, to my relief, that the bathroom was stocked with toothpaste, a new toothbrush, soap, fresh towels, and washcloths, all ready and waiting for whatever guest might appear. There was a full-length mirror on the back of the bathroom door. I stood naked with my back to the mirror and turned to see if there was a bruise. Bingo. There it was, a purplish bruise about the size of a half dollar. I also noticed how wide my behind was getting. I'd have to work on that.

I showered, letting the hot water hit my bruise in the hope of relieving the pain, then put my clothes on from the night before. Although I had tried to lay them neatly across a chair, they were wrinkled all the same. I walked out of the room and was met with the aroma of brewing coffee. There was a stairway at the end of the hallway that led down into the kitchen. I followed the smell.

Bernie's kitchen was the only room in the house that I felt comfortable in. The floors and countertops were done in hunter-green ceramic tile. The cabinets were rich dark cherry wood. There was a center island cooktop, and overhead was a rack hung with copper pots. Wicker baskets lined the tops of the cabinets. A brass-and-enamel baker's rack held large glass jars of pasta in different shapes and colors, beans, spices, and Bernie's collection of cookbooks.

There was a woman sitting at the kitchen table.

"Good morning," I said quietly, trying not to startle her.

"Kendra?" She stood and smiled. As usual, Diane Gibson, Bernie's sister-in-law, was dressed to a tee. She was wearing a cream-colored linen skirt, worn tight and short, and a navy silk sleeveless blouse. Her long hair was tied away from her face with a navy-and-cream polka-dot scarf. Her caramel-colored complexion looked as flawless and as radiant as expensive make-up could get it. A pearl necklace and pearl-drop earrings graced her neck and ears. Her shoes were navy Italian woven-leather pumps.

Diane looked every inch the widow of a successful businessman. She'd been married to Bernie's brother Ben for almost twenty years when he died suddenly of a heart attack last year. Even though I knew she was in her forties, Diane didn't look a day over thirty. Needless to say, I always feel like a potato next to Diane, even when I'm not dressed in wrinkled clothes from the night before and old tennis shoes. But I'd be damned if I was going to let her know how I felt. I strutted into the kitchen like I was dressed in a designer gown.

"Bernice said you stayed with her last night," she said coolly, pulling out a chair for me to sit in. "I just made some coffee. Do you want some? You know, I really wish she had called me. She could have stayed with me if she didn't want to be alone. I mean, what is family for?" I opened my mouth to comment when she started talking again.

"I just couldn't believe it when she called this morning and told me what happened. Lord, what is this world coming to?" She leaned forward and stared at me expectantly as if I were about to spout some monumental tidbit of wisdom.

Finally given the chance to speak, all I said was, "Yes, I will have a cup of coffee."

Clearly disappointed, Diane got up and walked to the cabinet and took out an earthenware mug. She was pouring me some coffee when Bernie walked into the kitchen. She was dressed in a blue caftan and was carrying the newspaper. She tossed it on the kitchen table.

"I looked through the entire paper and not one word

about what happened to Jordan!"

"I'm not surprised," I said, picking up the paper. "It was so late by the time the police arrived, the paper had probably already gone to print."

"You should be glad it hasn't hit the paper yet," Diane said, handing Bernie and me steaming mugs of coffee. I proceeded to heap spoonfuls of sugar and creamer into mine. Diane watched me with a mild look of distaste on her face and went on. "Before you know it, everyone and their mama will be over here telling you how sorry they are for your loss and bringing more food than you can eat in a year. Nothing but phonies, the whole bunch of them. They just want to get a look at the inside of your house," she said bitterly.

Bernie and I exchanged glances but said nothing. It was common knowledge that Diane wasn't well loved in Willow. She liked to think that it was because people were jealous of her and of how much she had. In reality it was because she's self-centered, arrogant, and a snob. She had a way of subtly insulting people with a smile on her face, making them think that she couldn't possibly have meant it the way it came out, when of course she had.

Thinking of all this now, I realized I wasn't in the mood for Diane and that I'd better leave before she made one of her smart-ass remarks and I had to slap her. She was already eyeing my clothes with a look of half-concealed amusement.

"Bernie, are you going to be okay?" I asked, getting up from the table. "I need to go home and change before we go to the police station, and I have to make arrangements for someone to cover for me at the restaurant."

"Oh, and how is your uncle's little restaurant doing? I see he's still in business. Good for him. You know, I'm going to have to go in there one day. I'm so used to eating at the country club that I never go anywhere else," Diane said with an innocent smile. I ignored her.

"Thanks for staying with me last night, Kendra," Bernie said quickly when she saw the look on my face. She came over and gave me a big hug. "I'll walk you to your car," she said, putting a hand on my back and gently guiding me out of the room and out of slapping distance of Diane.

"Don't pay her any mind," she said as we walked out of the front door. "I think the only way Diane can feel good about herself is to put other people down, and it's only gotten worse since Ben died."

"Never mind about her," I said. "I'm worried about you. Are you going to be all right? I can always come back and stay with you as long as you need me to."

Bernie gave me a sad smile and hugged me again. "Thanks for offering, but I'll be all right. I lived here by myself after Mother died. I can do it again. Listen, Kendra, I need for you to do me a small favor." Her look of discomfort let me know that this favor might not be so small.

"I was thinking about what you said last night, and you're right. I'm going to tell the police that I suspected that Jordan was involved with Vanessa but..." She looked away from me. I knew there was a catch. "I don't want the police to know that I knew for sure that they were involved and that I've known for two weeks."

"But why?" I asked. A feeling of uneasiness was coming over me.

"Please don't ask me to explain right now. I'll tell you about it, I promise, but not now." Her eyes were pleading with me but I couldn't be sympathetic. She was asking me to withhold evidence and that could land both of us in jail.

"You mean you want me to lie to the police, and you're not gonna tell me why! Bernie, you're putting me in a hell of a spot. What reason did you give for going to the house in the first place?" I demanded.

"I told them that Jordan told me he was going over there sometime yesterday to check on a stopped-up sink, and when he didn't show up at the recognition program, I had you drive me over to see if he was there because he had my car. Please back me up," she pleaded.

Thinking back on what I'd told Detective Mercer, I realized I'd already lied when asked about Jordan's reason for being at the house. But that didn't mean I wanted to dig myself in deeper.

"All right, Bernie," I finally said, hoping like hell that I wasn't going to regret it. "But if you don't tell me the reason for this, and if it's not a good one, I'm going back to Mercer and tell him the truth." I left after making arrangements to meet her at the police station later that morning.

After going home and changing into jeans, a T-shirt, and sandals, I headed over to Estelle's, my uncle's restaurant. Estelle's was named after my grandmother, Estelle Mays, and has been in business for the past five years. I've yet to get up the nerve to ask Alex if he named his restaurant after Mama as a tribute to her or because she cosigned for his business loan. I know for sure that it wasn't because she had taught him how to cook. My grandfather, when he was alive, had been very strict about male and female roles. Men worked and provided for their families and were the heads of the household. Women had babies and stayed home to take care of the house. To him it was that simple. Alex isn't a trained chef, just an extremely good cook who, when asked how he got to be that way, always insists that anybody who can read a cookbook and follow instructions can cook.

Estelle's is located in what used to be known as the business district—a five-block area of downtown that until twelve years ago had been a rundown mess of abandoned buildings. Many of Willow's major companies have long since gone out of business or have relocated. My mother used to tell me stories of how when she was a little girl, downtown Willow had really been something and that no one would be seen in anything but their best clothes if they were going to be downtown for any reason. A concept I can hardly imagine now.

Kingford College, whose campus is right next to the old business district, bought several of the old buildings and renovated them, using some of them as rental properties for faculty and students.

In recent years, downtown Willow has been able to recapture a little bit of its old glory. Estelle's sits right across the street from the old city hall building, which was bought years ago by the college and now houses its admissions, financial aid, and personnel offices.

In its former life, Estelle's had been a dress shop on the first floor and a dance studio on the second. Alex had bought the entire building after he was laid off from his factory job after twenty years. The main part of the restaurant was on the first floor. Alex had a small stage built on the second floor, had kept the mirror-lined walls, put in a bar, and had live music on the weekends.

I glanced through the large picture window in front and saw that Gwen Robins, my uncle's girlfriend of the past eight years, was sweeping the floor in preparation for the restaurant's eleven o'clock opening. When she saw me, she all but knocked over a table in her rush to greet me.

"Is it true what I heard about Bernie Gibson's old man?" she asked breathlessly as she clutched my arm.

"Well hello to you too," I said, pulling my arm out of her grasp. At five-ten and almost two hundred pounds, Gwen can be a little intimidating.

"How did you find out?" I asked, answering her question with a question.

"Come on, Kendra, you've lived in this town long enough to know how news travels, especially bad news. My friend Myra lives on Archer right across the street from Bernie's place. She called me first thing this morning. She saw you there. Is it true that his head was cut off?"

This was yet another aspect of the Willow grapevine. The information was usually ass backwards and upside down when it circulated. I told Gwen what happened, only leaving out minor details such as my pitiful attempt at heroism, my sore back a nagging reminder.

"Damn," she said, shaking her head. "Well, you know what they say, if you play you pay."

"So you think he was killed because of Vanessa Brumfield?"

"I think he was killed because he was a dog, plain and simple," she said.

"Now, I know you don't think Bernie did it?" It's a thought that hadn't crossed my mind until now. In light of Bernie's recent request, I didn't like where my thoughts were taking me.

"I don't put nothin' past nobody anymore, and who said anything about Bernie? What about that white girl? What's her name, Vanessa? He was found in the house where she was staying. My money's on her."

"She could be dead, too, for all we know," I reminded her.

"Myra said that girl's husband has been over there a couple of times and that they were arguing up a storm one night. Myra had to go over there and tell them to knock it off or she was calling the police!"

"When was this?"

"A couple of weeks ago. Why?"

"Just asking," I said. I couldn't help but wonder if Vanessa's husband had known about her and Jordan. Was it possible that he could have found Jordan in the house when he'd gone to see Vanessa and killed him in a jealous rage? But that didn't account for Vanessa's whereabouts. It didn't seem feasible that he would have killed them both and then left only one body in the house. Provided Vanessa was dead, that is. It did ease my mind that there could be other people who wanted Jordan dead besides Bernie. If only she hadn't asked me to go along with that lie.

"Where's Alex?" I asked, pushing the whole mess out of my mind for the time being.

"He's at the market. He should be back any time

now." I watched as Gwen checked her make-up in the chrome napkin holder on one of the nearby tables. She wouldn't be caught dead without her makeup. I doubted even Alex had ever seen her without it.

"Well, what do you think?" she asked, turning to me and shaking her hair. Gwen considered hair to be the ultimate accessory. She owned a closetful of wigs and wore them to suit her mood. Today she was sporting a blue-black chin-length bob. I could always tell when she was in a bad mood because she wore what we at the restaurant secretly refer to as her diva wig, which was an auburn, shoulder-length pageboy.

"Girl, you know you look good, and you know you don't need me to tell you that."

She smiled broadly. Regulars at Estelle's are always teasing Alex and asking him when he's going to marry Gwen. He just laughs and says that there is no way he could afford to keep her in hair and make-up. In actuality, I think that fun-loving Gwen values her freedom too much to marry Alex.

"I need someone to cover for me while I'm at the police station this morning."

"Sorry, honey. I'd cover for you but I got an appointment to get these raggedy nails done. I'm only here until Alex gets back." She looked at the offending nails with a frown.

"Evilene is supposed to come get her check this morning. She's scheduled to work this afternoon.

Maybe you could get her to trade with you. But don't hold your breath."

I knew exactly what she meant. The person in question was Joy Owens, the other hostess besides Gwen and me. Joy is an art student at Kingford College. I'd always heard that artists were temperamental, but Joy takes it to another level. She's moody almost to the point of being psychotic. Gwen swears the girl is possessed. In fact, the only time I've ever known Gwen to wear her diva wig for a week straight was when Joy first started at the restaurant and Gwen had to train her.

Joy's employment has been a major bone of contention between Gwen and Alex. I once asked Alex why he'd hired Joy, and all he would say was, "She's had a hard life. I'm just trying to help her out." He refused to say any more, and I didn't ask again.

I sat at one of the tables and waited for Joy. I watched as Gwen finished sweeping and wrote out the specials of the day on the white easel by the front door. My mouth watered as I read that Cuban black bean was the soup of the day and that a choice of fried catfish or chicken with hush puppies, slaw, and fries was the specialty.

There were few people out on the street that morning. Most of the students at the college left this week to go home for the summer. Summer session didn't start for a few more weeks. Permanent residents of Willow start coming out of the woodwork about this time of the year, because the college kids are gone and they feel as if they have their town back, even if it's only for a brief time. This was always a slow period for the restaurant. Estelle's, with its black-and-white-checked tile floor, jukebox, and exposed brick walls that house artwork by locals and students at Kingford, has become a very popular place.

I supposed that this was how Alex had met Joy. One of her paintings is hanging in the restaurant. As much as I hated to admit it, she's extremely talented. But the theme of her work is very dark and not exactly my cup of tea. My taste in art runs toward more upbeat themes like flowers and landscapes.

Joy's painting is entitled *The Bird of Prey* and depicts a huge black bird against the night sky with its head thrown back to reveal the blood red inside of its mouth. The wingspan takes up the entire picture from one end to the other, and clutched in its sharp talons, dangling limply, is a dead dove. It's not exactly a painting that would stimulate the appetite of the diners, which is why it hangs at the top of the stairway that leads up to the bar.

I wondered what sob story Joy had fed on Alex to get him to hire her. It must have been a doozy if he is still willing to keep her on when she is barely civil to the customers and can't get along with any of the other employees.

The bell above the door tinkled, bringing me out of

my thoughts and announcing the arrival of Evilene herself. Barely five feet tall, Joy was dressed in denim overalls, a blue-and-red striped T-shirt, and high-top tennis shoes. Burgundy-tinted bangs peeked out from beneath the brim of her baseball cap. She looked more like an escapee from a *Little Rascals* movie than a twenty-one year-old art student. I half expected a white dog with a black eye to come trotting in behind her. She was also wearing something I'd rarely seen on her, a smile. I noticed for the first time how pretty she was. The smile softened the lines that had already etched themselves into the smooth brown skin around her mouth and gave it a hard look.

"Well, well, well, it must be a man!" boomed Gwen in her loud voice, having also witnessed the minor miracle.

"What are you talking about?" Joy asked warily. Her eyes darted back and forth between us as her smile slipped a notch.

"I mean a man, honey. You do know what one is, don't you? That big smile must mean that either a good one has just come into your life or a bad one has just left. Or maybe you just got lucky last night. Now which is it?" Gwen asked teasingly.

Joy, the smile now completely gone from her face, gave Gwen and me a look of pure hatred. "If either of you had any business of your own to worry about, maybe you wouldn't have to wonder about mine!"

Having said that, she stalked back to the locker room.

"I don't know what the hell her mama was thinking when she named that child Joy," Gwen said solemnly. We both looked at each other and burst out laughing.

"I hope you know you probably just teased her out of doing me a big favor," I said, wiping tears of laughter out of my eyes.

I walked back to the locker room and decided to take my chances anyway. The locker room was nothing more than the old changing room left over from the days when the restaurant was a dress shop. Joy was standing by her locker looking at her paycheck, her usual frown back on her face. When she saw me, her lips curved into a sly smile.

"I heard your girl Bernie killed her man."

I was thrown for a minute but hoped I didn't let it show. The grapevine was working overtime on this one.

"Well you heard wrong. Bernie didn't kill anyone."

"That's not what I heard," she said in an almost singsong little girl's voice.

"All right Joy, just what did you hear?" I was getting annoyed and didn't care if it showed.

"I heard she caught him with another woman and smoked both their asses." Her hands were on her hips as if she was daring me to tell her anything different. I was tired of the whole thing, and it was getting late. Joy would just have to wait until she read tomorrow's paper to get her facts straight.

"Look, I don't have time to get into this with you. I need you to cover my shift while I go take care of some important business, and I'll work for you this afternoon." I hoped the direct approach would be better than trying to be nice to the little troll.

The direct approach worked a little too well, I thought later that evening as I sat in the Red Dragon Chinese restaurant with Lynette, her fiancé Greg Hull, and my blind date Drew Carver. Joy had happily agreed to work for me from eleven to four, and I got stuck working her four-to-eight shift, which barely left me any time to get ready for my date. As a result, I ended up wearing a dress that had fit just fine two months ago when I last wore it. But now I felt like a five-pound sausage in a two-pound casing.

I didn't have the time to iron anything else to wear and was wearing a girdle underneath my control-top pantyhose. I didn't have to worry about eating too much and looking like a pig because I could barely breathe. On top of that, I had a splitting headache, courtesy of Mr. Drew Carver.

I'll be the first to admit that when I laid eyes on the man, I was more than a little excited. One glimpse of that smooth ebony skin; that tall, muscular body; and that killer smile and I was halfway to being in love. Then the man opened his mouth and it was all over. His good looks were swiftly eclipsed by his negative attitude. At first he started out doing a simple soft-shoe routine on my nerves, but that soon gave way to a full-scale chorus line complete with encores.

He complained about the prices being too high, the time it took to get our meals, the portion sizes. The only time he wasn't being critical was when he talked about himself and his career. He was a bank manager and took it and himself very seriously.

"So, Kendra, Lynette tells me you're a teacher. What subject do you teach?" asked Drew after he spent five minutes picking imaginary lint from his shirt. It was the first time he'd asked me anything about myself. Up until now, he had shown less interest in me than he had in his food, which he'd already declared was inedible.

"I teach English in an adult literacy program," I said a little defensively, bracing myself for a put-down.

"How commendable," he said like I was a two-year-old who just peed in the potty. "We need more black teachers. I almost went into teaching myself, but I find banking much more rewarding." And with that I was dismissed as he returned his attention to Greg, who he'd spent most of his time talking to all evening. I was very tempted to strip off my girdle and give it to him to contain his swelled head. I turned and glared at Lynette who at least had the decency to look embarrassed as she mouthed a silent "I'm sorry."

My discomfort and overall disgust over the waste of

a perfectly good evening was almost enough to make me forget my visit to the police station earlier in the day. I spent almost two hours with Detectives Harmon and Mercer. They kept stressing details and how important it was that they know everything that I could remember about last night.

I couldn't help but wonder if they knew that I was lying about why Jordan was *really* at Vanessa's and that Bernie was aware of the real reason as well. I couldn't figure out why Bernie didn't want to tell the police the truth about Vanessa and Jordan. What possible difference could it make whether Bernie knew for sure or not? And just how did she find out? Somehow she'd never gotten around to telling me that.

I did find out that Jordan had been killed somewhere between nine and eleven yesterday morning. The cause of death was repeated blows to the head with a blunt object. The murder weapon hadn't been found. I also found out that Vanessa had taken two days off from work Thursday and Friday. But she was still missing. Bernie was still giving her statement when I left to go back to the restaurant. She owed me an explanation, and I intended to get it as soon as possible.

I looked around the restaurant at the other diners laughing and having a good time. Smiling couples leaned close to each other with their faces illuminated in the soft glow of the lanterns that lit each table. I wished I was someplace else, anyplace but where I was.

I always loved coming to the Red Dragon under normal circumstances; besides Estelle's, it's the only other decent restaurant in town that isn't a franchise.

My eyes continued to wander around the dimly lit room until they came to rest on a man sitting alone at the bar. His back was to me but I could see his reflection in the mirror behind the bar. He looked to be in his early thirties. He was dressed in gray dress pants and a white dress shirt. His burgundy tie was loosened. He was brown skinned, average looking, not hard on the eyes but not exactly fine either. I couldn't help but notice his mouth. His lips were full and sensual, and he wore a neatly trimmed mustache. I watched him take a sip of his beer and wondered what that mouth would feel like all over my body. He looked up and our eyes met in the mirror. I quickly looked away, embarrassed, as if he could read my mind.

Lynette slid close to me in our booth and hissed in my ear, "That's the last person in the world you need to be making goo-goo eyes at."

"Who is that?" I whispered, glancing over at Greg and Drew who were still deep in conversation. Lynette looked at me and rolled her eyes.

"Carl Brumfield. You know, Vanessa Brumfield's soon-to-be ex-husband or widower as the case may be."

I knew that Vanessa had married a black man, but I'd never met or seen him before now.

"How do you know him?" I was suddenly very

curious about the owner of that mouth.

"He has an account at the bank. I've talked to him a couple of times when he's come in. Seems nice; never has much to say or maybe he's just not into sisters," Lynette said, shrugging.

Lynette's a personal banker at Willow Federal Bank, which is how she met Drew Carver, who is one of the bank's branch managers. Lynette also met her fiancé Greg working at the bank. Greg's an accountant and a much better match for Lynette than her first husband, Lamont Gaines. Her marriage to Lamont brought a temporary halt to our friendship ten years ago.

The summer after we graduated from high school, Lynette had run off and married Lamont, who was a year older than we were and in the air force, stationed in Texas. She told her mother she was spending the night with me. Everyone thought I was in on the plot. Her mother even stopped speaking to me for a while. I was as surprised as everyone else when I found out that Lynette had forfeited a full academic scholarship to Kingford College to run off and become Mrs. Lamont Gaines. It took a long time to straighten out the mess Lynette had left behind.

The marriage, as predicted, was a disaster. It didn't take long for Lamont to realize that he hadn't finished sowing his oats, and he didn't let a little thing like marriage keep him from doing so. Five years later,

Lynette moved back home with four-year-old Lamont Jr. and one-year-old India and filed for divorce.

I was out of college by then and was home looking for a job. During her marriage, Lynette had written to me a couple of times asking me to try and understand and forgive her for using me the way she had. I never responded. I can be pretty hard-hearted when I want to be. It wasn't until we ran into each other at a garage sale after her divorce that I decided enough was enough, and we renewed our friendship. It was like we were never apart.

I looked over at Carl Brumfield, who was ordering another beer, and wondered how he was handling the possibility of his ex being either a murder victim or a suspect. I remembered Gwen telling me that he had been arguing loudly with Vanessa. What had it been about? Was it the same old arguments that people getting a divorce went through? Who was going to get what and who was to blame? I couldn't imagine ugly words coming out of a mouth like that. *But,* I thought wryly, looking over at Drew, *looks can be very deceiving.* I'd been wrong about men too many times to mention. Did he know about Vanessa and Jordan, and if he did, did he care?

The evening came mercifully to an end. Drew at least had the good manners to walk me to my car. Once at my car, he started fumbling in his pants pocket. Surely his arrogant ass wasn't about to give me his phone number. Instead, he handed me his business card.

"Kendra, if you ever have any banking needs, such as a car loan perhaps," he said, looking at my little blue Nova with amusement, "please don't hesitate to call me. Willow Federal Bank is firmly committed to helping the black community with all its banking needs. We even offer special financing," he said, briefly looking me up and down.

I stared at him in amazement and then started laughing.

"Don't worry, Drew," I said, leaning against the hood of my car.

"If I ever need help from a self-absorbed, uptight, arrogant ass such as yourself, you'll be the first person I call."

He gave me a dirty look, mumbled something under his breath that rhymed with witch, and walked quickly across the parking lot to his silver Miata.

As I was sitting in my car in the parking lot, using Drew's business card to pick cashew chicken out of my teeth, I decided that it had been far too long since I had a good beer. I'd certainly earned it after the day I'd had. If I just happened to strike up a conversation with Carl Brumfield, then so be it. What harm would it do? I didn't stop to think about it.

I pretended to search for my car keys in my purse as Lynette, Greg, and Drew drove off in their separate cars. I made a mental note to call Lynette and cuss her out the next day.

I went back into the restaurant and sat as comfortably on a bar stool as my tight dress would allow. I ordered a beer and looked around slowly, not wanting to appear too obvious. Carl Brumfield was sitting a couple of stools away and didn't give any indication that he was noticing much of anything or anybody.

"Hey, baby," said a reedy-sounding voice on the other side of me.

I turned and saw an elderly man who looked to be in his seventies. He was dressed in a green-and-black plaid suit with a polyester shirt opened just enough to reveal grizzled gray chest hair. The hair on his head—what was left of it—was slicked back with sickeningly sweet-smelling hair pomade that was clashing furiously with what smelled like Old Spice. He was grinning at me with large white teeth that looked too big for his mouth and couldn't be anything but dentures. Strangely enough he looked very familiar.

"Can I buy you a drink?" he asked, gesturing toward the highball glass in his hand.

Oh, Lord, help me. I just got rid of one fool, now here was another one trying to hit on me. "No, thank you," I said and turned away, hoping he'd get the hint, which, of course, he didn't.

"Aw, come on now, just one drink. I don't bite."

I sure the hell hoped not because I wouldn't have

stood a chance against those teeth. I turned and looked at him again and then realized who he was. I smiled wickedly. He looked as if he couldn't believe his luck and grinned harder.

"My name's Bert," he said and extended a hand that shook slightly.

I ignored his hand and turned completely around on my bar stool, which wasn't easy.

"Don't I know you?" I asked with exaggerated interest. This was going to be too much fun.

He squinted at me in the dim lighting for a few seconds, trying to place me. "No, honey, I don't think so. 'Cause I would sure remember a fox like you."

He obviously had no idea that his vocabulary was as outdated as his clothing. I went in for the kill.

"Sure you do. Don't you go to the Saint Luke's Baptist Church?"

He sputtered on his drink, which he'd been greedily gulping as he stared at my cleavage.

"You remember me, don't you, Mr. Ivory? I'm Kendra Clayton, Estelle Mays's granddaughter. Doesn't your wife play bridge with my grandmother?"

I thought the man would swallow his dentures. His mouth started moving almost a full minute before any words came out.

"Er... ah... yeah, I remember you now. You're Estelle's granddaughter, that's right," he said as he moved off his bar stool and started slowly backing away.

"It's been nice seeing you, sir. I'll tell my grandmother you said hello," I said brightly.

"Yeah, you do that," he said as he beat a hasty retreat. I couldn't wait to tell my grandmother that bossy Donna Ivory's husband—dressed like Huggy Bear no less—had tried to hit on me in the bar of the Red Dragon. I hoped she'd get a kick out of it and not be too mad at me for not calling or coming by for the past few days. Maybe I'd make one of my rare appearances at St. Luke's tomorrow and surprise her. I'd stopped being a regular churchgoer years ago and only went occasionally to please my grandmother.

I heard a deep-throated chuckle to my left and turned around. Carl Brumfield was looking my way and laughing. His eyes were crinkled and his full lips were curved into a smile, revealing perfect straight white teeth. His face was transformed from ordinary to extremely attractive. His laugh was infectious, and I joined in even though I didn't know what we were laughing about. He got up off his bar stool and came over to me.

"Sorry," he said, sitting down next to me, "I couldn't help but overhear. That old guy is probably pissing in his pants right now. Although," he said, looking at me appreciatively, "I can't blame him for trying."

So much for him not being into sisters. I took a sip of my beer and caught a glimpse of his left hand. No wedding ring. He was going through a divorce, though technically he was still married.

"What did you do, ditch your blind date?" he asked casually.

"Was it that obvious?" I was inwardly pleased that he'd been checking me out too.

"Oh yeah. Quite obvious." I watched as he absentmindedly traced the rim of his glass with a finger.

"And how did you get to be such an expert on blind dates?"

"Well, when you're the younger brother to two older sisters, you can't help but get fixed up on a lot of blind dates. Everyone seems to think they know what you need better than you do."

"Ain't that the truth?" How in the world could Lynette have thought I'd hit it off with Drew Carver?

"Of course, sometimes when you think you've gotten what you need, life has a way of showing you that you haven't got a damn thing." He said it with such bitterness that I set my glass down and looked at him. Was he talking about his divorce or Vanessa's disappearance?

"Ouch, where did that come from?"

"Sorry, don't pay me any attention," he said, smiling again. "I was just thinking out loud. My name's Carl Brumfield." He extended his hand.

"Kendra Clayton." I shook his hand; it was cool and dry.

"So, Kendra, do you live here in town or did you just come here to meet your hot date?" he asked with just enough sarcasm to let me know he was joking.

"As a matter of fact, I do live here in town. I teach English at Clark Literacy Center. How about you?"

"I'm from Columbus. I recently moved back. But I graduated from Kingford College, and I lived here for about three years after law school while I was married." He said the last part with a hint of a frown.

"So you're divorced then?" I asked, playing dumb and feeling a little guilty for pretending I knew nothing about the man.

"Not quite." He looked into his glass of beer. "We're supposed to go for our final hearing on Monday. But something's come up."

He could say that again.

"A change of heart maybe?" I asked and then realized by the look he gave me that maybe I'd overstepped my bounds.

"No," he said quickly, looking away. "It's nothing like that."

"It must be a very painful process to go through. At least that's what I hear."

"It's hard when you realize no matter what you do or how bad you want something to work that it's over. A divorce is the one thing we've agreed on in a long time. It's all right though. We've actually become friends." His body was slumped in defeat.

Good friends who were seen "arguing up a storm" as Gwen had put it. They had been so loud that the police were almost called. Maybe his idea of friendship and mine were different. Was Carl Brumfield so anxious to be rid of Vanessa that he had killed her? Maybe Jordan walked in and tried to come to her aid and was bashed in the head for his trouble. It suddenly dawned on me that this man might not be very understanding if he knew I was playing games. Maybe it was time I got my nosy butt home where it belonged. But nosiness to me was like smoking is to smokers; it was a hard habit to break. And they don't have a patch for nosiness.

"So it's nothing serious then?"

"God, I hope not. I don't know why I'm so worried though. Nessa, my ex, always seems to land on her feet. Yeah, she always comes out of every situation smelling like a rose. And always gets exactly what she wants," he said with a sad little laugh.

"Is that why you're in town tonight, because of your wife?" I was getting bold now, but he didn't seem to mind my questions.

"Yeah, but it was a waste of time. There's nothing I can do. I haven't seen or spoken to her in more than a week. Why don't we change the subject?" he said, suddenly perking up. "Can I buy you another drink?"

"No, thanks. It's time I got home. It's been a long night." I eased my way down off the barstool.

"Well, it's been a pleasure talking to you, Kendra. Maybe I'll see you here again sometime."

"Maybe," I said with a big smile. As I walked away, I could feel his eyes on me and added an extra sway to my hips. I knew I needed to quit but figured what the hell. He was the most interesting man I'd met in a long time and that wasn't saying much, considering my earlier date. It would be just my luck if he was mixed up in this crazy mess.

He was a hard man to read. One minute he seemed sad over his impending divorce and the next minute relieved by it. And I didn't quite buy that "we're still friends" stuff. It seemed like he was trying to convince himself that there was still a relationship there. I didn't quite know what to think of Carl Brumfield other than the fact that he had a killer smile that could easily melt my panties. And I couldn't help but feel a little sorry for him. Whatever had gone wrong in his marriage to Vanessa, he seemed genuinely disappointed. I just hoped my sympathy wasn't misplaced.

I arrived home around midnight. As I walked up the steps to my apartment, I saw two yellow eyes glowing in the darkness. Perched on my top step was Mahalia, Mrs. Carson's Siamese cat.

"Shoo," I hissed in a loud whisper. I was still mad at the damn cat for almost killing me the week before. I had been in a hurry to get to work one morning and had tripped over Mahalia as she lay stretched out on the step, sending me almost headlong down the steep stairway. I'd been able to save myself by clutching the wooden railing as I fell against it. I got a handful of splinters and torn pantyhose in the process.

Mahalia gave me a disdainful look, stretched, and then made her way slowly down the steps. I wish I had a rock to speed up her departure.

My apartment looked like a disaster area. Clothes, shoes, and underwear were flung all over the place from my frenzied preparation for the date from hell. As tired as I was, I couldn't go to sleep with the place a mess.

I bent over to pick up the clothing and pain flared up in my back. I went to the bathroom to get some aspirin. It was in just as bad a shape as the rest of the apartment. The skirt and blazer that I'd worn the night before were lying on the floor. As I picked them up, I heard the crunch of paper. I looked in the pocket of my blazer and found a folded white envelope. It took me a few seconds to realize that this was the wet envelope that I'd found the night before by the back door of the house on Archer.

It had completely dried. There was nothing written anywhere on the outside of the envelope. I opened it. Inside was a single sheet of white paper. Typed in uppercase letters and punctuated by an exclamation point was a single word typed in the middle of the page: *murderer!*

FOUR

"You say you found this by the back door between the step and the shrubbery?" asked Detective Trish Harmon, who was eying the envelope in question. It was now enclosed in a plastic bag.

I was sitting on my couch Sunday morning wondering what I'd done wrong in a previous life that I was having to be questioned again for the third time in three days. I had called the police first thing the next morning about the note. Not that I'd gotten any sleep after reading what I had found. Between the note and my back pain, any plans that I had had for a good night's sleep were shot to hell. It was as if the anger that had punctuated that single word had come off the page and permeated the air in my apartment.

I had tried to call Bernie after I called the police. If she was home she wasn't answering her phone. I left a message on her machine to call me as soon as possible. I wasn't surprised that I hadn't gotten a hold of her. The story about Jordan's murder, complete with a picture of Jordan cheesing for all he was worth, was splashed across the front page of the Sunday paper. After reading my name in the article, in which I was described as a witness at the scene of the crime, I quickly took my own phone off the hook.

"May I ask why you took the envelope and why you took so long to bring it to our attention, Miss Clayton?" asked Detective Harmon before I could answer her first question.

"It was in the pocket of the blazer I wore Friday night. I stuck it in my pocket and in the excitement forgot about it. I found it again last night and read it. Look, I told you all this on the phone before you came over. I called you first thing this morning, and I don't appreciate being made to feel guilty."

"It was not my intention to make you feel guilty unless, of course, you have something to feel guilty about."

She was sitting on the edge of my recliner leaning forward as if the act of sitting back in the chair would detract from the efficient image she was trying to convey. Her clothes were as drab and lifeless as they'd been on the other two occasions I'd spoken to her. Today she was wearing a gunmetal gray suit, the skirt of which was pleated and fell almost to her ankles, giving me a glimpse of flesh-colored pantyhose and black flats. Her brown hair was cut mannishly short and was streaked with gray. Her sharp-featured face was devoid of any make-up, making her as pale as death. Her expression was one of practiced neutrality, which made me wonder if she ever had an unguarded moment. I was surprised to notice for the first time that she was wearing a plain white-gold wedding band. I had a hard time imagining this woman as anyone's blushing bride.

"If I had anything to be guilty about, I sure as hell wouldn't have called you." My face flushed with anger.

"Let me assure you that removing evidence from a murder scene is a criminal offense. Are you sure you don't have anything else to tell me? Because I'm trying to figure out why I shouldn't arrest you right now."

I could think of a few things I'd love to tell her, starting with the run in her hose. But I decided now wouldn't be the best time.

"How many times do I have to say this? I didn't intentionally take the envelope. It just happened. What reason could I possibly have?"

"Time will tell, Miss Clayton. Time will tell." She finally sat back in the chair and gave me a hard intense look. She was trying to make me squirm. She was about to succeed before I decided I had a question of my own.

"Do you think that the murderer could have left that note?" I asked in an attempt to deflect her away from me.

"I'd be willing to guess, going by where you found it, that it wasn't left in that spot intentionally. It's possible that it could have been dropped there by accident. It's also possible that it has no connection to the murder. We don't know how long the note lay there before you spotted it."

"Now, let me get this straight. A man is murdered and a note with the word *murderer* is found outside of the house where the murder was committed and you think there's no connection?" Could I be hearing this right?

"All I'm saying is that it's possible. I'll take this to the station and have our lab take a look at it. Hopefully they'll be able to give us some more information."

"Has there been any news about Vanessa Brumfield?"

“Actually, we've spoken to a woman who was out walking her dog on Archer Street early Thursday morning and claims to have seen Vanessa Brumfield being picked up at her house. This person also said she was sure Mrs. Brumfield had what looked like an overnight bag with her. That combined with the fact that she took two days off from work would indicate that she might be out of town. We've left instructions with her family and her place of employment for her to contact us as soon as possible."

"So you don't think she's involved in any way?"

"We're looking at all possibilities at this time, Miss

Clayton," she said, rising from the recliner.

"Will you let me know what you find out about the note?"

"Oh, I will definitely be getting back to you about this mysterious note," she said, heading for the door.

"Can I ask you a question?" I asked suddenly as a thought came to me. She paused, indicating that she was waiting.

"How did Vanessa's family react to all of this? I've heard that she wasn't on speaking terms with her father on account of her marriage."

"They were very concerned, of course. They gave no indication that there was any estrangement. Her father was especially concerned."

That was strange. I'd heard that her father had put her out of the house when he found out she was involved with a black man and hadn't had anything to do with her since.

I headed over to my grandmother's house around noon. The sun was shining and the temperature, having moved back and forth between very warm and jacket weather for the past few weeks, had finally settled on a nice seventy-five degrees.

I thought about calling first and then decided against it. I knew she was probably mad at me, and trying to talk to her on the phone when she's mad is an experience I don't like to endure. It usually consists of me rambling about nothing in particular while the heat of her angry silence on the other end singes my eardrum.

Mama still lives in the house on Orchard Lane that she and my grandfather shared for almost the entire fifty years of their marriage. It's a two-story brick house with a wraparound porch. I turned into the steep gravel drive that wound up to the house and came to a stop in front of the detached garage. There had been talk of Mama selling the house and moving into an apartment after my grandfather died but that never came to pass.

I walked around to the backyard where I figured she'd be working in her vegetable garden. It hardly seemed like the same place where I'd spent so much of my childhood. When I was a child, there had been a big cherry tree in the back of the yard along the fence. I had spent countless hours under that tree every summer with my nose in a book, or playing freeze tag and hide-and-go-seek with my sister and the neighborhood kids.

The backyard was empty. I walked up on the porch and knocked on the back door before walking in. Mama was standing with her back to me at the counter by the sink. The kitchen was newer than the rest of the house with gleaming white countertops, oak cabinets, and blue and white tiles on the floor. Mama had made the blue curtains that hung in the windows. She kept all of the appliances shining so brightly that anyone walking into the kitchen on a sunny day when the curtains were open was in danger of being blinded. She decorated the kitchen herself, and it was her pride and joy. There was food cooking on the stove and the smell was making me swoon. The aroma of collard greens and frying chicken was filling the air. I'd yet to eat.

"Hi, Mama."

"Oh, it's you," she said, turning toward me. I could see that she was mixing something in a ceramic bowl. "Haven't seen or heard from you all week but I should have known you'd show up to eat today." She turned away from me and reached for a cake pan that was sitting on the counter next to her and poured the contents of the bowl into it.

She was dressed in baggy jeans and a floral-print T-shirt. It was still strange for me to see her dressed this way. Up until my grandfather's death a few years ago, she never wore anything but skirts and dresses. My grandfather didn't like women in pants. In fact, my mother never wore pants until her senior year in high school and that was only after years of pleading.

Mama was wearing her short white hair pulled back from her face with a blue elastic band; this, too, was a change. Mama is part Native American on her mother's side and she'd had hair almost to her waist and always wore it pulled back in a bun at the nape of her neck. After I got mine cut last year, she followed suit and now her hair is about an inch longer than mine. It's pure white and makes a startling contrast against her red-brown skin.

I look more like Mama than I do either my mother or my father. My mother and uncle Alex are both tall and thin like my grandfather, as is my younger sister, Allegra. Mama and I are short and have had to fight our weight all our lives. I have clothes in my closet that range anywhere from a size six to a sixteen. Right now I'm somewhere in the middle. Judging from the way that dress fit last night, it would seem I'm headed toward the top again.

"It smells good," I said lamely as I lifted the lid on the pot of greens and took an exaggerated whiff. The steam almost burned my cheeks. Mama looked at me and gave me one of her famous 'you poor, stupid child' looks and nudged me out of the way so she could put the cake in the oven.

"All right, Mama. I'm sorry. I was busy this week."

"So I've heard, Miss Witness at the Scene of the Crime," she said, gesturing toward the newspaper spread out on the kitchen table. "Donna Ivory called me yesterday to tell me all about it, although half of what she said was wrong as usual. I kept expecting to hear from you, but I guess I was expecting too much," she said with a weary sigh, as if dealing with me had taxed all of her energy and had left her drained. This woman could give classes on how to dish out guilt.

Like a scared mortal trying to appease an angry goddess, I offered up the story about Delbert Ivory hitting on me at the Red Dragon. That at least earned me a chuckle that gave way to laughter on both our parts as I played the story up for all it was worth.

"I always knew that man didn't have good sense. If he did, he never would have married Donna. I don't know how he puts up with her. Least now I know why he broke his neck to avoid me at sunrise services this morning. He should be ashamed of himself. Of course, if you came to church more often, he would have known who you were."

I should have seen that one coming a mile away.

She walked over to the table and picked up the newspaper. "What in the world has Bernie Gibson got you mixed up in?"

I told her everything, only excluding the part about my having gone along with Bernie's lie. Mama was big on helping friends in need, but she was also adamant about not getting caught up in other people's dirt. I for one couldn't think of anything dirtier than murder.

"I saw that Jordan Wallace strutting around town like some peacock. I knew he was bad news the minute I laid eyes on him." Mama has made this claim about many a person, but when asked to pinpoint the precise reason for her opinion, is never able to give any solid evidence other than beady eyes or a weak chin. But in this case I'd have to agree with her. "How's Bernie doing?"

"I really can't tell to be perfectly honest. I think

she's more horrified about what happened to him than she is upset at his loss. I mean, let's face it, it's not like she lost her soul mate." It shocked me to realize that I felt so coldly about Jordan's death. I might have felt differently if I'd noticed even one redeeming quality in him.

"That surprises me, especially with them being engaged and all."

"Engaged! Who told you that?" I asked.

"Well, it's in the paper plain as day."

I snatched up the front page of the paper and started to reread the article.

"No, Kendra, the obituary section," she said, handing me the right section. When I'd read the paper this morning, I was so caught up in the glaring headline and had been so preoccupied with the note that it had never occurred to me to read the obituary section. It took me only a second to locate it. I saw that it was accompanied by a smaller version of the same picture that was on the front page. It was also very brief.

Jordan Wallace, 42, of Willow died unexpectedly Friday, May 18, 1998. Mr. Wallace was born April 10, 1956, in Cleveland, Ohio, and had resided in Willow for a year. He was a 1976 graduate of Morehouse College and was self-employed as a business analyst. He is preceded in death by his parents and is survived by his fiancée Bernice Gibson of Willow. Funeral services are pending.

Bernie hadn't lied when she had said she didn't know much about Jordan's family. How could you have lived with a man and not at some point have been told his parents' names? As for the engagement, maybe she wanted to legitimize their relationship in the eyes of the public. Maybe she felt survived by a fiancée sounded better than survived by a live-in girlfriend. Or rather, girlfriend with whom the deceased had resided.

"Well, this is the first I've heard of any engagement."

"Maybe it's all a figment of her imagination. The man's dead and not here to tell anyone any different. If she says they were engaged, who's going to prove that they weren't."

“I don't think Bernie was so desperate that she'd go and invent some phony engagement." At least I didn't think so.

"You're forgetting that I knew Bernie's mother. I was one of the few people who was still speaking to Althea after she made her big move out to the Knoll. I've known Bernie since she was a little girl. Believe me, all that woman has ever wanted since she was little was to get married. Was always running around with some white sheet wrapped around her, pretending to be a bride. You can ask your uncle Alex. She was always after him to be the groom. I’ve never seen him run as fast as when he knew Althea was coming over and bringing little Bernie with her." She chuckled at the memory. "Bernie put Althea through a lot of grief right after she graduated from college and was working in her mother's real estate office. She was running around with—"

Before she could get another word out, the back door opened and in walked Alex and Gwen. Damn! Just when things were getting good. I felt like I was about to get a whole new insight into my friend that might clear up some questions that were beginning to bug me. Now it would have to wait.

Alex and Gwen were dressed in identical red-and-black Nike warm-up suits and tennis shoes. Gwen was wearing a short brown wig in a feathery pixie cut.

"Ms. Mays, your son about killed me this morning!" said Gwen breathlessly as she plopped into a kitchen chair and fanned herself vigorously with a section of the newspaper.

"How's that, Gwen?" Mama asked as she turned the chicken over.

"With all this walking, that's how," Gwen said, glaring at Alex.

"We both agreed that we needed to lose some weight. How are we supposed to do that by sitting around?" Alex responded calmly. "You'd think we just ran a marathon the way you're acting."

"No, *you* decided that *you* needed to lose some

weight. You've been dragging me around for company or so you claim!" Gwen is always convinced Alex is trying to get her to lose weight.

I looked at my uncle and had to admit he had a bit of a gut. I didn't see what the big deal was myself. He still looked in pretty good shape to me. Alex is a tall man about six-two, slender, bald, and with Mama's smooth red-brown skin, he hardly looked his forty-five years. He's always been very athletic, playing basketball and softball. But, like me and everyone else in the family, he's hooked on Mama's cooking. He eats here most Sundays. He also has the calm, serious nature of my grandfather, who thought long and hard before he committed himself to words.

"Heard anything from Bernie?" Gwen asked.

"No, but I think I'll stop by to see how she's doing later on."

"This murder is all anyone in the shop could talk about yesterday," Gwen said.

"The shop" was actually B & S Hair Design and Nail Sculpture, owned and operated by Gwen's oldest nephew, Bruce, and his wife, Sheila. Bruce is one of four hair stylists in the shop, and Sheila and two other women do nails. I used to frequent the shop once a week on a regular basis until a year ago. Now I go every four to six weeks for a trim.

"So what are they saying at the shop?" I asked.

"Well, everyone is pretty much in agreement that

Jordan had it coming. Half think Bernie did it and the other half think Vanessa Brumfield did it. I did find out something I didn't know though," Gwen said with a satisfied smirk. "According to Natasha Woods—she's the new manicurist at the shop—Vanessa and Bernie weren't the only ones Jordan was messing with. She saw him a couple of times with some real young chick. She said she saw them twice, and they were arguing both times. Now ain't that a trip?"

"Just because she saw them together doesn't mean anything was going on. Did Natasha know who the girl was?" I asked.

"No, she was too far away, and the girl had her back to her both times."

"But she saw enough to run her mouth about something that may or may not be true. Now see, that's how shi—" I caught myself just in time to see Mama cut her eyes at me. "That's how stuff gets started," I finished.

"Uh, I don't recall ever seeing you covering up your ears when the 'stuff' starts going around." She playfully swatted me on the arm with the now rolled-up section of the newspaper, making me feel like a bad dog.

"Kendra, what do you think happened?" Alex asked.

"No clue," I said. But I did know that Bernie wasn't telling me something and that something had caused her to lie to the police. Even though she had promised to enlighten me, I'd yet to hear from her. I was beginning to worry that getting an explanation would be as hard as pulling teeth with tweezers.

Then there was that weird note I found. Who dropped it in the backyard? I was assuming that it hadn't been left there on purpose. Maybe it was. It was found in the yard of a house occupied by Vanessa Brumfield, and she was nowhere to be found. She could have pretended to leave town, then snuck back and killed Jordan. She could have left the note to further confuse things. Then there was the question of why. What would cause either Bernie or Vanessa to kill Jordan? Was it true? Was there someone else besides Vanessa that Jordan was involved with? Did Bernie know about this person as well? I thought back on Jordan's body, his smashed head, and all that blood. Whoever killed him must have been enraged and must have kept hitting him long after he was dead.

"Well, if I didn't know any better, my money would be on Denton Cox," Alex said.

"Who?" Mama, Gwen, and I said simultaneously.

"Denton Cox is Vanessa's father and was my old boss at Hampton's," he said like we should have known this was common knowledge.

Hampton's was a company that manufactured truck parts where Alex had worked for years and had been laid off from about a year before it went out of business.

"I didn't know that," I said.

"Yeah, he's one of those white men who smile in your face, slap you on the back, and compliment you on a job well done. Was always sweet-talking you into working overtime, then acted like he didn't want to pay you for it. Then as soon as you were out of earshot he'd be dropping the N word left and right. Boy, what I would have given to be a fly on the wall when he found out who his precious daughter was marrying." The gleam in his eye told me it would have been a scene he would have treasured for life.

"So why do you think he would have killed Jordan?" Gwen asked before I could.

"Well, he basically disowned Vanessa after she got married. Then she separates from her husband and they file for divorce. There were no children as far as I know. So, this makes Daddy very happy and he's willing to forgive and forget. But what he doesn't know is that Vanessa is messing around with yet another brother. Somehow he finds out and is furious enough to kill."

"But you said you knew he couldn't have done it. How?" I asked.

"I ran into a buddy of mine from Hampton's last weekend. We got to talking and Cox's name came up. He asked me if I knew if it was true about Denton Cox being in the hospital. I hadn't heard anything about it, so I asked around and found out that Cox is in the hospital, been there a couple of weeks."

"What's wrong with him?" Mama asked.

"He's dying of cancer. He's not expected to make it through the end of the month."

I left Mama's around four and decided to head over to Bernie's. I had a lemon cake with me that Mama had made for me to take over. I was instantly reminded of Diane's remark about people bringing over more food than you can eat in a month when someone died and had to laugh. It was certainly true but you can hardly fault folks for trying to be thoughtful during a difficult time.

Fifteen minutes later, I pulled my little blue Nova into the circular drive behind a silver Mercedes that I recognized to be Diane's. I almost turned around and left. I wanted to talk to Bernie alone, plus I didn't feel like being bothered by Ms. Attitude. But, maybe there was a chance to talk alone, after all. The front door opened and Diane came out carrying an overnight bag.

Whatever her irritating qualities were, I had to admit that she had style. Today she was wearing a hot-pink suit, the skirt of which was short and tight as usual. The blazer was long and if it had been buttoned up, would have almost hidden the skirt. Her pink-and-white sling-back pumps added about three inches to her height. Although this wasn't an outfit I could see myself wearing in my forties, I had to admit she had the body to pull it off. Bitch!

For a split second I saw a look of irritation flicker across her face when she saw me. It was quickly replaced by a phony smile. She took a pair of sunglasses out of her pocket and put them on. Her hair was loose around her shoulders, and she flicked a piece of it out of her face.

"If you're looking for Bernie, she's not here," Diane said, setting the bag on the ground by her car.

"She's staying with me for a few days. I just feel that at a time like this she needs to be surrounded by her family. She and Trevor are all I have left, and we need to stick together." She sounded as if she had rehearsed that little speech for my benefit. Because if anybody knew better, it was me.

"I couldn't agree more, Diane," I said with equal insincerity. "How is Bernie?"

"Not too good. She's been having trouble sleeping, which is understandable. She'll probably be all right after the funeral when she can put all this behind her."

"When is the funeral?"

"Well, they're releasing the body to the funeral home on Tuesday. So, I imagine it will be toward the end of week. Maybe Thursday. The sooner the better as far as I'm concerned."

"Do you know how things went at the police station yesterday?" I asked.

"Okay, I guess. She didn't say much about it. Why?"

she asked, pulling her sunglasses down slightly and peering down over the tops of them at me. In the bright sunshine I could see lines around her eyes that I'd never noticed before.

"Is there any reason why there would have been a problem?"

"No," I lied. "I was just wondering how everything went and if they have any leads on a suspect."

"Like I said, she didn't say much about it," she said dismissively as if the subject suddenly bored her.

"I'm late for a meeting, and I have to take these clothes over to Bernie. Hey, could you do me a big favor, Kendra, and run these things over to her for me?" she said in a breathy little girl's voice that she probably reserved solely for getting people, especially men, to do things for her. I was so taken aback by it that I looked around quickly thinking that maybe a member of the opposite sex had walked up behind me. If it weren't for the fact that I wanted to talk to Bernie alone, Diane would have been out of luck.

"Yeah, I'll take the bag over."

"Thanks, Kendra, you're a lifesaver!" With a phony flash of teeth and a toss of her hair she was in her car and tearing out of the driveway, leaving the bag sitting on the ground.

I drove the three blocks to Diane's sprawling ranch on Blue Spruce Trail. I'd only been there once before, back during my days as a high school English teacher.

Diane's son, Trevor, had been my worst nightmare. When he wasn't being disruptive and cutting up, he was sullen and inattentive. I had mistakenly thought that by having a meeting with his parents I could get them on my side and together we could turn his behavior around. Ah, the delusions of a naive young teacher.

I had been invited to their house, which I thought was a good sign. I was wrong. While Ben Gibson was slightly more reasonable than his wife, I got the distinct impression from both of them that they felt their son's behavior was not only the fault of the school's but mine as well. Their child could do no wrong. If he was being disruptive, it was because he wasn't being challenged enough by the curriculum, not because he was spoiled, lazy, and disrespectful. They promptly pulled him out of school and enrolled him in a private boarding school around the Columbus area, which didn't hurt my feelings a bit. It was only then that I started enjoying my job a little, and then I was laid off. Imagine my delight when I became friends with Bernie and found out who her brother and sister-in-law were.

I turned into the long winding driveway that led to the house. It sat back from the street and was almost completely hidden by trees and hedges. The house itself was a huge Spanish-style stucco ranch. The yard had been landscaped to within an inch of its life, complete with a small fountain in the middle of which sat a mermaid, reclining on a rock, with water shooting out of her mouth. Money obviously doesn't buy good taste. A wrought-iron gate, which was strictly for decoration, surrounded the house, complete with a buzzer-and-intercom system, which I buzzed. After about a minute, a woman's voice that I vaguely recognized as Bernie's answered.

"It's Kendra, Bernie," I answered. I tried to ignore the fact that it seemed as if she'd hesitated a little too long in buzzing the gate and letting me in. The gate swung open and I drove through, parked, and walked down another short pathway to the front door. Before I could knock, one side of a set of heavy oak double doors opened. "Hey, girlfriend," Bernie said without much enthusiasm.

I had to admit she did look tired. She had dark circles under her eyes, and her face had a pinched look. She was dressed in black leggings and an oversized, slightly wrinkled, white T-shirt that hung almost to her knees. Her feet were bare, and I noticed her toenails were painted bright red. Her hair was pulled back in its usual perfect French roll. Not a hair was out of place. She stepped aside to let me pass and eyed the bag I brought with a quizzical look.

"I stopped by your house and ran into Diane. She asked me to bring this over to you. She was late for a meeting, or so she said."

"I think Diane has a boyfriend, though she won't admit it. Lord, Kendra, she's about to drive me crazy. I told her I don't know how many times that I was fine at home; then she started doing her whiny little girl routine, and I was willing to agree to anything to get her to shut up. Ben used to fall for that mess all the time. I swear I don't know how he put up with her."

"Well, I've got just the thing to take your mind off Diane." I held out the cake tin. "Mama sent over one of her lemon cakes."

"Ooh! Follow me. I could probably eat the whole thing by myself. The only food in this house is a head of wilted lettuce, a can of coffee, and some rice cakes."

I cringed as I followed her down the hallway. As we walked through the family room, I noticed how it had changed since the last time I had been there, almost four years ago. The decor was now a southwestern theme. The gleaming hardwood floors were covered with Indian-print rugs. The walls were white stucco. Two large potted cactus plants flanked either side of the fireplace. A white couch was draped with an Aztec-print throw in shades of orange, brown, and black. There were also several pieces of Indian sculpture. It was a beautiful room and looked very warm and inviting. I followed Bernie into the kitchen, which was another matter. It was completely white and very sterile looking with chrome and white appliances. No plants, dishrags, or potholders; not even a dirty plate or cup in the sink to show that this room was alive.

I set the yellow flowered cake tin down and at once

noticed how out of place it looked. Bernie got two plates—white, of course—out of the cabinet and handed me a knife to cut the cake. I sliced two thick pieces.

"Let's eat outside. This kitchen depresses me," Bernie said.

She led the way through a set of French doors just off the kitchen and out onto a stone patio. We sat down at a maroon-and-gold striped canopied table. We sat in silence for a few minutes savoring the moist lemony sweetness of the cake. I watched Bernie as we ate. She was being pleasant enough, but I could tell she hadn't been thrilled to see me. I was beginning to wonder if the real reason she was staying here was so she could avoid me.

"So, how'd it go yesterday?" I asked.

"Fine." She wouldn't look at me. I knew this was going to be like pulling teeth.

"Then there was no problem with your explanation about why you went to the house?"

"I told them just what I said I would, that I went there to get my car from Jordan. I also said that I was beginning to get suspicious about all the time he was spending over there, which is why I let myself into the house when there was no answer at the door."

"What I can't understand is why you don't want the police to know that you knew for sure that they were involved. What difference could that make?"

For a minute I didn't think she was going to answer me; then finally she sighed and spoke.

"Kendra, I did something stupid a long time ago. Something that could give the police reason to suspect me if they find out that I knew about Vanessa." She saw the look on my face and continued. "Now hold up! I didn't kill him, even though I was mad enough to when I found out what he was up to. So don't look at me like that!" she said defensively.

"Well, are you going to tell me what you did? I mean I did lie and withhold information from the police. I'd like to know why in case this comes back to bite me in the ass!" We glared at each other for a few seconds; then she got up from the table and stood facing away from me.

"When I graduated from college, I still didn't know what I wanted to do with my life. I had a degree in home economics. Mother really hated that. She always wanted me and Ben to take over running the real estate company when we finished with school so she could cut back and do some traveling. Ben was all for it. I wasn't. I couldn't find a job and had to live at home. Mother told me that in exchange for room and board I had to work for her until I found another job. I think she was hoping I'd learn to like the business and want to stay on and get my real estate license." She turned around and came back to sit at the table.

"That's where I met Raymond Hodge. He was one

of my mother's real estate agents. Raymond was eleven years older than me. He was handsome, dressed real nice, and talked a good game. Jordan reminded me a lot of Raymond," she said wistfully.

"I was a naive twenty-two-year-old who never had a real boyfriend and didn't date much. So when Raymond started paying me attention, I was flattered. We started seeing each other. I was so happy because I couldn't believe a man like Raymond could ever be interested in me. He told me he wanted to marry me. I said yes and we became engaged. We'd been hiding our relationship from my mother because Raymond said she would think he was too old for me and that she would try and break us up. God, I was a fool!

"Raymond lived in Dayton. He told me he lived with his sister and brother-in-law, which was why I could never come over to see him. He said he didn't get along with his brother-in-law. I believed everything he told me, not because it made sense, but because I wanted to believe in him." She looked at her empty plate and then at me.

"What went wrong?" I asked, even though I knew what she was going to say. I'd heard this same story in many different forms from other women.

"He was married, that's what went wrong! All that time he was married and hiding it from everyone, not just me. He lived with his wife, and his brother-in-law lived with them. One of the other agents saw him and his wife at a club one night and asked if she was Raymond's girlfriend. It all came out that she was his wife. The agent came back to work and told us all about it. No one knew I was seeing him, so I wasn't completely humiliated. Later that night, I confronted Raymond about his wife and he broke down and started crying. He said he loved me and he knew I wouldn't have had anything to do with him if I knew he was married. He said he was in the process of divorcing his wife so he could marry me. He even offered to show me the divorce papers he had had drawn up by his lawyer."

"Let me guess," I said, interrupting her, "you believed him."

"Hook, line, and sinker," she said with a tight smile. "Actually, he was telling the truth about the divorce. He was divorcing his wife. But it wasn't for the love of me. It was for the love of my mother's money, which he thought he could get his hands on by marrying me. His wife knew there was another woman, and when she found out it was me, she went straight to my mother and told her. My mother and I got into the biggest fight we'd ever had in my life. She was so hurt and disappointed. She threatened to fire Raymond if I didn't stop seeing him. I knew how much he loved his job, so I said I wouldn't see him again.

"I couldn't stay away from him, though. We were planning to elope and then all of a sudden everything changed. He wouldn't have anything to do with me. I was stunned. Every time I wanted to talk to him about it he blew me off. Finally, I confronted him in the office one night when he was working late. Kendra," she said, shaking her head, "he was like a different person. He was so cold and nasty. He told me the real reason he wanted to marry me and that Mother had made it worth his while to leave me alone. Said it was easier to leave me alone and get paid for it than to pretend he loved me. Then he just turned his back on me like I was dismissed. I never felt so angry and hurt in all my life."

"What did you do?" If it had been me, I'd have cut him a new butt hole.

"Like I said, something stupid. I remember feeling really hot like I was about to burn up. I think I was even sweating. All I could think about was hurting him as much as he hurt me. I was standing by the receptionist's desk and my hand came to rest on a paperweight. Actually, it was just a big rock with some paint on it that our receptionist's daughter made at school. I grabbed hold of that thing and threw it with all my might at Raymond. It caught him right square in the back of the head. He just fell like he'd been shot. There was so much blood, and I couldn't get it to stop. I didn't know what to do."

I remembered her saying almost the same thing the night she called me when she found Jordan.

"Didn't you call for an ambulance?"

"No," she said defensively. "I called the only person

I could think to call: Mother. This was before she moved out here to the Knoll. The house wasn't finished yet, and she was still living in that little place next door to the office. Mother always was in her element during a crisis." I couldn't help but notice the resentment in her voice.

"So you took him to the hospital?"

"Mother sent me home. She said she'd handle it. I kept looking out the window trying to see what was going on and then the phone rang. It was one of Mother's clients going on and on about some problem with a house they'd bought. I couldn't get the woman off the phone. When I finally did tear myself away, I rushed to the window just in time to see Mother driving away in Raymond's car. I could see him slumped over in the passenger seat. I waited and waited and finally around two in the morning she came home in a cab. When I asked her what happened, all she would say was that she took care of everything and that Raymond wouldn't be causing any more problems."

"You mean to tell me she took him away and didn't say where or what happened?" I asked in amazement.

"She told me to go next door and clean up the mess and that was it. For years afterward, whenever I would ask her about it, she would tell me the same thing. To tell you the truth, Kendra, I don't know what happened to Raymond. His wife showed up at Mother's kicking up a fuss. She wanted to know where he was or what we'd done to him to be precise. She filed a missing person's report and the police came around asking a lot of questions. I was so scared."

I sat back and took in all that I'd just been told. Fool that I was, I thought—or rather hoped—that Bernie's explanation would ease my mind. Instead I felt even more confused. Now I understood why Bernie didn't want the police looking too closely at her or any motive she might have. They would connect her to Raymond Hodge's disappearance. But who's to say they wouldn't anyway?

"What did your mother tell the police?"

"That Raymond never showed up for work and that no one had seen him. They had no reason not to believe her and after a while they stopped looking."

"Did the police know about you and Raymond?"

"Of course they knew. His wife made sure they knew about it. Now can you see where I'm coming from? For the second time in my life something bad has happened to a man I've been seriously involved with. It's only a matter of time before the police make a connection, and when they do, it's not going to look very good for me."

"Bernie, there's more to it than that. What about opportunity? You were at work Friday morning and Jordan had your car. Archer Street is several blocks away from the literacy center. How were you supposed to have killed Jordan and gotten back to work on foot before anyone noticed you were gone?" I reasoned.

She thought about what I'd said for a minute but still didn't look convinced.

"If the police want me to be guilty, then they'll find a way for me to have done it. It would sure make things easier for me if Vanessa were guilty, and if I didn't do it, that could only leave her."

It would solve her current problem but I didn't have the heart to tell her that it could also rake up old questions of what really happened to Raymond Hodge. The answer to that one died along with Althea Gibson. Why did Althea refuse to tell Bernie what happened? Could she have just been shielding her from the knowledge that Raymond died of his wound or that possibly Althea herself finished off what Bernie started? I suspect that whatever happened, Bernie's mother saw it as a prime opportunity to gain control over her daughter. Bernie must have felt a debt of gratitude to her mother for getting her out of a bad situation.

"Kendra, if you don't mind, I would rather not talk about this anymore."

"Sure," I said, and then a thought came to mind. "Bernie, just how did you find out about Jordan and Vanessa?" She gave me a look of pure annoyance.

"I got an anonymous note in the mail."

Another note? What the hell was going on?

FIVE

Monday morning I woke up evil. I thought of a million reasons not to go to work. I thought back to the look on Bernie's face when I told her about the note I had found. I thought she was going to spew lemon cake all over the patio. Could the two notes be connected? I know how people could be when they know your man is cheating. They can't wait for you to find out about it, even if they have to tell you themselves. Maybe that's all the letter was about. I tried to get Bernie to tell the police about the letter and she said no. She'd thrown it away, or so she claimed. When I tried to get her to change her mind, she asked me to leave.

I'd pretty much made up my mind to call in sick when it dawned on me that this would be the last full week of classes at the literacy center. We would have a four-week break, during which I would not be paid, and then resume for an eight-week summer session. I thought about all my bills and the fact that I'd already used most of my sick leave when I had the flu back in January. I dragged my butt out of bed. My back was still bugging the hell out of me, which didn't make my mood any better. Lynette had sprained her back a few months ago, and I wondered if she had any painkillers left. I had to call her anyway. I still owed her a cussing out.

Less than an hour into my workday, I wished I had called in. Dorothy Burgess, my boss, was on a rampage. She's usually pretty cool and laid-back. She only gets this way once a year around the time she has to get the yearly report ready for the State Board of Education. Our funding rides on that report, so I guess she has the right to get a little crazy. She'd already lit into me about some attendance sheets that she needed for statistics and couldn't find. I have to admit I wasn't very diplomatic about it. Maybe if I hadn't spent the weekend dealing with the police, Bernie, and a horrible blind date, I'd be in a more helpful mood. As far as I was concerned, I'd earned my bad mood and planned on savoring it.

Rhonda Hammond, the program's math instructor, walked into the room. I knew she must have encountered Hurricane Dorothy because she was red in the face, mumbling angrily, and rubbing the fingertips of her right hand together, something she always does when she needs a cigarette. Rhonda's a heavy smoker and always smells like cigarettes and Liz Claiborne perfume, a combination that reminds me of a dirty ashtray filled with flowers.

"I don't have to ask where you just came from," I said.

"I just keep telling myself five more days till Bermuda." She sat down at her desk and ran her hands through her short blond hair. Rhonda's husband's a doctor, and they were going to celebrate their tenth wedding anniversary in Bermuda.

"Oh, I forgot to tell you, Dorothy's taking up a collection to send Bernie some flowers. Boy, I couldn't believe it when I read that in the paper yesterday. Do they have any idea who did it?"

"Not that I know of," I said with an air of finality. I was hoping she wouldn't ask me any more questions. As much as I like Rhonda, I was sick and tired of the subject of Bernie and the murder. Ever since I showed up at work, I'd been bombarded with questions. I'd decided when I got out of bed that I was going to stay out of it, stay away from Bernie unless she called me, and hope and pray the killer was caught soon.

I didn't even want to think about it anymore because every time I did, I imagined myself being arrested on a charge of obstruction of justice, and, as I'm being carted off to jail, Mama is there sadly shaking her head and saying, "I tried to tell you, girl, but you just wouldn't listen. A hard head makes a soft behind." That must have been her favorite thing to say to my sister and me right before she whipped us. I looked at the clock and groaned. Classes hadn't even started yet. It was going to be a long day.

The rest of the day went by slowly. Attendance was low, which didn't surprise me since this was the last week of class. I was able to get a lot of lesson plans done. I wanted to be prepared when Dorothy came charging down to see what I had planned for the summer program. As expected, she came to my classroom around eleven thirty after the morning session was over. But it wasn't to see any lesson plans. She had two visitors with her, Detectives Harmon and Mercer. I took one look at them and wanted to cry.

They made such an odd pair. Charles Mercer, florid, overweight, rumpled, and friendly. Trish Harmon, thin, neat, humorless, and completely professional. I was surprised she went by Trish and not Patricia. I told the Laurel and Hardy of the Willow police force to have a seat. I was well aware that Dorothy was probably lurking in the hall somewhere trying to hear everything. I watched as Mercer squeezed himself into one of the desk chairs. Trish Harmon ignored him and got straight to the point.

"Miss Clayton, we need to speak to you about your relationship with Jordan Wallace."

"My relationship with Jordan? We didn't have a relationship. He was Bernie's boyfriend, not mine." Of all the things they could have asked me, this was the last thing I was expecting.

"Then can you tell us the nature of an argument you had with Jordan Wallace approximately one month ago in the parking lot of Estelle's restaurant? An argument in which you threatened to kill Mr. Wallace."

"What!" I said in amazement and then I remembered. How could I forget? It had been late one Friday night when I had filled in for one of the servers. I hate waiting tables but could hardly pass up the chance to earn some extra cash. I was leaving to go home and was at my car about to unlock the door when I felt a hand on my shoulder. I turned and was quickly pulled into a clumsy embrace by a very drunk Jordan. I tried to pull away but he held me tightly against him. He had two big handfuls of my ass and was breathing his beer breath in my face, telling me to relax and to stop being so stuck-up.

I lost it. I started calling him everything but a child of God. I managed to break free by stomping on his foot. Then I started beating him with my long beaded key chain. He called me a crazy bitch and said it was no wonder I didn't have a man. He started walking back toward Estelle's where he must have been drinking up in the bar. It was then that I yelled out that I would kill him if he ever touched me again. He responded by throwing a rock at me, missing, and cracking someone else's windshield.

I started to leave the person a note with Jordan's name and phone number but I chickened out and just went home. I wanted to forget about it. I never told Bernie what happened. Jordan took her away for a romantic weekend that she probably paid for. Bernie was so happy—she talked about that trip for weeks afterward. I didn't have the heart to tell her.

It seemed kind of funny now. So much so that I started laughing. I noticed that Harmon and Mercer were looking at me strangely. So I filled them in. Mercer looked away but not before I saw a smile on his face. Trish Harmon didn't see any humor in my story at all. Her thin lips were pursed in disapproval.

"Then you're not denying you made the threat?" Harmon asked, ever the professional.

"Well, no, I'm not denying that I made the threat. But I didn't mean it. I was mad. Look, I don't know about you, Detective Harmon, but I don't like any man touching me without my permission," I said calmly. I knew this situation wouldn't be helped at all by being defensive. But inside I was seething. How dare they come here and ask me these stupid questions! I also knew that they could have only gotten this information from one person: Joy Owens. She had come outside and was unlocking her bicycle during my encounter with Jordan and had witnessed the whole thing. I could just kill her.

"What my partner means to say is that when we get

information like this during a murder investigation, it's our job to look into it, Miss Clayton," Detective Mercer said kindly, speaking for the first time. I got the feeling that Charles Mercer saw me as a potentially hysterical female and was treating me as such with his calm-yet-firm voice. His tone reminded me of when I stepped on a rusty nail as a kid and had to get a tetanus shot and of the doctor whose words calmed and soothed me right before he jabbed a big needle in my arm. This visit had that same feel to it.

Harmon, who hadn't liked my last comment one little bit, continued on. "Did you have any other violent encounters with Jordan Wallace in which you threatened his life? It would be a good idea to tell us now before we find out on our own."

I pressed the palm of my hand against my forehead in mock concentration. "Now, let me see. I made an illegal U-turn last week; I also stole candy from a baby and kicked a puppy. But, nope, I haven't threatened to kill anyone lately." Only when I'm truly pissed do I become a complete smart-ass.

"Miss Clayton, someone you knew has been brutally murdered, and we would really appreciate your cooperation," Charles Mercer said calmly, playing the good cop to Harmon's bad one.

"Is that so? I could have sworn that's what I was doing when I called you about that note. By the way, what have you found out about it?"

Harmon looked like she was about to burst a blood vessel. "You are in no position to make any demands. You trespassed on a murder scene, you removed a piece of evidence from the scene, and you were witnessed threatening the victim's life. As far as this note is concerned, I'm beginning to wonder if you were the one who manufactured the note in order to divert our attention away from you and Ms. Gibson."

It was like I'd been kicked in the stomach. It never occurred to me that they would think I was responsible for the note. How did everything get so screwed up?

"We've found out nothing much about the note so far," Mercer said softly, giving me a look of pity. "Both the paper and the envelope were of cheap quality, the kind that can be purchased at just about any store. We're not prepared at this time to make any connection between it and Jordan Wallace's murder."

"That's it? What about fingerprints? Did you find any fingerprints?" I asked in a small voice. I felt like all the air had been sucked out of the room.

"Oh yes, we found a perfect set of prints on both the envelope and the paper," Trish Harmon said. "Both sets belong to you, Miss Clayton." She gave the first hint of a smile I'd ever seen on her face. I wanted to wring her skinny neck.

"Please don't plan any trips or leave town in case we have more questions for you," Mercer said as he hefted his bulk up out of the small desk.

They left me sitting at my desk feeling like a trapped rat on a sinking ship.

The rest of the day went by quickly enough. I wasn't at all unhappy when quitting time came. It didn't take long for the news to spread throughout the building that the police had been to see me and that I didn't look happy when they left. One by one, my coworkers, and even people I barely knew who worked for other programs housed in the Clark Literacy Center, were coming up to me and asking if I was okay and did I want to talk. Although I knew a few of them were genuinely concerned, most of them had that glitter in their eyes that people get when they drive past a car wreck or witness a fistfight—that strange mix of fascination and repulsion that draws people like flies to other folks' troubles. So much for staying out of it. It didn't seem as if I was going to be able to do that now.

I decided to go over to Estelle's and ask Joy what the hell she'd been thinking, even though I knew she'd just deny it. When I got there, Gwen told me Joy was outside taking a cigarette break. I walked toward the back door and saw that there was a piece of brick wedged in the doorjamb so it wouldn't close all the way. Alex hated for any of us to do this because the Dumpster wasn't too far from this door and it let flies in. Of course, Joy didn't care and did it anyway.

I walked through the door and saw Joy leaned up

against the fence opposite me. She was dressed in her work clothes—black pants with suspenders and a white blouse. Her burgundy-tinted hair was pulled back into a knot at the back of her head. Her bangs almost covered her eyes. She had a cigarette dangling from her fingers. She looked like a juvenile delinquent.

"I just came to thank you, girlfriend," I said nastily.

"What?" she said with her usual frown.

"Thanks for telling the police about what happened between me and Jordan Wallace in the parking lot last month. I really enjoyed them coming to my job and asking me a lot of bullshit questions."

I had expected her to get defensive. What I didn't expect was for her to laugh at me. But that's what she was doing. She was laughing hard and then she started coughing and choking on the smoke she forgot to exhale. When she was finished, she grinned at me, took another drag on her cigarette, and blew the smoke straight at me.

"So you got busted, huh?" she said with a smirk.

"Don't act like you don't know what I'm talking about."

"Oh, I know exactly what you're talking about. You and your friend's man with your hands all over each other. Yeah, I saw you all right, only I'm not the one who told on you. I got better things to do than to be telling the police anything, especially when it don't have shit to do with me."

"Since when have you ever let that keep you out of other people's business?" Joy is notorious for stirring up a mess wherever she goes, and I was sure that this time was no different.

"Hey, don't get mad at me because you got busted," she said, holding her hands up in front of her like we were about to play patty- cake. "You should consider yourself real lucky though. Your girl Bernie could have seen you and killed you both right there on the spot. Instead she just killed him." She flicked her cigarette on the ground and mashed it with her foot.

"Duty calls," she said, giving me a mock salute and then disappearing through the door.

I stood outside for a few minutes to think. I didn't believe her. Who else could have been there? It never occurred to me to ask Mercer and Harmon who told them. I started to go inside and couldn't. Joy had moved the piece of brick and I was locked out. I kicked the door.

I stopped at the store on my way home and wandered up and down the aisles, hoping something would interest me. I finally ended up with a bottle of my favorite Japanese plum wine and a roasted chicken from the deli. I was in the checkout line when I heard someone call my name. I turned around and saw Carl Brumfield standing behind me. He had on a navy blue double-breasted suit that he was wearing the hell out of.

Since he had been sitting most of the time the night we met, I hadn't realized how tall he was. He was smiling down on me with those perfect white teeth framed by that incredible mouth. "Saucy lips" as Lynette would say, meant for kissing. I caught a whiff of what smelled like Obsession for Men. Lord, have mercy.

"You must be in another world. I've been calling you for five minutes."

"Oh, I'm sorry. After the day I've had, I wish I were in another world. A world with no Mondays, no bosses with attitudes, and no friends with big problems."

"I hear you," he said, looking down into my cart. "I guess that accounts for the bottle of wine?"

"Yeah, it's been that kind of day." I was suddenly wishing I had worn the dress I almost put on this morning instead of jeans and a T-shirt. Of course, if I'd been dressed to kill I wouldn't have run into him.

"So what brings you here? You do all your grocery shopping in Willow?"

"I was in court this afternoon. The final hearing for my divorce," he said, watching me closely.

Had Vanessa shown up? And if so, where had she been? It dawned on me that Carl Brumfield probably knew who I was by now, and I was suddenly very uncomfortable.

"So how's it feel to be a free man again?" I asked, not quite able to look him in the eye.

"Not completely free yet. We'll get a call from the

court in a week to ten days, then it will all be over."

So, she had shown up. I was aware that Carl was watching me, and his smile was barely hanging on.

"You know, I should be really mad at you. Why didn't you tell me you were friends with Vanessa's landlady? The paper said you were a witness at the scene. How come you never said anything?"

"I guess I didn't quite know how to bring up the subject of a dead man in your ex-wife's house in casual conversation. I really didn't mean to be evasive. Am I forgiven?" I gave him my best doe-eyed innocent look.

"On one condition." His smile had returned to its full wattage. "Have dinner with me Friday night."

Hell yes, my mind screamed. But my mouth said, "Okay, I'd really like that." We exchanged phone numbers, paid for our purchases, and he walked me to my car. It didn't hit me until later that he might be using me for information just as I'd used him. I knew what answers I was after. But what was he after?

"Look, how many times do I have to say I'm sorry?" Lynette said later that evening as we sat in my tiny kitchen eating roasted chicken, mashed potatoes with gravy, and green beans.

"If it weren't for that pitiful date Saturday, you wouldn't have met Carl Brumfield," she said, waving a chicken leg in the air. "And I hope you know you ain't half slick. I saw you go back into the restaurant when I was sitting at the traffic light. I hope you don't blow this, Kendra."

"Whatever," I said, my mouth half filled with mashed potatoes. "It's just a date, Lynette. He didn't ask me to marry him. I think you're more excited about this than I am. And I thought you said I shouldn't be making eyes at him, remember."

"That was before I knew he was so close to being a free man. And you know when a wife goes missing and there's a dead man in her house, the first person they look at is the husband. But from what you said, she was just out of town for the weekend."

"Yeah, which makes me wonder what in the world Jordan was doing over there in the first place."

"You don't think... Naw, even he wasn't that big of an asshole," Lynette said.

"What?"

"You don't think he had the nerve to be meeting another woman. Maybe he knew Vanessa was out of town and decided to use the house to hook up with some other chick."

"It's possible. I wouldn't have put anything past that man." I filled Lynette in on what Gwen heard at the shop about the possibility of a third woman. Would Jordan have had the nerve to meet another woman in the house where his other woman lived? I was getting tired just thinking about all the plotting and planning that would have involved. That would certainly be grounds for murder in most women's eyes.

"Now that makes me wonder if he had a key, and if he didn't, who let him in?" I said, carving another piece of chicken.

"Bernie was at work and Vanessa was out of town. So that leaves the mystery woman," Lynette said.

"Yeah, but if he was screwing someone else besides Bernie and Vanessa, why not go to her house? Why risk going to Vanessa's?"

"Maybe she has a husband or a boyfriend."

"Why not a hotel?" I asked.

"Hell, I don't know, Kendra. Maybe the idea of doing it in someone else's bed turned them on. Folks are freaky these days. Don't you watch *Jerry Springer?"*

"Not if I can help it," I said, laughing.

We cleaned up the kitchen and took the bottle of wine and our glasses into the living room. I knew I'd have a headache in the morning but didn't care. Between our jobs, her kids and fiancé, Lynette and I didn't get a chance to get together for girl talk very often.

"You miss the kids yet?" Lynette's ex-husband, Lamont, had the kids for a month every summer. They'd left for California the day before.

"Nope," she said, then taking a sip of wine added, "not yet anyway. Ask me in a week or two."

"Were they excited about going?"

"You know how kids are. They act like they can't

wait to get away from me whenever they're not getting their way. They couldn't wait to get out there to see their daddy's new house. He's got that big new job now, so I think they figure he's going to spend a lot of money on them. I didn't tell them about Daddy's new wife. He can tell them that himself. I imagine when they come home they'll tell me how mean Daddy was and how they couldn't wait to get home. They're spoiled. As much as I appreciate Ma letting us stay with her, she spoils those kids rotten."

"And of course you don't have anything to do with it," I teased.

"Of course not," she said with a wink.

We drank almost the entire bottle of wine and talked until midnight. If it weren't for our jobs, we would have probably talked all night. I walked Lynette to the door and as I opened it, I saw a flash of gray like a puff of smoke shoot down the steps.

"I see Mrs. Carson still has that raggedy cat. That thing must be as old as she is."

"Don't talk about Mahalia. You'd think that cat is one of her children. She treats it a lot better than she treats her kids. She even buys Mahalia presents when she hits the numbers."

"Oh, I almost forgot," Lynette said, reaching into her purse and pulling out a bottle of pills. "Be careful with these, girl, they're strong. I never took them during the day because they knocked me out. They'll take care of your back pain, though, and anything else that's hurting."

I took the pills and watched her go. I wouldn't be taking anything tonight. The wine had given me a nice buzz, and I wasn't in any pain at the moment. But, the morning wasn't far off.

The next two days dragged by slowly. Our attendance at the center remained low. Bernie had come back to work but was keeping a low profile and avoiding me. I'd heard from someone else that Jordan's wake and funeral were going to be on Thursday. Dorothy had decided to cancel afternoon classes then so we could all attend.

I was functioning in a daze for the most part because of the painkillers I'd gotten from Lynette. I'd taken only one on Tuesday night and ended up oversleeping the next morning and being late for work. I was exhausted all the next day. But, true to Lynette's word, my back felt great.

Carl had called me, and we made plans to have dinner at one of my favorite restaurants over in Springfield—Cedar Street Restaurant. I was excited about the date because it would be great to be in the company of an attractive man, and it would also give me an opportunity to get some more information about him and Vanessa.

There had been a brief account in the paper about

how Jordan's murder investigation was going. Apparently, Vanessa had been visiting friends in Dayton for the weekend and didn't have any clue as to why Jordan Wallace would have been in the house. According to the article, the police didn't have any suspects. No one in the neighborhood had seen anything out of the ordinary that morning. I knew Vanessa hadn't told the police about her personal involvement with Jordan. It was only a matter of time before they found out. I kept wondering if Carl had known. What I did know was that I didn't like the fact that, thanks to Joy, the police were looking at me for any reason. I smiled when I thought about my date and then realized I still had Jordan's wake and funeral to get through.

It rained on Thursday. *Fitting funeral weather,* I couldn't help thinking as I sat on a hard wooden chair at the Walker and Willis Funeral Home that afternoon. Reverend Robert Merriman was delivering the eulogy to a half-filled room of people, most of whom had never met Jordan Wallace. The wake had been held an hour before and had been attended by mostly friends and coworkers of Bernie's and a few close friends of her mother's. It was a closed-casket ceremony with the same picture of Jordan that had been in the paper sitting in a wreath of flowers in front of the casket.

Bernie had put on a brave face as she sat in the first row ahead of me. She was dressed in a charcoal-gray suit, and every few seconds she would wipe away a tear with a white lace hanky. As she did so, Diane, who was sitting next to her, would pat her gently on the back. I couldn't help but wonder how Bernie really felt. She'd been ready to end her relationship with Jordan. Hadn't she told me the night she found him that she'd wanted to end things with Jordan once and for all? Killing someone was definitely once and for all.

I looked around the room. Detectives Mercer and Harmon were sitting in the back taking everything in, especially Harmon. I was sure she was making a mental note of everyone who'd come to the funeral. The one thing that had amazed me was that Jordan had no relatives there. I'd read in the paper that his parents were dead. There were no brothers or sisters listed as survivors. Was Jordan an only child or did Bernie just not know? What about cousins or aunts and uncles? Could Jordan have a family out there who didn't know one of its members had been murdered? I couldn't ask Bernie. She was just barely speaking to me. I guess reluctantly revealing a secret that you desperately wanted to forget has a way of putting a damper on a friendship.

The service was brief. It had to be. There wasn't much to say about a man who most of us, including Bernie, barely knew. The minister had talked about the precarious nature of human life and living it to its fullest. I had a feeling that Jordan had done that and mostly at the expense of other people. There would be an even briefer graveside service in the morning, which I did not plan on attending.

I was sitting between my boss, Dorothy, who was wearing a disgustingly tight dark green dress, and our program's secretary, Iris Reynolds. Iris had been out sick all week and had just come back to work that day, which was a relief to us all. Her sub had been hours away from being run off the premises by an angry mob of pissed-off students and employees with me leading the pack. The woman must have been a graduate of the Eat Shit and Die school of charm. I didn't want to think about how many prospective students she'd run off with her less-than-lovely phone etiquette.

The service was over and people were leaving to go to Bernie's house for the usual post-funeral swine fest. I'd been wondering if I should go. In the end, my stomach won out as it always does. I was also in desperate need of a bathroom. I'd been holding it since before the service began. After telling Iris and Dorothy that I'd see them at Bernie's, I went off in search of a bathroom. As I left the room, I spotted Detective Trish Harmon. We nodded at each other solemnly, befitting the occasion. Then once past her, as I rounded the corner, I flipped her the finger. Hey, what can I say? My level of maturity slips on me now and then.

The Walker and Willis Funeral Home had once been one of the finest homes in Willow. Back in the days when Madison Street, on which the home sits, was the ritziest street in town. Blacks mostly populated the east side of town or wherever they could get anyone to sell them a house. In the mid-to-late fifties, when realtors and contractors started building up the north side of town, many whites moved north, and the south side of Willow slowly became predominately black.

Edmond Willis and Hugh Walker ran separate funeral homes and had been competitors in servicing the black community of Willow for years. But when their grandchildren Roger Willis and Leticia Walker, both only children, fell in love and got married after both inherited the family business, they combined both funeral homes into a large one. The house that they moved their combined business to was an old mansion that sits back from the street. The house was made of brick that has been painted white with black shutters and a mansard roof. The place has three floors. The ground floor and the basement are used for the business. Roger, Leticia, and their children occupy the second and third floors.

I found a powder room at the end of a long hallway. When I came out, I noticed another parlor across the hall smaller than the one Jordan's funeral had been in but every bit as nice, with the same maroon carpet and lace curtains. The sign posted on a wrought iron easel by the door said "Elfrieda Barlow" and listed visitation hours. I peeked in and saw a mahogany casket opened to reveal an elderly black woman in a blue suit. No one else seemed to be present. I felt sad. Didn't this woman have a family? The visitation hours were half over.

"Hello," said a cheerful voice behind me, making me jump. I turned and saw an attractive, light-skinned woman who looked to be in her mid fifties. Her thick black hair was streaked with white and piled high on her head. She wore bright red lipstick on her wide smiling mouth and had on a sharp black-and-white Donna Karan suit that I'd seen at the mall for more money than I pay in rent a month. Her suit matched her hair.

"I didn't mean to scare you, honey," she said in a soft voice with just the hint of a Southern drawl. "I'm Winette Barlow. Did you know Elfrieda?" she asked, gesturing toward the casket.

"No, ma'am. I'm sorry I didn't. I was here for the Wallace funeral. I didn't mean to intrude."

"No harm done, honey. I probably should have done without the visitation. Elfrieda didn't exactly like people very well. The only ones who showed up today were friends of mine. But, she was my sister- in-law. She was my late husband's older sister, and he would have wanted me to make sure everything was done properly," she said, smiling.

"Was she sick very long?" I was at a loss for words.

"Oh, honey, she wasn't sick. She died of a stroke in her sleep. I found her when I came back from visiting my brother in South Carolina. She lived with me, you know. Such a sad life," she said, shaking her head. Her smile softened a bit. "I know what everyone thought, but she wasn't a bag lady," she said, lifting her chin defiantly. I watched her walk over to the side of the casket and bend to adjust the lapel of the blue suit.

I went and stood by her and looked down into the casket. The occupant looked like she had just lain down for a nap after church. Her short gray hair was styled away from her face in finger waves and her hands were folded at her waist. Her blue suit looked a little big and I had to wonder if it was something she'd worn in life.

"Why would anyone think she was a bag lady? Didn't you say she lived with you?" I asked quietly as if the woman in the casket might wake up from her nap.

"Well, Elfrieda was eccentric. But it wasn't her fault, you see. She was a perfectly normal person up until her accident years ago. She was an educated woman, had a good job at Wright Patterson Air Force Base. One night she was coming home late from work and nodded off at the wheel. She crashed into a tree. It's a wonder she survived. Sometimes I think it would have been better if she had died 'cause she was never the same afterward. She had a severe head injury that left her brain damaged. I thought it would have been better if she was institutionalized, but Henry, my late husband, wouldn't hear of it.

"We did the best we could. She would disappear for

days at a time, wandering the streets at all hours. It was all we could do to keep her fed and in clean clothes. Things had gotten a little better in the last few years since we finally got her on some medicine that worked for her. She was still a handful though. I felt so guilty leaving her here when I went to South Carolina, but my brother was recovering from heart surgery, and I went to take care of him. I couldn't look after them both. I had a home health nurse come check on her every day."

As she spoke, it suddenly dawned on me who it was that I was looking down at, Crazy Frieda. Winette Barlow was right. Everyone in town, including me, did think she was a bag lady. I hadn't recognized her without her matted hair, dirty face, and dirty clothes. She could usually be found wandering the streets of Willow muttering to herself or shouting obscenities at passersby. She was rarely without her shopping cart full of cans that she rummaged through the trash for. She'd scared me to death on more than a few occasions when I'd taken trash to the Dumpster at the restaurant.

I never knew anything about her except her name—or rather the name everyone in town called her—Crazy Frieda. No one paid much attention to her. She was harmless and most people were content to ignore her and let her rummage for her cans. She may as well have been invisible. Looking down at her now, I felt very sad. I never thought that she might have a family who loved her or had a normal life once. I never thought about her at all.

While we were looking down into the casket, an elderly couple arrived to pay their respects. As soon as I saw who they were, I was itching to make my getaway.

"She looks good, Winnie, real good," Donna Ivory said, looking down into the casket. She looked over at me and her slightly bulging eyes opened wide.

"Kendra, I almost didn't recognize you. You've picked up weight, haven't you?"

Now, maybe I'm being overly sensitive, but to me, the one thing worse than commenting publicly on someone else's fat is to make them own up to it by asking questions like the one I'd just been asked. I had to practically pinch myself to keep from saying, "Why yes, Mrs. Ivory, I have, and you look like you're giving the seams of that suit of yours a workout as well." But, I didn't. I took the high road and said, "Yes a few pounds maybe."

She laughed a shrill high-pitched laugh as if to say, "A few pounds, my ass."

Delbert, who had been signing the guest book, came over and stood by his wife. He had traded his geriatric pimp suit from the other night for a respectable brown cotton-poly blend that he looked like he was sweating to death in. He looked everywhere but at me and finally started making small talk with Winette Barlow, all the while glancing nervously at his wife and me. I wasn't about to say a word. Considering who he was married to, I figured he must already be in hell.

Donna Ivory stood several inches taller than her husband and must have outweighed him by at least a hundred pounds. Her eyes bulged slightly and her neck was almost nonexistent, making her look like a frog. Her thinning hair was naturally red and was teased to strategically cover her scalp more effectively. Her feet looked stuffed into the thick-soled black orthopedic shoes she was wearing. She was dressed in a shiny-black polyester suit and a sky-blue ruffled blouse that did nothing to enhance her sallow yellow skin and freckles.

"You cut off all your hair too. I about had a heart attack when I saw your grandma's hair. I still can't believe Estelle could do such a thing. She had such beautiful hair. I swear with all you girls running around bald-headed, I can't hardly tell the girls from the boys. Ain't that right, Delbert?"

"Yes, dear," Delbert Ivory said reflexively as if he'd trained himself to give the right responses by listening to the inflection of his wife's voice. I doubted he'd even heard what she'd said.

I'm not too bald or too fat for your husband to make a pass at, I thought nastily. Winette Barlow caught my eye over Donna's broad shoulder and winked at me.

"I think she knew her time was near, Winnie," Donna said, looking down into the casket.

"Why do you say that?" Winette asked with a slight

frown.

"Well, the last time I saw her she was in the alley behind my house. I saw her when I was doing the breakfast dishes. She always came by every Thursday morning 'cause I left cans out for her. Let it be said that Donna Ivory does her part to help the homeless."

"She wasn't homeless."

"Of course not, dear." Donna gave Winette a patronizing pat on the shoulder. I thought Winette was going to burst a blood vessel. Her face was bright red and her lips were tightened into a thin line. If Donna noticed, and I don't see how she couldn't have, she didn't comment. I waited patiently for a chance to make my escape.

"Like I was saying, I saw her in the alley just pacing back and forth. I didn't pay her any mind 'cause I've seen her do strange things before. I looked out ten minutes later and she was gone, and she never did take those cans."

"What was so strange about that?" Winette asked icily.

"I said she always came by on Thursday to get the cans. When I saw her, it was Friday morning."

"The poor thing probably just got her days mixed up, that's all. Stop being so melodramatic, Donna. You're always trying to make a big deal out of nothing," Winette said.

Donna's eyes bulged dangerously; then she gave a

smile that would have made a shark shudder.

"I know you're just upset, Winnie. Why else would you be so rude when all I came to do was give you my support and say how sorry I am for your loss? Being a Southerner just as you are, Winnie, it's the only proper thing to do. Ain't that right, Delbert?"

But Delbert was no fool. When things started heating up, he beat it across the hall to the restroom, where if he was smart, he would stay as long as possible.

I took advantage of the sudden silence and tension in the room to say my good-byes and get the hell out of Dodge.

As I walked past the room where Jordan's funeral had been, I glanced in and noticed everyone had gone. Even the casket had been removed. I spotted a flowered umbrella underneath the seat that Iris had been sitting in. It was the same one she'd arrived at the funeral with. I grabbed it so I could give it to her.

SIX

There were twice as many people at Bernie's house as there had been at the funeral. I stood in line with my paper plate, greedily eyeing the food-laden table that had been set up buffet style in the dining room. People were still bringing food. It seemed as if the doorbell was ringing every five minutes. Much to my surprise, I saw Alex—along with Joy—bringing in meat-and-cheese trays from the restaurant.

After filling my plate, I took it and went to the kitchen to eat. It, too, was filled with people. I went out back and found a spot on the low stone wall that encircled the patio to sit and eat. I was savoring some strawberry pie when a young black man came and sat down next to me. He was about eighteen and had a short Afro, a hint of a mustache over his upper lip, and a ghost of a goatee on his chin. He was dressed casually in baggy khaki Dockers, a denim shirt, and black Filas. He was grinning at me goofily as if there was some big joke that I was missing.

"Don't tell me you don't recognize me, Ms. Clayton. I was only your favorite student."

"Trevor Gibson, well isn't this a surprise," I said sarcastically. "So, where have you been all this time? Making some other teacher's life hell?"

"Aw, don't be like that, Ms. Clayton. You know you loved me. I kept you on your toes, didn't I?"

And almost made me choose another profession, I thought. "Seriously, though, how have you been? You should have just graduated from high school, right?"

"Yeah, I graduated two weeks ago. Man, I'm glad to be back. When my parents pulled me out of school here and put me in that wack private school, I didn't think I would make it. Then when my dad died last year, I told my mom I was dropping out. She told me if I stuck it out, she'd buy me a Jeep. So, here I am. Mr. High School Graduate driving a phat Jeep Cherokee."

"Are you going to college?"

"I wasn't planning on it. I was gonna go to the army. But, my mom said if I'd think about going to college, she'd take my girl and me to Jamaica for Christmas. She must really want me to go to school bad to make an offer like that. She can't stand Yvonne. She'd be happier if I'd started kickin' it with one of those stuck-up rich bitches from school."

I gave him a look that I hoped conveyed my disapproval of his term for women. He gave me a challenging look, letting me know that nothing much had changed since I last saw him. I had a feeling that Diane's desire for Trevor to go to college had more to do with keeping up with her rich friends at the country club than with wanting him to get a good education. I also had a feeling that Trevor was milking this for all it was worth. If he did something Diane didn't like, she would bribe him into doing what she wanted. I looked at him and saw the same devilish glint in his eye that I had seen when he was in my class. He knew exactly what he was doing.

A young girl who looked to be about Trevor's age came over to sit next to him and linked her arm possessively through his. She kissed him on the cheek and threw me a "this is my man" look. I almost laughed out loud.

She was brown skinned and wore shiny pink lipstick the color of cotton candy. Her hair was braided into spaghetti-thin braids that fell to her shoulders. She had a diamond stud in her nose and was wearing a short-sleeved, white satin bare midriff top with a leopard- print miniskirt and black high-heeled sandals. I vaguely wondered if there was a store at the mall called Hoochies where one could buy such clothing. Someone had neglected to tell the child that this was a post-funeral gathering and not a house party.

"This is my girl, Yvonne," Trevor said, proudly putting his arm around her. "Yvonne, this is one of my old teachers from high school, Ms. Clayton." I thought I heard an emphasis on the word *old.*

"Hi. You can call me Vonnie," she said, giving me a big grin that revealed dimples and a gap between her two front teeth.

"Why don't you go hook us up some food, girl."

"Okay, baby," said the eager-to-please Vonnie. She got up and twisted off in the direction of the kitchen. Trevor stared at her butt as if hypnotized. Diane had her work cut out for her if she was going to try and pry those two apart.

"Did you know your aunt Bernie's friend Jordan?"

"You mean my aunt Bernie's gigolo. That's what my mom called him," Trevor said casually.

Damn, there was no beating around the bush with this generation.

"Don't look at me like that, Ms. Clayton. Everybody knew what was up with that. Don't act like you didn't know."

"How well did you know him?"

"I didn't know him at all. I met him at my dad's funeral last year. He was getting his hustle on all right. I think he thought he was Denzel or somebody the way he stood around flashing those teeth when aunt Bernie wasn't around. Then acting like he was all concerned when she was around. It's crazy, man. Now here we are about to put *his* ass in the ground. That's a trip."

I couldn't have agreed more.

I made the rounds and mingled with everyone. I was looking for Iris to tell her that I had her umbrella, but I couldn't find her. I did have to agree with Diane on one account. Most of the people were openly gawking and making appreciative comments about the house. I knew there was no way all of these people could have known Jordan—or Bernie for that matter. I noticed that a long table that usually sat against the wall in the foyer underneath a large mirror had been moved in front of the marble staircase to prevent people from going upstairs.

I glanced up the staircase as I went by and noticed that the door to the guest room at the top of the stairs, where Jordan had been sleeping, was ajar. I stopped and looked again. Someone was in there.

I went around to the kitchen and went up the back stairway. I figured it must be Bernie. I hadn't had a chance to say much to her so far today and was hoping we could talk in private. There was a bench positioned across the top of the steps that had been pushed aside. I walked into the room and flipped on the light, startling the person in the room who was down on hands and knees looking under the bed. But to my surprise it wasn't Bernie. Joy Owens was looking at me with a mixture of anger and annoyance.

"I was looking for the bathroom," she said belligerently before I had a chance to say a word.

"And you think it's under the bed?"

She stood slowly, all the while glaring at me. For a split second I almost felt guilty for walking in on her.

"How the hell should I know where it is in this big-ass house?"

"Big-ass house or not, I don't know anybody who has a bathroom under a bed. What are you really doing in here?"

"I said I was looking for the bathroom. My earring popped off when I walked in, and I thought the back rolled under the bed. Not that I owe you an explanation. This ain't your house."

"There's a bathroom downstairs off the kitchen."

"Whatever," she said, brushing past me on her way out of the room. I looked at her ears as she passed me and noticed that she wasn't wearing any earrings.

"Oh, and Joy," I said, turning around to catch her before she got out the door.

"What!"

"If anything in this room turns up missing, I think we'll know who to come looking for."

"Fuck you," she said and was gone. What a charming girl.

I looked around the room for the first time. Despite having gone to stay with Diane, Bernie had managed to find the time to clean it up. Not only was the room now spotless, but also every trace of Jordan had been removed. All of the clothes and shoes that had been scattered all over the room were gone. I walked over to the closet and opened it. It, too, was empty, as were all of the dresser drawers. Out of curiosity, I looked under the bed. Nothing. I wondered if I should tell Bernie about catching Joy in here and then decided against it. I figured there was no real harm done.

After coming back downstairs, I finally spotted Iris. She was standing by the buffet table talking to Miguel Ruiz, the literacy center's English-as-a-second-language instructor. Miguel is from Mexico and reminds me a little of Benjamin Bratt. He taught high school Spanish by day and English at the center three nights a week. He was looking sexy as ever in his black jeans and white shirt. He'd loosened his tie and was holding a food-laden plate, which he kept looking at longingly while Iris chatted. She was practically in the poor man's face and had seriously invaded his personal space by at least an inch.

Everyone at the center knows what a big crush Iris has on Miguel. But then again, most women at the center have had a crush on Miguel at one time or another, myself included. Iris's crush is one of the more enduring ones. Even though Miguel is newly married, Iris is still hoping that one day he'll come to his senses and fall in love with her.

"Hola, Kendra," said a relieved-looking Miguel

after spotting me. I felt for the man. Iris is as sweet as she can be and a very efficient secretary, but having a conversation with her can be a trying experience. She has no tact and is not afraid to talk about anything. I still remembered her cornering me at last year's Christmas party and talking to me for almost an hour about the consistency of her dog Cupcake's bowel movements before and after being dewormed. I felt then the way Miguel was looking right about now, queasy.

"Hey, you two. What's up?"

"Oh, Kendra, I was just telling Miguel about my awful bout with stomach flu. I thought I would just die. I mean the way it kept running out both ends of me. It was so draining. Just when I thought I had nothing left in me, here would come another onslaught. Poor Cupcake didn't know what to think. I'm sure she thought her mommy would never get well."

"Miguel, I think your wife is looking for you," I said, looking him in the eye.

"Thanks for telling me." He gave me a relieved, knowing look and took his plate and what was left of his appetite and rushed out of the room.

Iris watched him go with longing. I decided I better get straight to the point before she started telling me about her recent illness. I'd already eaten, which would make the story even worse.

"Iris, I'm glad I caught you. You left your umbrella

at the funeral home. I brought it with me. It's out in my car."

"Oh, I didn't even realize I'd left it! It's not even mine. It's Bernie's umbrella. This is the very reason I can never keep an umbrella. I'm always leaving them someplace." Iris's face had reddened, giving her a rare burst of color.

"I'm sure you just forgot because it didn't belong to you, and you weren't used to having it. I always do that when I borrow stuff from other people. It's a wonder anyone will lend me anything anymore."

"I didn't borrow it. Bernie left it in my car last Friday. You know how Dorothy gets this time of year. She was ranting and raving because someone forgot to go pick up the programs from the printer. I wasn't feeling well. If it hadn't been for the recognition program, I wouldn't have even come in that day. Bernie was such a sweetheart. She piped right up and offered to go pick them up for me. I let her use my car because she didn't have hers that day. Wasn't that sweet of her?"

Warning bells were going off in my head. The blood was pounding so hard in my ears that I almost couldn't hear.

"Yeah, that was really nice of her. You remember about what time that was?" I asked breathlessly.

"It was during the morning session. Maybe around nine o'clock. I don't think it was much after I got to work that morning," she said, her brow creased in concentration. "I don't remember exactly. Why?" She was looking at me strangely. "Kendra, are you okay? I hope you're not coming down with what I had because, let me tell you, it was no fun. I..."

I politely stood and listened to Iris tell me about the dirty details of her illness. I probably would have thrown up if I'd been focusing on what she was saying and didn't have other things on my mind. Bernie had been away from the center around the time of Jordan's death. She never even mentioned it to me. I wondered if anyone else knew. Dorothy probably thought Iris went to pick up the programs. It had been a madhouse last Friday. It wouldn't have been hard to slip away unnoticed.

"Do you remember what time she came back?" I asked, interrupting Iris.

She looked at me for a few seconds. "No, not really. I mean, I was in the gym helping set up tables and chairs. You were there yourself, Kendra, remember? When I got back to my desk to go to lunch at eleven thirty, my car keys and the programs were on my desk. Not that I was very hungry. I was in and out of the bathroom every five minutes. I didn't come back after lunch. Just between you and me," she said, leaning close to me, "Dorothy said she understood about me being sick, but she's been acting funny toward me ever since I came back to work. She was telling me about that awful sub that worked for me. You'd have thought it was my fault the woman was so horrible the way she's acting."

"Iris, did the police talk to you?" I asked, then wished I hadn't when I saw the shocked look on her face.

"The police! Good God, no! Why would they want to talk to me?" Her cheeks were positively flaming. I didn't think she had that much color in her.

"No reason, Iris. I just wondered with all that's happened with Bernie if maybe they talked to anyone else at the center." I wasn't doing a very good job of cleaning it up. But Iris seemed to buy it. Her normal sallow color was returning.

I excused myself and went to look for Bernie. I found her in the kitchen talking to Diane. Diane was wearing a black Ann Taylor coatdress that surprisingly came to her knees, instead of two or three inches above, and a beautiful triple-strand pearl choker with a diamond clasp in the shape of a butterfly. Her hair was pulled back into a ponytail with a mother-of-pearl barrette. She and Bernie were standing with their backs to me and didn't see me when I came in.

"This isn't the time, Diane. We can talk about this later. The business isn't going anywhere. It'll still be here when I get back," Bernie said with a sigh. She sounded pissed.

"Well, we need to get this taken care of pretty soon, Bernie. They're not going to wait around forever. We'd be fools not to take them up on this offer. You've never had any interest in Gibson Realty. I can't understand why you're dragging your feet on this."

Bernie spun toward Diane to give an angry reply and spotted me in the process. Diane also turned and they both gave me an annoyed look. Between the two of them and Joy, I was really starting to get a complex.

Without even speaking to me, Diane announced that she had to find Trevor and his tramp and left the room in a wake of Opium perfume.

"I seem to be developing a talent for coming in at the wrong time."

"No, actually you saved me from giving that bitch a piece of my mind. I knew she had a reason for wanting me to stay with her that didn't have anything to do with wanting to be there for me and all that other bullshit she's been feeding me."

"I wondered about that myself," I said, slightly amused at the fact that Bernie was turning into such a potty mouth. Or maybe I was just seeing the real Bernie.

"We've had an offer from a larger real estate company in Columbus to buy Gibson Realty. Diane and I are co-owners. Neither of us can sell without the other's consent. I'm not ready to give mine yet, and Diane's been bugging the hell out of me for days to sign the papers."

"You thinking about selling real estate?"

"No, not at all. It's just that it's the only thing I have left of my mother and brother. They both loved that business and put so much of themselves into it. It's not going to be easy to let it go. I can't seem to get Diane to understand that."

"Diane's never struck me as being the sentimental type," I said. Knowing Diane, she was probably mentally calculating how many little short tight skirts she could buy with the money.

"Didn't Ben leave her provided for? Why's she so hot to sell the business?"

"Ben left Diane more than enough to live on. But Diane's always been foolish with money. Most of it goes on her back or to spoil that rotten nephew of mine. You should see the Jeep she just bought that boy. If I were him, I wouldn't want to go to college either. Why should he when his mama will buy him anything he wants?"

"I overheard you say 'when I get back.' Are you going somewhere?"

"A college friend invited me to visit her in Seattle. I was thinking about going just as soon as this business with Jordan's murder is wrapped up. I just hope and pray it's soon."

This was the most Bernie had talked to me in days. I knew I had to bring up the umbrella but I hated to. It almost seemed like old times for a minute. I decided it was now or never.

"Iris wanted me to return your umbrella to you. She said you left it in her car last Friday when you used it." I held my breath and watched closely, praying that any expression or reaction might give me the slightest clue. I was disappointed. She looked right back at me completely unfazed.

"No big deal. I have plenty of umbrellas. I didn't even miss it." We stared each other down for what seemed like an eternity. Bernie looked away first.

"I hope you didn't think I was going break down and confess, did you?"

"I didn't—" I began. She held up her hand and stopped me.

"Before you even ask. Yes, I used Iris's car to go pick up the programs at the printer's. Yes, I drove past the house on Archer. Yes, my car was parked outside. No, I didn't stop. No, I didn't kill Jordan." She crossed her arms and stared at me with a self-righteous look that I wanted to slap off her face. If she was hoping I felt stupid, she'd be disappointed. I had a right to know, a right that was given to me when she asked me to go along with a lie. Instead of slinking off embarrassed, I asked, "Why didn't you stop?"

"Because I thought or hoped he was there telling Vanessa it was over between them and that he and I were getting married. I gave him an ultimatum: either give up his chick on the side or get the hell out of my house. That's why he moved into the guest bedroom. He sulked around the house for a few weeks acting like a man falsely accused. Then a couple of days before he died, he did a complete turnaround.

He was really nice to me and he apologized. Said we should get married. I told him he'd have to tell Vanessa 'cause that was the only way I'd believe he was sincere."

I didn't have the heart to suggest that maybe his needing to use her car had something to do with his turnaround. "Did he say he was going to tell her that morning?"

"No, he just said he'd see me later that night at the recognition program. I didn't plan on going past the house that morning. I just ended up there. When I saw my car parked in front of the house, I was hoping against hope that he was breaking things off with her."

"That's why you didn't want to leave Friday after the recognition program?" I asked.

She nodded.

"I was so sure he'd show up. I guess when he didn't, I just couldn't believe he'd lied. How do you think I feel knowing that when I drove by he was either already dead or being murdered?" Her eyes were filled with tears that were threatening to spill.

I was always amazed at Bernie's capacity to love a man who'd treated her the way Jordan had. I knew love caused people to do strange things. I just hoped that it was really love that had caused Bernie to act the way she had after the recognition program and not guilt. As mad as I'd been at her for the past couple of days, I couldn't help but feel sorry for her. I hated to see her so miserable.

"Hey, I know something that might cheer us both up," I said, putting my arm around her shoulders and giving them a squeeze. "Let's go out and get a drink later, okay."

"Yeah, let's go to the Spot," she said, perking up considerably.

My heart sank. The Spot was a local watering hole called the Spotlight Bar and Grill. The Spot had been an institution in Willow since before my parents were born. It was located in a seedy little building that wasn't much bigger than my apartment. I'd only ever been there once—with Bernie when we first became friends. I hadn't been impressed with the expensive, watered-down drinks and all the cigarette smoke. I'd vowed that it would be my last visit. But, I could stand it just this once if it would cheer Bernie up. Famous last words.

I met Bernie at the Spot a few hours later. I was still in my funeral clothes, but Bernie had changed into a gold Capri pantsuit. I felt dowdy by comparison in my black skirt and gray silk blouse. When we opened the door, we were greeted by a thick cloud of cigarette smoke and loud laughter. Marvin Gaye's "Got to Give It Up" was blasting from an ancient jukebox in the corner. It was crowded and we had to squeeze our way up to the bar. There was no place to sit, and after paying for our drinks we stood by the bar sipping them. We practically had to scream at each other in order to have a conversation. My eyes were watering and my throat was getting scratchy from all the smoke, but Bernie looked like she was having the time of her life, bobbing her head to the music. She gulped down the last of her drink and grabbed me by the arm, pulling me toward a small table by the bar that had just been vacated. It felt good to sit down, and I slipped my pumps off under the table and looked around.

The Spot attracted a very diverse clientele. Aging players trying to mack and party girls who looked like they'd stayed at the party too long were elbow to elbow with Spandex-encased sweet young things looking for their next baby daddy and junior thugs doing their best to look and act hard.

"Damn, it's good to get out. I've felt like a prisoner all week long," Bernie said, smiling and looking more relaxed than I'd seen her since before Jordan's murder. I noticed that everybody was looking at us and figured they were wondering if a murder was in their midst. Thankfully, Bernie didn't seem to notice the attention we were attracting.

"I'm glad you're having fun. If you want, we can go to some other places too," I said hopefully.

"Oh this is just fine, Kendra. This is just what I

needed." Great, it appeared I was stuck there for the evening.

I excused myself and went to stand in the long line to use the one dingy little restroom that was for both men and women. When I got back to our table, about twenty minutes later, Bernie had been joined by a chubby, orange-suited, gold-chain-wearing man with processed hair who looked about her age. The two of them were laughing like they were old friends, so I figured they must know each other.

"Kendra, this is Lewis Watts," Bernie said, introducing us. I shook Lewis's hand and sat down.

"What'll you two beautiful ladies have to drink? I'm buying," Lewis asked us, although he was staring at Bernie the whole time.

"I'll have a whisky sour," said Bernie.

"Rum and Coke," I said. As Lewis headed up to the bar, I noticed he wasn't much taller than the garden gnome in Mama's backyard.

"It's nice you ran into a friend," I commented to Bernie.

"Girl, I just met him five minutes ago. He's sharp, isn't he? I've always been a sucker for a man who knows how to dress."

She couldn’t be serious. Sharp? The man looked like a pumpkin with a perm. I was starting to get an uneasy feeling. Bernie had just buried her fiancé. The last thing she needed was to get caught up with some new man. Before I could comment, Lewis was back with our drinks.

"That was quick," said Bernie, beaming at Lewis.

"I spend a lot of money in this joint, baby doll. They know they better serve me quick if they want to keep me coming back," he said smugly.

"So, Lewis, what do you do for a living?" I asked, trying to make conversation.

"I'm on disability. Got a bad back. But don't worry. It don't keep me from handlin' my bidness, if you know what I mean," he said, winking at Bernie who giggled like a schoolgirl.

Talk about too much information. It occurred to me that all this time I had been wondering how a woman as nice as Bernie could become involved with a man like Jordan. She wasn't just a sucker for well-dressed men. Now I knew that Bernie was just a sucker for any man who showed her the slightest bit of attention. I watched her for the next hour as she flirted and acted like a bubblehead.

We listened as Lewis told us how all he needed was a good woman to take care of him and how he was worth it because he was a good man. Bernie was mesmerized. I could almost see the wedding bells in her eyes. At one point, I bent under the table to retrieve one of my pumps and saw that Lewis's big meaty hand was massaging Bernie's knee. Bernie didn't appear to have learned any lesson from the whole Jordan fiasco. I had to get her out of there before she ended up engaged to this fool too.

It didn't take much effort on my part, as I was starting to feel queasy. I'm not much of a drinker, and the drinks I'd had were not mixing well with all the food I'd eaten after the funeral. Plus, all the secondhand smoke I was inhaling made me feel like I was about to toss my cookies in Lewis's lap.

"Ooh, Kendra, you don't look so hot. Are you all right?" Bernie asked, rubbing my back.

I was afraid to open my mouth, so I just shook my head no. Bernie gently pulled me to my feet.

"Lewis, it was nice meeting you, but I better take Kendra home. You take care and thanks for the drinks."

Lewis gave Bernie a big grin and told us to have a nice evening. However, when I waved good-bye to him, he glared at me like I'd farted in church. By the time Bernie got me to the door, I looked back and saw that Lewis had wasted no time in scouting a new conquest and was now grinning at a well-preserved matron holding court at the bar. Once outside, I felt the cool rush of fresh night air on my face and promptly threw up in the bushes.

SEVEN

B&S Hair Design and Nail Sculpture was packed as usual. I sat in the crowded reception area along with a dozen or so other women who were waiting for their turn to be beautified. The familiar scent of chemicals filled the air. There was a TV set mounted on the wall in a corner above the receptionist's desk. A talk show was on and those who weren't reading *Jet, Ebony,* or *Essence* were watching Nadine tell her husband Earl how she wasn't sure their daughter Misty was his child. The topic of this particular show was "I've Got Something to Tell You." It should have been called "I Want to Humiliate Myself and Loved Ones on National TV."

Curtained doorways flanked opposite sides of the reception area. Through the black-curtained doorway to the left was the hair salon run by Bruce Robins, Gwen's nephew. Through the silver-curtained doorway to the right was the nail salon run by Bruce's wife Sheila. My nails were what had brought me to the shop on a dreary Friday afternoon. I wanted a manicure for my date with Carl Brumfield later that night. At least that was the official reason. I really wanted to talk to Natasha Woods about the woman she'd seen Jordan arguing with. Since Natasha hadn't yet built up a clientele, it wasn't hard to get a last-minute appointment.

As I sat there pondering just how I could get Natasha to tell me what she'd seen, the curtain to the hair salon parted and out stepped Bruce Robins with his fine self. I couldn't help but notice the almost audible crackle of electricity as every woman in the room took notice of Bruce. He was dressed casually in faded jeans and a black T-shirt. Even his feet, which were shod in leather sandals, looked good. Bruce always looked like he needed a shave. On most men that would have been real raggedy. On Bruce it was sexy as hell. I've actually known more attractive men, but Bruce exuded a charm and sensuality that made every woman who sat down in his chair feel as if he were all theirs—that is as long as they were getting their heads worked on.

He spotted me and frowned slightly.

"Didn't I just cut you?" he asked, running a caressing hand over my hair. Warmth spread through my body that made me feel very needy. He had indeed cut my hair a week earlier, the day before the recognition program.

"I won't be visiting your side today. I need to get my nails done."

"Really, I didn't think you were into nails. You've never struck me as the two-inch-long-nails-with-glitter type," he said, sitting down next to me.

"You're right about that. I'm not up for the care and feeding of any nail tips just yet. A simple French manicure will do for now."

"Who's your appointment with?"

"Natasha Woods."

"Tasha's cool," he said, running a hand over his scruff. "She likes to run her mouth a little too much, but Sheila says she's good."

That's just what I wanted to hear. I wanted her to run her mouth, the more the better. Five minutes after Bruce led his next appointment away, a heavyset girl came through the silver curtains and called my name. I walked back just as a tearful Earl was telling Nadine that he'd always suspected Misty wasn't his child and this suspicion had lead him to an affair with Nadine's mother, Wilma. Whoever had coined the phrase the truth is stranger than fiction had unknowingly predicted TV talk shows of the future.

Natasha gestured me toward the table in her booth and sat down on the other side.

"So what we doin' today?" she asked and looked very put out when I told her that all I wanted was a

French manicure. "We're runnin' a special on acrylic nails this week," she said hopefully.

She finally got to work on my nails after I explained that I was a simple woman who didn't live an acrylic-nails lifestyle. Simply translated, this meant that I was too poor and too lazy to be bothered with my nails on a regular basis. As long as they were clean and trimmed, I was happy. Besides, I'd rather spend my money on the other luxuries in life like food and shelter. She seemed a little put out but she'd get over it.

Her own nails were about three inches long and were painted metallic silver with black zigzagging stripes. They matched the silver smock that she and the other nail technicians wore. Her hair was styled in a French roll that was almost conical with long tendrils that framed her face and hung almost to her shoulders. The tendrils were dyed blond and looked a little strange in contrast to her dark brown hair. I noticed a gap between her two front teeth, making her look like someone else I'd met recently.

"Do you have a sister named Yvonne?"

"Yeah, you know my baby sister Vonnie?" She was grinning now. I'd obviously been forgiven for my lack of nail ambition.

"She goes with a friend of mine's nephew, Trevor Gibson. I met her yesterday."

"Yep, that's Vonnie. Wherever Trevor is, Vonnie ain't too far behind. I told that girl she needs to chill as far as that boy's concerned and start thinking about her future. Trevor Gibson's gonna go off to college or the service and leave her butt behind. You know how kids are; they don't listen to nobody."

I thought this was funny seeing as how she didn't look much more than twenty herself.

"You must not like Trevor."

"He's all right. It's his mom I can't stand. Girlfriend be trippin'. Can't stand Vonnie. Doesn't think she's good enough for her son. Trevor don't take up for her the way he should. And I can't stand for anybody to be messin' with my little sister."

I knew she meant what she said because she got a little too carried away with the orange stick she was using to push back my cuticles and stabbed me.

"Ouch!"

"Oh, I'm so sorry," she said, looking around quickly to make sure no one was watching as she rubbed my finger. I wasn't bleeding, so I assured her it was okay.

"How does she mess with her?"

"Real stupid shit. She'll lie and say Trevor ain't home whenever Vonnie stops by, like she can't see his car parked in the driveway. Won't give him messages. Vonnie sometimes leaves notes in the mailbox that he never gets. But last week Vonnie came home cryin' 'cause his mom made some tacky-ass comment about making sure she don't get pregnant 'cause there won't be any money in it for her. Like Vonnie's just some hoochie lookin' to get paid. I was ready to go tell that bitch off, but Vonnie didn't want me say nothin', so I left her alone."

"That's a shame," I offered for lack of anything better to say. Though I couldn't figure out which was more the shame—Diane's treatment of Vonnie or Vonnie pinning her hopes on the likes of Trevor. I wondered how fast he'd kick her to the curb if Diane made it worth his while.

The conversation was starting off in the right direction. I just had to figure out how to bring up the subject of Jordan and his mystery woman. As it turned out, I didn't have to.

"Vonnie told me she was at Trevor's aunt's house after the funeral of that man who got killed. I told her she didn't need to be going over there until they catch who did it. Now that's some scary shit."

"Meaning?"

"Well, everybody keeps saying either that white woman did it or Trevor's aunt. But I wouldn't be surprised if all three of them ganged up on his ass and killed him."

"All three of them?" I said, feigning ignorance. I was about to hit pay dirt.

"Yeah, girl. There was a third woman. I saw him arguing with her myself."

"Damn. Did you know who she was or hear what they were arguing about?" I asked casually.

"Naw, they were too far away to hear what they were saying. I saw them twice. The first time I didn't see her face, but the second time I saw it for just a second."

"Did you recognize her?" I asked.

"I had never seen her before then. But yesterday I saw her in that restaurant over by the college."

"You mean Estelle's?"

"Yeah, that's it. I saw her in there."

"Really, was she eating alone?" I had to calm down a bit because I was rapidly losing my nonchalant demeanor. I didn't want her to know that I had any other interest in her answer other than simple nosiness. But Natasha had a willing audience in me and didn't seem to be at all curious about my interest in the so-called third woman.

"When's the last time you had your nails done?" She was looking at my nails with a frown as she continued to work on my cuticles.

"Ten years ago for the prom. I wonder whether she had anything to do with the murder?" I needed to steer her back to the topic at hand.

"Who? Oh yeah, that other chick. Could be. She sure looked and acted mean enough to kill somebody. I was ready to kill her myself by the time I left that restaurant. If it weren't for the fact that they got da bomb potato skins, I wouldn't have gone back. I even complained to the owner and he gave me a free dessert, cheesecake. It was good too."

"What?" I was a little confused. "You mean the woman who you saw works at Estelle's?"

"Yeah, little runty-lookin' hostess with burgundy-tinted hair. Pissed me off. She kept seating people ahead of us who hadn't been waiting half as long as we had. Then when we finally got called she didn't even speak to us. Wouldn't say hi, bye, kiss my ass, or nothin'. We barely got up from the waiting area before she started walking back to the table. Didn't bring any menus. We had to finally go up and get our own."

Joy Owens. I couldn't believe it! What in the world could she have been arguing with Jordan about? I wouldn't have thought they even knew each other. Could they have been seeing each other? I just couldn't picture it. I doubted Joy was ever pleasant enough for anyone to want to get close to her, except to slap her, of course. But she had been snooping around in Bernie's house. What had she been looking for? I also wondered how many free desserts Alex had given away because of Joy, and why was he so hell-bent on keeping her on at the restaurant.

"Were they arguing both times you saw them?"

Natasha stopped what she was doing a second and thought about it. "I think so," she said finally. "The first time I saw them they were just talking in that little park over by the college. Like I said, I didn't see her face that time. I recognized her the second time by her hair.

Don't nobody dye their hair that played-out color no more," she said in disgust. I left the shop a half hour later with a fresh new manicure and more questions than I had when I came.

Seven o'clock rolled around fast. It had taken me forever to decide on what to wear. The rain of the previous couple of days had made it muggy out. Nothing looks less appealing than trying to look cute while sweating like a pig. I finally decided on a long sleeveless batik- print cotton dress in shades of olive green, cream, and gold. The long loose style hid a multitude of sins and made me look almost svelte. Almost. Chunky-heeled leather mules and gold jewelry completed the look. I had just sprayed on my favorite vanilla-scented perfume when there was a knock at the door.

Carl had obviously taken the muggy heat into consideration as well. He looked very cool in a thin gauzy white shirt worn untucked over casual black slacks. I caught the same familiar scent of Obsession for Men worn just heavy enough for me to catch a subtle whiff when he moved.

"You look good," he said. "Smell good too."

"Thanks. You too. Did you have any trouble finding the house?"

"Not really. Is the woman downstairs your landlady?"

"You met Mrs. Carson?"

"I knocked on the door downstairs by mistake. She seems like a nice lady. I actually got here ten minutes ago, but she got to telling me about her high blood pressure, and I had a hard time getting away."

"Yeah, she's a talker all right. I used to think she was just lonely when I first moved here. But her family's over here all the time."

High blood pressure my ass. She just wanted to get a good look at my date. As we walked down my steps to Carl's car, I glanced in Mrs. Carson's window and saw that she was on her phone. I figured she had probably called Mama and was giving her the lowdown on Carl. I knew I was in for a lecture about dating a still-married man, not to mention a man who had a link to Jordan's murder. There was always the off chance that neither one of them would realize who he was. However, I was never that lucky when it came to those two.

Mama and her good friend Annie Ruth Carson were like an information-gathering tag team when it came to any event or anybody they felt they needed to know about. Mama could always be counted on for the well-placed phone calls here and there, while Mrs. Carson's contribution was the latest beauty shop and church gossip. It always got them the desired results. I was doomed.

The fifteen-minute drive to Springfield was a fairly

quiet one. Carl and I made small talk about the weather and our jobs. I wanted to wait until later before I brought up the subject of Vanessa. Good food and drinks in a relaxed setting had a way of loosening the tongue. I couldn't help but notice the skeptical look on Carl's face as we pulled into the crowded parking lot. Both the neighborhood and the outside of the restaurant left much to be desired.

"I know it doesn't look like much," I told him as we walked toward the two-story redwood building that resembled a barn, "but you won't be sorry."

"I'm not hard to please. As long as I can get a good steak, I'll be happy," he said, holding the door open for me.

"Not bad," he said, looking around the restaurant in surprised admiration after we'd been seated. Upon entering the restaurant, most people were immediately struck by the contrast between its relaxed understated elegance and the ordinary, almost seedy, neighborhood.

Carl ordered New York strip with mushroom sauce, and I ordered the stuffed pork chops. Once our orders had been placed, he sat back in his chair and looked at me with that killer smile.

"All right, I want to know all about you, Kendra Clayton, and don't hold anything back."

"Well, I don't tell anybody everything," I said teasingly, "So I'll give you the condensed version." There wasn't much to tell, but I would never let him in on the fact that my life, thus far, had been as uneventful as a car wash on a rainy day.

"I was born and raised in Willow. I'm twenty-eight years old and the oldest daughter of Ken and Deidra Clayton. Get it, Ken and Deidra? My name is a combination of my parents' names. Cute, huh? Anyway, I'm big sister to twenty-five-year-old Allegra, the aspiring actress-model-singer." Or whatever else will allow her to do what she does best, which is being the center of attention. I didn't bother to tell Carl that because it would just sound like sour grapes, which it is. Just a little.

I've always been a little jealous of Allegra for having the guts to take off for L.A. right after high school with little more than bus fare and her dreams. We all thought she'd be back in a week with her tail between her legs. We were wrong. She's been in Los Angeles for seven years now. She still hasn't gotten her big break. However, she's managed to support herself with little help from the rest of the family. Thus far her professional work has consisted of magazine ads for toothpaste and feminine-hygiene products, being the object of a homely singer's desire in a music video, and as a dead-on-arrival accident victim on an episode of *ER.* That combined with her full-time job as an interior decorator's assistant has kept her going.

I finished telling Carl about myself, which took all of two minutes, and listened as he told me about himself.

"Not much to tell. I'm thirty-two and the only son of Charles and Martha Brumfield. Born and raised in Columbus. Two older sisters, Anita and Monica. I graduated from Kingford College and got my law degree from the University of Dayton. I work for the Franklin County prosecutor's office. Pretty boring stuff actually."

"I wouldn't say that. What made you decide to go into law?"

"Well, I could say it was a burning desire to see justice done and to be part of the legal system. But that would be a lie. I had a degree in business management that I didn't know what I was going to do with, and my girlfriend at the time wanted to be a lawyer in the worst way. I helped her study for the LSAT and signed up to take it myself for the hell of it and—"

"Let me guess," I said, interrupting him, "you got a higher score than she did and decided to go to law school."

"Yeah," he said, grinning. "In between feeling bad for her and guilty for having done better, I was pretty damn proud of myself."

"So what happened with the girlfriend?"

"She retook the test and got a much better score. She got accepted to a school out of state. We kept in touch for a little while. But you know how long-distance relationships can be. It didn't last very long.

Absence didn't make our hearts grow fonder."

I didn't know but I nodded in commiseration anyway.

"Last I heard she was corporate attorney in the Chicago area."

"You ever thought about going into private practice?" I took a sip of my iced tea and watched Carl frown. I'd obviously hit a nerve.

"I'm sorry. I'm being nosy. I didn't mean to pry."

"No, that's a perfectly innocent question. It's just that the whole private-practice issue became a real problem between me and Nessa."

Ordinarily I would be put out at the mention of my date's ex. Not that I have a problem acknowledging the fact that anyone I go out with has had prior relationships. It's just no fun listening to a guy talk about his ex all evening. Plus, it's been my experience that the way a man talks about the women in his past, especially if he's got nothing but bad things to say, speaks volumes about the man himself.

As of that moment, I really liked Carl and I wasn't ready to start experiencing any of those infamous red flags that we women read about in all the women's magazines. Although, common sense told me that being connected to a murder should be enough to keep me away from this man. Then again, I was connected to Jordan's murder, too, no matter how reluctantly. If it weren't for this fact, I would have changed the subject real quick. Instead I put on my sympathetic face and psyched myself up to hear all about Carl and Vanessa's failed marriage.

"How so?" I asked.

"I didn't go into law to become a rich man. Don't get me wrong. Lots of money has its appeal. That's just not my main motivation. I'd like to go as far as I can and become a judge one day. I didn't grow up poor. I mean, we weren't rich, either. My dad's a high school principal and Mom's a nursing-home administrator. We weren't hurting when I was growing up. Vanessa, on the other hand, had it kind of rough as a child. Her mother died when she was ten and her father was a foreman at a truck-parts factory. Vanessa always dreamed of living in a big house out in Pine Knoll."

"So, what better way to get there than by being married to a lawyer in a lucrative private practice?"

"Of course," he said with a tight smile.

"She didn't think that a judge could put her in a house in Pine Knoll?"

"Eventually, yeah, but she didn't want to wait for that to happen, if it happened. So you can imagine how disappointed she was when she couldn't talk me into going into a more lucrative form of law."

"How'd the two of you meet?"

"We met at a fourth of July barbecue given by a mutual friend. We hit it off right away and were married within a year."

"You know I went to high school with Vanessa. We weren't friends, but I'd always heard that her father was a racist."

"You heard right. When she first told me about him I didn't take it seriously. I figured it would be no problem to win him over. I mean, I'm well-educated, professional, come from a good family. But all that didn't mean a damn thing. Denton Cox would have rather seen his daughter married to a white ax murderer than to a successful black man."

Our food came and I watched Carl dig into his steak with gusto. I took a bite of one of my pork chops and wondered if Carl had known about Vanessa and Jordan. Instead I said, "I heard Vanessa's father's dying."

"He's got prostate cancer. He doesn't have much longer."

"She must be devastated."

"She is. They were real close up until she married me. He remarried a year or so ago and his wife Edna tried to get them back together. Denton was willing to forgive and forget as long as Vanessa would admit that her marriage to me had been a mistake. She refused to do that at first. We had our differences but things weren't that bad. Then all of a sudden everything changed. One minute we were talking about having a baby, the next minute she moved out of the house and filed for divorce."

"What happened?"

"Oh, I have an idea. She won't admit to it but I know I'm right."

I waited for him to elaborate, but he had turned his attention back to his meal. The subject was closed for the time being. We ate in companionable silence for a while and then Carl asked out of the blue, "So, who do you think killed your friend's fiancé?"

For a split second I didn't know who he was talking about. I'd forgotten that Bernie and Jordan were supposedly engaged. I thought for a minute before answering. I certainly couldn't say, "I think your soon-to-be ex-wife did it." Something told me that wouldn't exactly endear me to the man sitting in front of me. Instead I played it safe.

"I don't know, Carl," I said, looking him straight in the eye. "I can only say who I think didn't do it and that's Bernie." I said it but did I really believe it?

"Did they ever figure out what he was doing there in the first place while Vanessa wasn't home?"

"I don't know. Possibly to fix something. Does Vanessa have any idea?" I asked innocently.

"Actually, the only time I saw her was at our final divorce hearing on Monday. She was late, and afterward she was in such a hurry to get back to the hospital that I didn't get a chance to talk to her."

I looked at Carl as he cut another piece of his steak. Could he really be as clueless about Vanessa's involvement as he seemed? He was living in Columbus now, so I guess it wouldn't be impossible for him not to have known. I also had to wonder why in the world Vanessa would go away for the weekend when her father didn't have much longer to live.

"It was probably some nut. Some crazy asshole that was trying to rob the place," he said casually.

I wish it were that simple, but too many things just didn't add up.

"Well, the world certainly isn't on short supply of crazy folks," I said.

"I remember when Nessa and I first started dating, she was working in a health clinic over in Dayton that performed abortions. She had to walk through a picket line of right-to-lifers every single day and some of them got pretty ugly with her. One guy in particular, some weirdo named Russ Webster, took a particular dislike to her. Followed her home from work and started harassing her. Sent her notes. She was scared to death."

"What happened?"

"She got a restraining order against him, quit the clinic, and started working at Willow Memorial. Then as quickly as he started, he just stopped. We didn't question it. Just figured he'd found someone else to bother."

"What did the notes say?" I asked, suddenly feeling very lightheaded and excited.

"Murderer, baby killer. Crap like that. It really freaked her out."

"I'll bet," I said thoughtfully.

I was wondering if I should tell Carl about the note I found at the scene of Jordan's murder. Could Russ Webster have killed Jordan, mistaking him for Vanessa? Could he have broken into the house looking for her when Jordan arrived and Webster, mistaking him for Vanessa, clobbered him as he rounded the corner? Upon discovering he'd killed the wrong person, he fled, dropping the note he had meant to leave on the body. But that didn't explain why Jordan was at Vanessa's house in the first place. Another thought came to me. Had Carl dropped this little tidbit of information in my lap hoping I'd tell the police? How far was Carl willing to go to protect a woman he obviously still cared about? Would he lie for her? Was he still in love with her? Damn. I hate red flags.

EIGHT

"You can just poke that lip back in anytime now, missy. I didn't say you should never see the man again. Just wait a while until this murder business is solved. You can never be too sure just who you're dealing with nowadays. But, then again, if you want to worry your poor grandma to death, you just go right ahead and do what you want."

Mama was in rare form today. Not even my own mother had the power to make me feel like a spoiled child, a reckless fool, and a heartless hussy all in one breath. I'd stopped by for breakfast after a night spent tossing and turning. Brought on in part by all of the questions that were still churning in my mind. It also didn't help matters that Carl and I had shared a goodnight kiss that had curled my toes and left me fantasizing about all kinds of indecent possibilities.

I turned and caught a glimpse of myself in the chrome toaster oven on the counter. My lip was indeed stuck out just like a little girl who wasn't getting her way. I straightened up quickly and told Mama about what Carl had told me about Russ Webster harassing Vanessa.

"And that's supposed to mean what exactly?" she asked with her hands on her hips.

"Well, it could mean that Jordan wasn't the intended victim after all. Maybe this Russ Webster was after Vanessa again and killed Jordan by mistake," I said hopefully.

"How'd he get into the house? I read in the newspaper that there was no sign of a break-in. So, you think Vanessa Brumfield went away for the weekend and left her door unlocked for whatever lunatic that might want to stop by? Naw, baby, I think Jordan knew the person who killed him and that person must have let him into the house."

I didn't have anything to say to that. I hadn't thought about how the killer had gotten into the house. I was too busy trying to make it all work out in my mind, because it would mean that both Bernie and Carl were in the clear.

"Who all do you think have keys to that house?"

"Bernie and Vanessa definitely have keys. Jordan used to live in the house before he moved in with Bernie. It's entirely possible that he never gave his key back to Bernie. Vanessa could have given a key to someone."

"You think Carl could have been given a key?" she asked, as she slid another pancake onto my plate and sat across from me. I doused it with syrup and took a couple of bites, catching a drop of syrup with my tongue before it dripped on my shirt.

"I don't see why he would have been," I said a little too defensively. "Most women aren't in the habit of giving a husband they've walked out on a key to their house. I wonder if maybe she left an extra key hidden outside somewhere, like under a doormat, in case a family member or friend might want to get into the house."

"Speaking of family members, didn't that man have any family? Does anybody know where he was or what he did before he came here? Seems awful strange to me that anyone would just come to Willow to live when they had no job, friends, or family here. He didn't strike me as being the small-town type."

"All I know, is he was born in Cleveland and was raised by his grandmother in Columbus. His parents are dead. If he had any brothers or sisters I don't know about them. I don't get the impression that Bernie knows any more than that herself. She always told me that Jordan was a business consultant. I have no idea what businesses he was supposed to be consulting. I always wondered why, if he was so wonderful, he wasn't consulting Gibson Realty."

Mama sucked her teeth in disgust.

"Like I've always told you and your sister, it doesn't pay to be desperate when it comes to men. If Bernie had been thinking straight instead of jumping on the first man who smiled at her a minute too long, she wouldn't have been caught up in that man's web. She turned out to be just the fool he was looking for. The man's dead, and he's still causing her heartache."

She wasn't getting any argument from me. I wondered how I could find out about Jordan's background. Jordan's obituary had said he was a graduate of Morehouse. Gwen's brother Ed was a Morehouse graduate. He was around the same age as Jordan. Ed and his wife lived in New York City. But Gwen had mentioned once that a lot of Ed's things were still stored in their mother's basement. I wondered if he had any college yearbooks. I figured it wouldn't hurt to ask. In the meantime, I wondered what Vanessa might know.

I don't know what I was hoping to accomplish by going to Willow Memorial. Bernie once mentioned that Vanessa was a rehab nurse. The plan was to find out where the rehab unit was and wander around until I ran in to her. I didn't want to think about what I'd say after that. If I thought too far ahead I'd lose my nerve.

Willow Memorial is a big, squat, gray-brick building that has always reminded me of a prison. No matter how many flowers and trees were planted around the grounds, nothing could soften the effect of the cold gray brick.

I walked into the maroon-carpeted lobby and up to a large rectangular desk. A pleasant-faced sixtyish woman, whose name tag identified her as a volunteer named Maggie, told me that the rehab unit was in five north. She gave me directions on how to get there. I walked through the hospital following the blue arrows on the walls that pointed the way to the north wing. Soon I came upon a lounge area with a TV and some well-worn plaid furniture arranged around it. There was an elderly woman leaning heavily on a cane talking to a nurse who was guiding her to one of the couches.

"You should be coming out here to the lounge every day, Mrs. Gilman. The best thing you can do after knee surgery is to maintain a normal routine. That's why we want you to get dressed every day and come out here to eat with the other patients in the dining area." I could tell by the strain in her voice that this was an old subject.

"I don't want to eat with a bunch of old people. It's depressing. Mr. Tate won't put his teeth in when he eats and Mrs. Shockly drools. And every time I come out here to watch TV, that old man in the room across from mine is watching some stupid nature show on PBS. I don't give a damn about the mating habits of the tsetse fly! I haven't seen my soaps since I got here! Why can't I have a TV in my room?"

Off to the left of the lounge area was a nurses' station where two nurses were drinking coffee and looking on in amusement. Their backs were to me, so I could get close enough to hear what they were saying without them noticing.

"I told Mary it was her turn to deal with Mrs. Gilman today. I had her yesterday," said one of the nurses.

"Vanessa sure knows how to deal with her. She's the only one who can get her to come out of her room without a fight."

"It's too bad about her father," said the other nurse.

"I know. They released him this morning. There's nothing more they can do for him. He wants to die at home. Vanessa's moving back today to help take care of him."

"I'd be moving anyway if someone was murdered in my house! Does anybody have any idea what that man was doing there when she wasn't home?"

"Well now, I could be wrong, but thought I heard something about her being involved with him. I don't know what to think anymore."

"Better not let Adamson hear you say that. He'd have a fit if—"

They both turned and saw me standing there.

"May I help you?" they both asked automatically.

"I was looking for the cafeteria. I must have gotten lost," I said, smiling.

"It's on the other side of the building. Just follow the red arrows on the wall, and they'll take you right to it."

I thanked them and left.

I was hoping to catch Vanessa over on Archer before she moved out. I made my way through the hospital maze. It seemed as if there were more volunteers and employees than patients. I had tried after my grandfather died to get Mama to volunteer at the hospital so she could get out of the house for a few hours a day. She had flatly refused. She told me that the only reason for anybody to be in a hospital is if they were a patient, a visitor, or a paid employee. Even the free lunch given to volunteers wasn't enough of an incentive for her. That had shocked me since *free* was Mama's favorite word.

Every day her mailbox is filled with free samples and coupons for stuff she has absolutely no need for. Any free offer she sees on TV or in a magazine she snaps up as if her life depends on it. Once she got a package of free condoms. When I'd sarcastically asked her what she was going to do with them, she'd said she had planned on giving them to me but figured with the sorry state of my love life I had as much need for them as she did. The sad part is she was right. Instead, for reasons I've yet to figure out, she gave them to Alex. Gwen found them and, combined with her usual paranoia, swore he'd been cheating on her. They got into a big fight and didn't speak for a month.

I walked past a woman in a white lab coat who was pushing a cart. As I walked past, she whirled and called my name.

"Kendra Clayton, I know you're not gonna just walk past me and not speak!"

Startled, I turned around to see who it was. "Gigi?"

"Who else would it be?" she said, coming toward me, arms outstretched.

We hugged and I pulled back and looked at her in astonishment. The last time I'd seen Gina Gregory, or Gigi as she's known to family and friends, had been about seven years ago after I'd graduated from college. She'd been dating a minister or so he liked to call himself. Reverend Calvin Watkins of the House of Jesus Church, which actually was an old house two doors down from the Spotlight Bar and Grill. Gigi had sported no make-up and wore skirts past her ankles. No drinking, smoking, or fornicating. But I had a hard time believing that Gigi wasn't lifting those long skirts of hers for Reverend Cal.

Then again, Gigi always did have what I like to call a tofu personality. Meaning, like tofu, she was rather bland on her own. She got all of her flavor from the men she dated. When we were in high school it was

Gerald Tate, class president and preppy freak. The boy would have probably wiped his ass with Izod toilet paper if he could.

Gigi was right by his side with a 4.0 grade point average and a preppy wardrobe of plaid pants, button-down shirts, and loafers. After high school, Gigi had followed her preppy prince to Miami University where he promptly dumped her. We kept in touch throughout college, and I got the lowdown on all her exploits.

She wasn't alone for long. Next in line was Malik Witherspoon, campus activist and president of CBS—Concerned Black Students. It was good-bye loafers and plaid, hello Birkenstocks and dreadlocks, or at least an attempt at them. Judging from the picture she sent me, she only succeeded in looking as if a dried-up baby spider plant had taken root on top of her head. After Malik, there was a brief fling with a member of the football team. But since Gigi is rhythmically challenged and not gymnastically inclined, cheerleading was out of the question. Gigi's not one to stick around if she can't stand by her man in his every endeavor.

"Where have you been?"

"We were out in California for a while. Too many damned earthquakes. We brought our butts home."

"We?"

"Man, it has been a long time, hasn't it? I've been married going on three years now. We've got a little girl eighteen months old," she said, beaming.

"That's great, Gigi! So, are you a nurse?" I asked, gesturing toward the cart.

"A med tech. I work part-time in the lab. What about you?"

We stood and gabbed for about ten minutes. The only way I could tear myself away was to promise to have lunch with her later that day. We both agreed to meet at Estelle's at one o'clock.

I headed over to catch Vanessa before she was completely moved out, and I almost lost my nerve. I parked in front of the house. The red Mustang convertible was parked in the same spot in the driveway and a brown station wagon was backed up into the driveway behind it. As I walked up the driveway, I saw that the station wagon was almost filled with clothes and boxes. The front door of the house was propped open. I noticed a piece of yellow crime-scene tape hanging from the screen. Before I could knock, a young woman carrying a CD player came rushing out. Her head was down and we almost collided.

Vanessa Brumfield hadn't changed much since high school. She still had the same lean boyish figure and the same long dark curly hair. She let out a small gasp upon looking up and seeing me but recovered quickly.

"If you've come to look at the house, you'll have to come back later. As you can see, I haven't finished moving out."

"I came to see you, Vanessa."

She looked at me hard. "You look familiar," she said finally. "Where do I know you from?"

"Springmont High, Mrs. Vance's home ec class. I'm Kendra Clayton."

"Oh, yeah, I remember now. Listen, Kendra, I don't mean to be rude, but I don't have time for a high school reunion." She walked past me to the passenger side of the station wagon and put the CD player on top of a box on the front seat.

"Actually, I came to see you about Jordan Wallace."

"What about him?" She had stopped automatically at the mention of his name, and her cheeks turned pink.

"I was wondering if he ever talked about his past at all, or if you knew anything about his background?"

"What exactly does this have to do with you? Are you a police officer?"

"No, I'm a friend of Bernice Gibson's. I thought something in Jordan's past might hold a key to his murder."

"I barely knew the man. He came over here a few times to pick up the rent and to do some minor repairs. We certainly didn't know each other well enough to have any in-depth conversations."

I guessed that rolling around in the sack didn't leave much time for intelligent, let alone coherent, conversation. I say *guessed* because it had been so long since I'd participated in the act myself that it was a hazy memory at best. I should have known Vanessa wasn't going to volunteer any information that would point to any intimacy between her and Jordan. If she wanted to play it that way, it was fine by me.

"Why don't you ask your friend what happened to Mr. Wallace?"

"She thinks you did it," I blurted before thinking.

"Me! I was out of town. I have absolutely no reason to kill anyone, let alone someone I barely knew." She looked away from me when she made that last statement. Even she had to know how thin it sounded.

"It doesn't make any sense that he came here unless he thought you were home. Your car was in the driveway, wasn't it? He must have thought you were home."

"That car has been in the driveway for three weeks now. The transmission went out, and I don't have the money to get a new one put in. I've been driving my dad's car. He won't be needing it anymore." Her eyes filled with tears, and she quickly looked away. When she looked back at me, the tears were gone, replaced by weariness.

"Look, I'll tell you the same thing I told those detectives. I don't know why he was here. The last time I saw him was on the first of the month when he came by to get the rent."

"Why did you tell me to ask Bernie what happened to Jordan?"

"Because she called me a couple of weeks ago and

told me she was putting this house up for sale and that I'd have to move out at the end of the month. When I reminded her that I'd signed a yearlong lease, she freaked out and told me she knew all about me and Jor—ah, Mr. Wallace. I told her I didn't know what she was talking about. Like I said, I had no reason to kill him, but she acted like a crazy woman that day. She probably lured him over here and killed him and set me up."

"Do you know if Jordan had a key to the house?"

"No, but Ms. Gibson does."

Before I could ask anything else, an electric-blue BMW pulled in front of the house. A short, balding, pudgy man got out and came walking up the driveway. As he got closer I could see that he was in his early thirties and was dressed in jeans, a red polo shirt, and expensive-looking cross trainers that looked too clean to have ever been worn for exercise. I also recognized him as the man I'd seen in the birthday picture on Vanessa's refrigerator. Vanessa looked momentarily panicked, and then quickly pasted a smile on her face.

"Hi, hon," he said and planted a kiss on Vanessa's cheek. "Got here as soon as I could. I got tied up at the hospital at the last minute." He gave me a curious look.

"Oh, this is Kendra, a friend of mine from high school. She just came by to look at the house. She's looking for a place to rent."

"Ted Adamson," he said, extending a hand, which I

shook.

"I guess I'll be seeing you around, Vanessa," I said with meaning.

Vanessa turned her phony smile up a notch and replied, "Just contact Ms. Gibson and I'm sure she'll answer any questions you still may have."

"Nice meeting you," I told her friend and left. I saw that Ted Adamson's car had vanity tags that read "drted." Dr. Ted. How goofy can you get? I figured that this must be the Adamson that I'd heard the nurses at the hospital talking about. I wondered if he was the reason Vanessa had left Carl. He certainly looked like a man who could buy a house in Pine Knoll. I wondered how he would handle it if he knew that his sweetheart had been sleeping with her landlady's boyfriend. Not well I'd bet. He'd take his money and run. I wondered what lengths Vanessa would go to keep her involvement with Jordan a secret.

As I drove away, a thought suddenly came to me. I pulled my car into the alley that ran between Archer Street and River Avenue and got out. I walked quickly down the alley until I got to the fence that led into the backyard of Bernie's house. The fence was high enough that anyone approaching the house from the alley would have to open the gate to see through the yard to the driveway. I pushed the gate slightly and it opened enough for me to see into the backyard. The gate that led to the backyard from the driveway was almost completely obscured by overgrown hedges. I couldn't even see the car in the driveway from where I was, which answered another question. The killer had to have figured that Vanessa was at work and had approached the house from the alley, not noticing that her car was parked in the driveway. But if the killer was Vanessa or someone she had been in cahoots with, it wouldn't matter whether there was a car in the driveway. I looked around the alley and saw that some of the other houses behind Bernie's didn't have fences as high as hers. I wondered if anyone in those houses had seen anything the morning Jordan was murdered. I knew just how I could find out. But I'd have to wait until Monday to put my plan into effect.

I went home and cleaned my apartment. I usually tried to clean it once a week, whether it needed it or not, and today it needed it—badly. I lay down on the couch afterward for a couple of hours, trying to catch up on some of the lost sleep from the night before. I dreamed that I was in the house on Archer staring down at Jordan's body. But instead of his head being all smashed and bloody, he just looked like he was sleeping. I heard a noise behind me and turned to see a person walking slowly toward me. As they came closer, I could see the person had no face. I tried to scream but couldn't. I turned to run and someone grabbed my leg. I looked down and it was Jordan. His head looked like a smashed melon, and he had a viselike grip on my leg.

I woke with a start. I'd never been prone to bad dreams. This one had been enough to last me a lifetime. I lay there a while, almost too afraid to move. My heart was hammering hard. I've always considered myself to be a pretty straight arrow when it came to obeying the law. I've never even gotten a parking ticket. But I knew the nightmare came from my guilt over lying to the police. I didn't know how much longer I could keep it to myself. After a few minutes, I calmed down and looked at the clock. I jumped up after realizing I was supposed to meet Gigi for lunch in fifteen minutes. I had just enough time to fix my hair and put lipstick on. I was never so happy to get out of my apartment.

My lunch companion was already seated when I got to Estelle's. Gwen was wearing her diva wig and had a funky look on her face. I knew something was up, so I didn't try and engage her in any small talk.

Gigi was her usual bubbly self. She'd brought a picture album with her. My bad dream was soon forgotten as we started reminiscing and going through the album. There where a lot of pictures of us from high school. Gigi and I had been acquaintances all throughout our school years. It wasn't until our senior year in high school that we became good friends. This was mainly because she tutored me in algebra and because Lynette was too busy being in love with Lamont Gaines to be a good friend to anybody.

"This is my husband, Mitch," she said, pointing to a picture of a muscular brown-skinned man with glasses and a lopsided grin.

"And this is our baby, Sasha. She'll be two this fall." Sasha had Gigi's dimples and big brown eyes and her daddy's smile.

It would be impossible not to notice how happy Gigi was to be a wife and mother. I guess she finally found an identity she could stick with. I wondered if I'd ever feel that way. Not that it mattered much at the moment. I instantly thought about Carl and wondered what kind of a father he'd be. I quickly pushed the thought out of my mind. I'd only been out with the man once and was already wondering about his potential as a father.

"So, what's your last name now?" I asked.

"Lewis, Mrs. Mitchell Lewis. What about you, Kendra? Are you seeing anyone special? I'm surprised you're not married by now."

"You sound like my grandmother. I met someone last week. We've been out once. I'd like to see him again. He just got a divorce, so he may not want to get involved again so soon."

I told her all I dared about Carl and left out the part about him being possibly linked to a murder. That wouldn't be an easy thing to gloss over. I've been known to sugarcoat the men in my life. Unemployed became he's deciding what job offer he's going to take;

chubby became he's a big guy just like I like 'em; opinionated became he's very passionate about the things he cares about. What the hell could I say about murder?

Our food came and we put away the album. I dug into my tuna melt. It was a specialty at Estelle's and my favorite thing on the menu.

"Well, it's up to you to make him want to get involved, Kendra. You've got a lot to offer. When I met Mitch, I knew he was the one, and I set out to make him see that we'd be good together. You've got to do the same thing," she said with her mouth half full of chicken salad.

"How'd you two meet?" I asked to change the subject. If there's one thing I hate, it's friends who have found love and think they're experts on romance.

"I got into an accident over in Dayton a few years ago. A woman ran a stop sign and slammed into the passenger side of my car. I was shaken up, but she was banged up pretty bad. Mitch was one of the paramedics on the scene. Those biceps and his take-charge attitude got me all hot and bothered. Girl, I was trying to faint so I could get some mouth to mouth! I slipped him one of my business cards—that's back when I was selling Amway. He called a couple of days later and the rest is history."

A paramedic. I should have known that's why she was in the medical profession. I guess she was still the same old Gigi after all. We ate in silence. I looked up after a while and saw her staring at me.

"Well, aren't you going to tell me?" she asked almost indignantly.

"Tell you what?"

"You know, Kendra, the murder. The paper said you were there. What happened?" She was practically whispering, and her eyes were glittering with anticipation.

Most people I'd encountered since the murder had had the good grace not to ask. Now, my bad dream came roaring back into focus, making me close my eyes and shudder slightly. I instantly lost my appetite for the rest of my sandwich, which isn't an easy feat when it comes to food and me.

"Kendra, I'm sorry. I'm so damned tactless at times. Mitch is always telling me my mouth is going to get me in trouble one day."

"Well, don't worry," I said, taking a sip of my iced tea and pulling myself together. "Today's not that day. You just caught me off guard, that's all."

"It's just so unreal, you know? Besides," she said with a wicked gleam in her eyes, "I know something that I bet the police don't even know."

"What?"

She looked around dramatically, making sure no one was listening. The only people sitting near us were two blue-haired old ladies having pie and coffee three booths down from us. They looked ill at ease, like they were afraid a pack of rabid college students might attack them at any moment.

"You have to promise me you won't tell anyone what I'm about to say, 'cause I could lose my job. This is confidential information. Promise me."

"I promise, Gigi, just tell me!"

"I don't know about now, but as of about a month ago, Vanessa Brumfield was pregnant."

"What!" I screeched. I almost knocked over my iced tea.

My screech coincided with a blast of music from the jukebox, shattering the peace and quiet of the restaurant. George Clinton's "Atomic Dog" thumped loudly, causing the two old ladies, who were now convinced all hell was about to break loose, to toss money on the table and scurry from the restaurant, probably vowing never to stray from Denny's again.

"Are you sure, Gigi? Did you hear this at the hospital?"

"I was the one who ran the test. Her doctor sent blood work to the lab for a bunch of tests about a month ago. One was a standard pregnancy test. It was positive. I didn't even realize it was her until I saw her in the cafeteria a few days later. I didn't know her married name until I saw her nametag. I'd just started working at the hospital. Of course she pretended like she didn't recognize me. We were in all the same college prep classes together, plus National Honor Society. I couldn't help but look at her stomach. She wasn't showing at all."

She certainly didn't look pregnant when I'd seen her earlier in the day. I was shocked but not surprised. It made a lot of sense when I thought about it. I had wondered why Vanessa would take off for a weekend to "stay with friends" when her father was so ill. Especially since they'd recently reconciled. Now I knew why. Vanessa went away to have an abortion. It made perfect sense. But whose baby was it? Jordan's, Ted Adamson's, or God forbid, Carl's? She was involved with Adamson and Jordan. Had she been involved with both men at the same time?

Had she and Carl had one last roll in the hay for old times' sake before the divorce was final? Had that been what Gwen's friend Myra had seen them arguing about? Maybe Carl had thought it meant something while Vanessa didn't. I wondered who else could have known she was pregnant. Did she go to the same abortion clinic she used to work at? Could her stalker, Russ Webster, have found out and lay in wait for her in the house and killed Jordan by mistake? That still didn't explain what Jordan was doing in the house in the first place.

"Do you happen to know how far along she was?" I asked.

"No, I don't know anything about that."

"Have you told anybody else?"

"Are you crazy? I shouldn't have told you. Just make sure this stays between us, got it?"

Gigi finished up her lunch and we made plans to get together in the future. After she left, I sat and drank another iced tea. Gwen came over and sat with me.

"This may be my last day working in this place," she said melodramatically with her arms crossed. I'd heard this statement at least a million times. Gwen gets pissed at Alex and threatens to quit. Alex sweet-talks Gwen and she stays. I wondered what had happened this time.

"What's up, Gwen?"

"Either your uncle fires that little troll or I'm outta here for real this time! I don't know why I stay here anyway. Bruce offered me a job doing nails full time at the shop. Even offered to pay for me to go to school to refresh my skills since it's been so long since I've done them professionally." Gwen had been a manicurist about twenty years ago and always acted like it had been the career of a lifetime.

"What did Joy do this time?" I should have known it had something to do with Joy.

"I have plans tonight. Tonight is Myra's niece Shelly's bachelorette party. She's getting married next weekend. Myra's rented out the party room at the Red Dragon. They're even gonna have male strippers. I got a million things to do before tonight and that little tramp decides she ain't comin' in tonight. She called and said something came up and she has things to do. That's the second time this week she's pulled this shit. Alex just shakes his head and says he'll talk to her, and then when she comes in he don't say jack to her. If I didn't know any better, I'd say something was going on between them."

I wasn't even going to touch that one.

"What time does the party start?"

"Eight o'clock."

I looked at my watch. It was almost three. "If I come back at four and work until closing, will you work Monday for me?"

"Yeah, girl. You know you can count on me. Thanks, Kendra, you're a lifesaver." She got up to greet a party of five. Her mood was greatly improved. "Oh, by the way," she said, turning back to me. "I got that graduation program of Ed's you asked me about. I'll slip it in your locker on Monday. Just make sure you give it back. Ma's real sentimental about that kinda stuff."

I'd told Gwen when I asked her earlier that I had a friend who was trying to track down someone they graduated from Morehouse with back in 1976 and needed to find the exact spelling of the guy's name. She bought it and didn't ask any questions. I left the restaurant and tried not to feel like such a sucker. I don't know why Gwen didn't just come out and ask me to work for her in the first place. It's what she wanted all along anyway. But at least I had all day Monday to stick my nose where it didn't belong.

Business had picked up a little by six. The restaurant was almost half full. Alex was in his office. He and Gwen had had an argument before she left to go get ready for the party. I'd heard muffled shouts behind the closed door. Alex hadn't come out since. I wondered if Joy was aware of all the problems she was causing. I still couldn't imagine what she and Jordan could have been arguing about. Could it have been about bad service? Did Joy treat Jordan badly when he'd come into the restaurant? Was it something a free dessert couldn't fix and when he saw her in the park, he decided to give her a piece of his mind?

By eight o'clock, the restaurant was almost empty again except for a large party of teenagers that was spending the weekend at the college for early freshman orientation. Music blaring out of the jukebox and loud laughter made it seem as if the place was bursting at the seams with customers. Business would pick up again in another week when summer session started at the college. I told one of the servers to cover for me. I went back to see if I could pry Alex out of his office to keep me company while I had my break. I got two bottles of root beer out of the big fridge in the kitchen and knocked on the office door.

"It's open," he called out.

I opened the door and walked in. Alex's office is decorated in what I like to call principal office chic. He'd gotten his big gray metal desk and hard wooden chairs when the school board had had an auction of old classroom furniture. There was even a small blackboard on the wall behind his desk with work schedules written on it. An outdated Macintosh computer sat on one corner of the desk. He refused to buy a new computer, insisting that what he had suited his needs just fine. Black plastic letter trays stacked four high sat in the opposite corner. There were two metal bookcases filled with books on accounting for small businesses, restaurant management, cookbooks, and Walter Mosley and Stephen King novels. There wasn't a speck of dust anywhere. He kept his office like he wished he could keep his life, orderly. Being involved with Gwen didn't leave much room for order. They had almost nothing in common. I figured the sex must really be good. He looked up at me, or rather peered at me, over the tops of his glasses.

"Everything okay out there?"

"Just fine." I set his root beer down on his desk. When I was a little girl, Allegra and I would spend just about every weekend with Mama and Grandpa. Alex was still living at home then. I used to wait until Allie and my grandparents were asleep and then sneak downstairs, and Alex and I would watch low-budget scary movies and eat popcorn and drink root beer.

"So, what are you doing all closed up back here?"

"Trying to put together some new specials. I was thinking maybe some new specialty salads like a cheeseburger one with ground beef and cheese with toasted-bun croutons. What do you think?" I could tell he didn't want to talk about Gwen.

"Sounds good," I lied. "You think maybe we could hire another hostess? Someone to maybe fill in when one of us can't come in. It's getting harder and harder to spread the three of us around, especially when Joy ups and decides at the last minute not to come in."

"Actually, Debbie came in and talked to me yesterday. She's pregnant and doesn't want to be a server anymore with all the heavy lifting. But she can't afford not to work. She's going to start hostessing next week."

"Did you tell Gwen?"

"Yeah, I told her. But she's not going to be happy until I fire Joy. To tell you the truth, the way I'm feeling right now, if Gwen wants to quit and join the wild wacky world of nail sculpture, then so be it. I'm tired of all the bitching," he said with the sarcasm that everyone in the family swears I've inherited from him. "Besides, it might just help our relationship if we stopped working together."

I was stunned. Not just by what he said but by the fact that he'd said it at all. Alex isn't one to confide in anyone, least of all me. He kept everything inside and dealt with it in his own way. He must really be fed up to have made a statement like that. Unless, of course, Gwen was right and there was something between Alex and Joy. I shuddered to think that there could be.

"You'd rather see Gwen quit than fire Joy?"

"It's not just Joy. There are other problems. Joy is just adding fuel to the fire."

"Are you pleased with the job Joy's doing? How many free desserts have you had to give away because of her funky attitude?"

"I'm just trying to give the kid a chance. She's had it rough. Her mother committed suicide when she was fifteen. She went to live with her aunt. But she didn't have much time for her because she was working two jobs to keep her own kids in college. When I first interviewed Joy for the hostessing job, I didn't hire her. She must have lied to her aunt and told her she got the job because her aunt called me and thanked me for giving her niece a chance. Then she told me about Joy's background, so I called her back and hired her. I don't know if I was suckered or not, but the girl has a king-size chip on her shoulder about something. She never talks about her family. So, I figured it must all be true."

Whether or not Joy's aunt had known what she was doing, I knew that she'd really struck a nerve in Alex. Alex's best friend Jessie Milton had killed himself four years ago. They'd grown up together and had even worked together at Hampton's Truck Parts. But when they'd been laid off, Alex used the opportunity to start his own business while Jessie got depressed and started drinking. He'd get jobs and then lose them because of his drinking. His wife left him and took their two boys with her. A month after she left, Jessie closed himself up in his garage and left his car running.

Alex has felt guilty ever since. He was too busy getting the restaurant off the ground to notice that his best friend was in trouble. It was especially hard on him to see how the lives of Jessie's sons had taken a wrong turn. Their mother had taken them to Detroit to live, and they'd gotten mixed up with a bad crowd. Dell, the oldest, is currently serving a five-to-fifteen-year prison term for armed robbery. His younger brother Timmy is a crack head. I knew now that hiring Joy had little to do with Joy herself and everything to do with the guilt Alex still felt over Jessie and his sons.

"Don't you think that's all the more reason for her to do a good job? You took a chance on her and look how she repays you, by offending your customers."

"I'm wondering how much longer she's going to be working here anyway. I was the one who talked to her when she called earlier. She was real excited because she was going to meet with someone who was interested in buying some of her paintings. She said if she could sell the paintings for what she was asking, then she wouldn't have to work and she'd be able to take a full load in the fall so she can graduate on time."

"Well, I hope it works out for her." I meant that sincerely. Maybe she'd be a much happier person if she was doing something she enjoyed.

NINE

Monday morning I forced myself out of bed. I've never been good at getting up when I have someplace to go. It's especially hard when I'm off on summer break and I don't have to be anywhere. What I planned on doing this morning wasn't anything I had to do, but I wanted some answers, especially since my own ass was on the line, plus, I'm just plain nosy. I figured that going out and getting them on my own was the only sure way. I took a quick shower to wake myself up, then put on cutoff jean shorts, an Ohio State T-shirt, and my Nikes. I wolfed down a bowl of Cap'n Crunch and headed out. It was a little after nine o'clock.

The first place I went was the public library. I went to the reference section and got the most recent edition of the city directory. I turned to the section in the back of the directory that listed street addresses and the names of the people who lived at each address. I made a copy of the names and addresses on River Avenue, the three hundred block that runs directly behind Archer Street. I'd worked for the company that publishes the directory one summer when I was in college. It had been a miserable job going door to door verifying information in the summer heat. Most people were nice enough. Of course there were always the few who had to be difficult. I got eaten up by mosquitoes, chased by dogs, and had doors slammed in my face. Not to mention being scared half to death by a strange man who tried to lure me into his house with a big glass of ice water. All that excitement for minimum wage was more than I could stand. After about three weeks, I quit and worked the rest of the summer baby-sitting.

I figured I could endure it again just this once. I was only planning on going to a few houses: the ones that backed up to the alley and had a view of Vanessa's backyard. I parked my car on Archer and walked around the corner to River Avenue. The house directly behind Vanessa's, 315 River Avenue, had a fence as high as hers. I doubted they'd seen anything. Besides, the residents at that address were listed as Alice and Dave Parker, a laborer and a secretary, respectively. They were probably at work that Friday morning. Both residents on either side of them were listed as being retired. Lucretia Bentley at 313 and Walter Crawley at 317.

I took my sheets of paper that I copied from the directory and put them on a clipboard along with a pen. I put on my sunglasses because the sun was pretty bright by this time, plus I figured people wouldn't notice how shifty I might look and get suspicious. I walked up the cracked front steps of 313. It didn't look like anyone was home. The house was white with black shutters and black trim around the door. The mailbox was also black with the name "Bentley" written on a piece of white tape on the lid. I rang the doorbell and heard it echo through the house. I didn't hear any movement. The curtains were shut tightly, and I couldn't see into the house.

"She ain't home," yelled a voice behind me that made me jump ten feet. I turned and saw a woman in a blue housecoat with black flip-flops and curlers. She was walking a dog that looked like a cross between a poodle and a dachshund. It was a curly-haired dog with short legs. I walked down the front steps and the dog growled at me. The woman jerked the dog's leash and it shut up but continued to stare at me like nothing would make it happier than sinking its teeth into my flesh.

"She don't bite," the woman assured me. She had a gravelly smoker's voice. I stayed where I was, not taking any chances.

"You selling something?" she asked, looking me over suspiciously.

"No, I'm with the city directory. I'm verifying

information from last year."

"Oh yeah. I guess it is about that time of year again. Well, I can tell you that Lucretia Bentley still lives here. All her information's the same as last year. She's still retired and she's still a mean old heifer. You better be glad she wasn't home. She sprayed some Jehovah's Witnesses with her garden hose last week. She don't like strangers."

I pretended to consult my list and made a check mark next to Lucretia Bentley's name. I could see my bright idea start to fizzle before my eyes. I walked over to the woman, keeping my eye on the dog.

"I can also tell you about the Parkers next door here. They're the same as last year too. Except he got a new job at GM. They're supposed to be moving in a couple of months. I'll believe that when I see it. He's been promising her a new house for ten years."

I wrote down the information on my paper. "What about 317? I have down a Walter Crawley living there."

"Nope, he's dead. Died a few months ago. He was in his nineties and senile. His son and daughter-in-law moved in with him last year to take care of him. They're still living there. I don't know much about them 'cause they ain't real friendly. He's not bad but she's real uppity. Don't never speak."

"Do you know if they're home?"

She turned and looked while the dog sniffed my shoe and started barking. It probably knew I was a fraud. The woman jerked on the leash again. "There's a car in the driveway. I guess someone's home."

"Thanks a lot. Do you live on this street?"

"Yeah, Josephine Cooper, 322. All my information's the same too."

"Wasn't it awful about that man who got killed around the corner?" I asked for the hell of it.

"Sure was," she said, shaking her head.

"I was out walking Lady here that morning before it happened. I saw that white girl that lives there. Looked like she was leaving for a trip. Had a little suitcase with her. Got picked up by some woman. Course we all knew what that brother was doing over there with her. He was working on her plumbing," she said with a smirk and a wink. "I bet he surprised a burglar or something."

Or something, I thought. I thanked her and watched her drag her little mutt down the street. I walked up the driveway of 317. There was a late-model Buick in the driveway. The yard was very neat with an immaculate lawn and pink-and-white impatiens by the front door.

The small ranch house was brick in the front with white siding everywhere else. The front door was open. I looked through the screen door, which had a small tear in it, and rang the doorbell. When I saw who came to the door I almost fainted. It was Delbert Ivory, Donna's henpecked husband. He came to the door and squinted at me through the screen. When he realized it was me, I thought he might pass out.

"Mr. Ivory, what a surprise," I exclaimed. I was trying to figure out how I was going to play this off. He was the last person I was expecting to see. I prayed his wife wasn't home.

"Hi there, young lady," he said nervously. He opened up the screen door and looked up and down the street quickly.

"What can I do for you?"

"I'm working for the city directory this summer and I need to verify information for this address." I figured why ruin a good excuse.

"Is Walter Crawley at home?"

"He was my stepfather, and he passed away back in March. Donna and me live here now. He left the house to us. Would you like to come in?" He had regained his composure and had a sly gleam in his eye. I knew instantly that his wife wasn't at home.

"Sure, I'd like that." I stepped into a small living room, which was crowded with furniture. A big brown tweed couch took up most of the wall facing the door. A piano sat under the front picture window that looked over the front yard. The top of it was covered in family pictures. The wooden cross on the wall over the couch and the various ceramic figurines of Jesus and praying hands told me that this was a Christian home, even if the look Mr. Ivory was giving me wasn't very chaste. He gestured me toward a beige recliner that had a plastic cover on it. It made an obscene noise when I sat down.

"Now what was it you needed to know, sweetheart?" He sat down on the couch. He had directed the question at my legs.

"I just need to update information for this address. I had no idea that you and Mrs. Ivory weren't still living over on Harvey Street." Actually, Mama had probably mentioned it at some point, but the information was too useless for my brain to retain.

"We been here almost a year now. The house over on Harvey just got to be too much for us since the twins left home."

The twins were Donella and Donte, the Ivory's grandchildren who they raised after their daughter Donetta died of leukemia when the twins were nine. My mother had gone to school with Donetta. After a childhood and adolescence spent in strict religious upbringing, Donetta had gone to college at Kent State and had taken the sixties "free love" experience to the limit. According to my mother, Donetta had no idea who the twins' father was, a fact that Donna Ivory would rather cut off her arm than admit to. She told everyone that Donetta was married and that her husband was killed in the Vietnam War. Rumor had it, Donetta was told to go along with Donna's lie if she wanted any financial assistance from her parents.

I went to school with the twins. I've always been

amazed at how they had each taken on the exact characteristics of their grandparents. Donte was a loud, bossy, know-it-all just like his grandmother. He had a crush on me all throughout high school and had harassed me almost daily about my breast size. When I got an after- school job at the public library as a page, I caught him stealing the "Beauty of the Week" photos out of the *Jet* magazines and threatened to tell his grandmother. He left me alone after that.

Donella, on the other hand, was as meek and mild as her grandfather, but I knew she had a secret side that few people were aware of. I'd had a feeling right around the time we'd graduated from high school that Donella was messing around with one of the married deacons at the church, a fact no one would believe until she turned up pregnant. The baby's father was never mentioned. Instead, she was shipped off to relatives down South, and the baby was put up for adoption. Last I'd heard, she'd joined some strange cult out West.

"How are the twins? I haven't seen them in years."

"Donte's a minister up in Cleveland. He's married with two kids. Donella, well, we pray for her. That's about all we can do. I just hope she'll come to her senses and come home one day." He started grinning at me with his big white dentures and leaned closer.

"So, why is it that a pretty young lady like yourself isn't married yet? The young men 'round here must be blind."

I was more than willing to go along with that assessment. "The Lord hasn't blessed me with a mate yet like he has you, Mr. Ivory. How long have you and Mrs. Ivory been married?"

"Forty-nine years," he said with a grimace. I got the feeling that he wasn't feeling very blessed.

"You know, Mr. Ivory, I'm just thankful to be alive from day to day. You just never know what might happen to you. Like that Jordan Wallace who was murdered last week. That happened just around the corner and no one saw a thing."

"I know just what you mean. The police came 'round here after it happened. But Donna and I didn't see anything out of the ordinary that morning."

"I'm a little thirsty. Could I please have a glass of water?" I wanted to get a look at the kitchen window to see what kind of view it offered of the alley.

I followed Mr. Ivory into the kitchen. It was decorated with seventies-green appliances with bright yellow countertops. We'd had a similar kitchen when I was growing up. I was suddenly transported to the days of eating Trix cereal on Saturday mornings while watching *Scooby Doo* and *Josie and the Pussycats* on the portable TV that sat on our bright orange kitchen counter.

While Mr. Ivory was busy pouring me a glass of water, I took the opportunity to walk over to the kitchen sink and take a look out the window. The backyard was just as well kept as the front. The small patio off the back door had a barbecue grill on it and white plastic patio furniture. There was a bird feeder hanging from the large tree in the left corner of the yard by the back fence. In the opposite corner was a garden shed. The fence that separated the yard from the alley was a high chain-link one. Still, there was an excellent view of the alley and the back gate of the house on Archer.

"You know, they figure the killer probably came down the alley and approached the house from the backyard," I said.

"When my stepfather first moved here years ago, after my mother died, I made him get that fence installed. There didn't used to be a fence separating the backyard from that alley. I think most of the people who live on either side of this alley have had to put fences in." He handed me my glass of water and I took a long drink. I was actually thirsty after all. I guess it was all the lying I was doing.

"Do you get much traffic down this alley?"

"There's a car now and again. Usually it's just kids on bicycles and of course Crazy Frieda was usually roaming up and down the alley looking for cans. Most people left their cans out for her to collect. But you never know who might be coming down that alley at night.

Just then a horn sounded from the driveway. Mr. Ivory jumped at the sound. "Oh, that's Donna. She's back from the store and wants me to come out and help her bring in the groceries."

I wasn't in any hurry to see Donna Ivory and Mr. Ivory looked like he'd just been caught with his fly open. "Why don't I just go on out the back door and cut through the alley. My car's parked around the block, and in this heat I'd appreciate a shortcut. Thanks for the water." I didn't even wait for an answer and just walked out the back door. I didn't miss the look of relief on the poor man's face as he scurried to do his wife's bidding.

I quickly cut across the backyard and slipped out the gate. I headed down the alley and noticed bags and sacks of what looked like aluminum cans along the fences of a couple of houses. No doubt they were for Frieda. I figured people might not be aware that she was dead. It would be hard to connect Elfrieda Barlow, educated former career woman, to the muttering bundle of rags she became. A rumble from my stomach brought me out of my thoughts, and I headed back to my car.

I drove over to Estelle's for an early lunch. It was now almost eleven. There wasn't anybody around except Gwen, who was standing by the hostess station staring off into space. She didn't even notice me when I walked in.

"Earth to Gwen, come in, Gwen." She looked at me and burst into tears.

"Girl, what's the matter?" Since I'd known Gwen I'd

seen her cry exactly twice. Once when her father died and the other time when her dog Cleo got run over by a car.

"It's Joy," she said, barely able to get the words out.

Here we go again.

"Somebody ran her down last night while she was riding her bike. You know I can't stand that girl, Kendra, but I never wanted anything like this to happen to her. I wanted her out of here, but not like this."

I was stunned. "Is she alive?"

"Yeah, she's alive but it don't look good. Whoever did it just drove off and left her in the road." She pulled out a tissue from her skirt pocket and wiped her eyes.

"Where did it happen?"

"Out on Commerce Road."

"Commerce Road? What was she doing way out there?" Commerce Road was about as far out as you could get and still be in Willow County. It was practically a dirt road out by the fairgrounds. What could Joy have been doing out there?

"I don't know. Alex got a call early this morning from the police. They found his number in her backpack. He's at the hospital now. He had to call her aunt and give her the news."

"Do you want me to stay here so you can go to the hospital?"

"No, I don't think I could stand it. Alex called and said I could close the restaurant and go home if I want.

If I go home, all I'll do is think about Joy. I need to keep busy," she said with a shaky smile.

"I did remember to bring that graduation program. It's taped to your locker."

I thanked her and headed back to get it. I hurriedly flipped through the program, scanning the list of names in the W column. No Jordan Wallace was listed as having received a degree from Morehouse in 1976. It didn't surprise me. His carefully put-together lie of a life would have required a degree from a prominent university. And who's to say he didn't attend Morehouse? I gave Gwen back the program and headed over to the hospital.

When I got to the lounge across from the intensive care unit, Alex was there consoling an older woman who looked to be in her mid- fifties. Clara Mills was Joy's aunt, her mother's older sister. She must have dressed hurriedly because her denim skirt and white blouse were wrinkled and her thick graying hair was mussed. She looked not only emotionally drained but physically exhausted and had dark circles under her eyes. Alex introduced us but I may as well not have been there. She vaguely nodded at me and stared straight ahead.

"Her two daughters are on their way. Joy's in surgery now. She has some internal bleeding and a head injury." He shook his head, indicating silently that things weren't looking good. He gestured me over to the drinking fountain. Joy's aunt continued to stare into space as a single tear slipped down her cheek.

"I just can't believe it. How could this have happened? Gwen said Joy was out on Commerce Road. Is that true?" My dislike for Joy wasn't as strong as Gwen's but we both agreed on one point: she didn't deserve what happened to her, and I didn't want her to die.

"No one knows what she was doing out there. Some old man with a paper route found her about five this morning. I don't know how long she lay out there. It could have been all night," Alex said. His voice was thick with emotion.

"I can stay here with Mrs. Mills until her daughters get here if you want to go get some coffee or fresh air." I knew that Alex hated for people to see him without his emotions in check.

"Thanks," he said and headed down the hall.

I walked back into the lounge. I noticed for the first time that it smelled like stale cigarette smoke. Some of the furniture had cigarette burns in it. I would have thought that being across the hall from a place as serious as the intensive care unit, the lounge would have been a more cheerful place with brighter colors, instead of this drab tweed-and-plastic decor.

"Can I get you anything, Mrs. Mills?" I asked. She shook her head no and looked down at her hands in her lap.

I picked up an old copy of *People* magazine and half-heartedly started flipping through it.

"How do you know my niece?" she asked suddenly in a surprisingly deep voice for a woman.

"We both hostess at my uncle Alex's restaurant."

"Are you a friend of hers?"

"No, ma'am, I'm not."

The older woman sighed heavily.

"Joy's never been good at making friends. She runs everyone away. I can't blame her for that though. It's all her mother's fault. I loved my little sister but she was an unfit mother. Rita never wanted Joy. She was too busy running around with some man to be any kind of a mother. She was always putting her boyfriends before Joy. The only time she paid any attention to that child was when she wanted to impress somebody and didn't want them thinking she was a bad mother. And if it wasn't some man, it was her business. Men and that damn coffee shop of hers. Everything came before Joy."

"I understand Joy's mother is dead."

"Committed suicide when Joy was barely fifteen. It was an overdose of sleeping pills. All over some man. The woman never did have a bit of sense. When things got bad she always took the easy way out, leaving everyone else to clean up the mess."

I got the impression that everyone else meant her and her alone.

"So, you took Joy in?"

"She moved here from Cincinnati. She hates it here. I did the best I could. Of course, the damage was already done. Joy was a sullen, moody, and argumentative girl. She loved to pick fights and start trouble. It was like she wanted everyone to be as miserable as she was. It got to the point where she'd become a problem in my home. I thought seriously about putting her in foster care. Then her art teacher at school recognized her talent for painting and really encouraged her. After that, things changed. She was never sweetness and light but she was a lot better. Now it may be all over," she said with a sob.

I started to go to her and put my arm around her when two young women hurried into the lounge. I could immediately see the resemblance. They quickly came to the older woman and embraced her. Mrs. Mills introduced me to her daughters, and I left them to hope and pray in private.

I met Lynette for lunch at Wendy's across the street from Willow Federal Bank where she worked. I gave her the rundown on everything that had been happening.

"Have you heard from Carl?" she asked.

"No, but it's only Monday. It's too soon to start considering myself blown off. Mama thinks I should stay away from him anyway until Jordan's murder is solved," I said, spooning some Frosty into my mouth.

"Do you know how many murders go unsolved? Then what are you supposed to do? Kendra, call that man. He and Vanessa are getting a divorce. Why would he want to kill Jordan?"

I didn't mention anything about Vanessa being pregnant.

"I just wish I knew more about Jordan's past. There has to be a key to this somewhere."

"Why don't you ask Bernie?"

"Bernie hasn't been very forthcoming on the subject of Jordan. Besides, I don't think she knows much more herself."

"What about possessions? Where are all his private papers and things?"

"I really don't think the man had much by way of possessions. Nothing except clothes, shoes, and that car of his. The police probably have everything that he owned..." It suddenly dawned on me that Jordan's car had been in the shop at the time of his death. Could it still be there? Was there any valuable evidence in it? I knew that Jordan had used Frank Z's Auto Body once when he had a fender bender several months ago. I'd run into him when I was picking up my car. Someone had rear-ended me in the parking lot at work. It wouldn't hurt to go to Frank Z's and check it out.

Frank Z's was on Fairmont Street. The garage itself is

next to the house where Frank Zucker and his family live. It's a small business run by Frank, his son, and his brother-in-law. They're the best auto body repair shop in town but they're expensive. The person who hit me had great insurance, otherwise I wouldn't have been able to afford Frank Z's.

I parked in front of the house and walked around back to the garage. I looked to see if I could see Jordan's car anywhere. It was a navy blue Jaguar that had been his pride and joy. Bernie told me he wouldn't let anyone drive it, including her. It was an older model, a classic. I spotted Frank Zucker emerging from the garage in dirty white overalls. He was a short, squat, white man in his late sixties with a bushy mustache and thick snow-white hair. He smiled when he spotted me.

"How can I help you, miss?" He didn't seem to remember me. Good.

"A friend of mine is selling his car. He said he already had about a dozen people interested in it and would be letting people look at it after it was out of the shop. I wanted to be first in line with an offer, so I decided to come see it while it was here." I should have come up with a better excuse before I came. It sounded stupid even to my ears.

"Your friend should have called first to let me know. I don't usually let people wander around my garage. This is an auto body repair shop not a showroom."

"Oh, I understand that. I guess I also wanted to know what was wrong with it. He's going to add the repair cost to the price of the car."

"Whose car is it?"

"Jordan Wallace. He has a navy blue Jag."

"Oh, that car," he looked at me quizzically. "Miss, were you aware that the owner of that car was killed a week or so ago? The police impounded that car last week."

I feigned shock. "Are you serious! I've been out of town for a couple of weeks. Just got home this morning. I had no idea."

"Yep, got himself murdered. Had a beautiful car though. It was a pleasure working on it." I heard a phone ring back in the garage. "Excuse me, I have to get that." I watched him sprint off to get the phone. He could move fast for an old guy.

I should have known the car was gone. I walked back to my car. There was a boy crouched down next to my car on the driver's side. At first I just saw the top of his head. As I approached, he looked up at me. His face was ablaze with acne. He was dressed in dirty jeans and a black T-shirt. He looked about sixteen. I stopped dead in my tracks, uncertain about what to do and what this kid wanted. For a minute I thought he was slashing my tires.

"Ma'am," he whispered, "could I talk to you a second, please?" He gestured for me to crouch next to him. I looked at him like he was crazy.

"Just pretend like you're tying your shoe," he said, looking around cautiously.

Against my better judgment I crouched next to him.

"Are you a friend of that guy who got killed?"

"Yes. What's this about and why are we crouching like this?" I asked, feeling like a complete idiot.

He pulled a black leather case from behind him and set it next to me.

"This belongs to him. The dead guy. I ain't no thief. It's just that my car got broken into a while back and they got my CD player and all my CDs. I just borrowed that guy's CD's to listen to while I was working. He had some pretty cool tunes. Next thing I know, he's dead and the cops came and got the car. I never got a chance to put the case back. Please don't tell my grandfather, he'd kill me." The kid was almost in tears.

"What's your name?"

"Josh Zucker."

"All right, Josh, your secret's safe with me." I picked up the case and stood.

"Thanks, lady," he said, standing and looking around. He started to walk away when I stopped him.

"Hey, do you know what kind of work he was having done on his car?"

"Yeah, somebody took something, probably keys, and scratched the word *murderer* on the hood. Kinda spooky, huh, since he got killed? It was pretty deep too.

We had to strip the entire car and repaint it so the paint would match. They don't make the original paint anymore. I don't understand why anyone would mess up a sweet car like that."

I went back to the hospital to see about Joy. She was out of surgery and was still listed in serious condition but was hanging on. Alex had gone back to the restaurant. Joy's aunt went home to rest. Her daughters were still at the hospital. Candace Mills and her sister, Rachel, looked just like their mother. But, where Clara Mills looked tired and frumpy, her daughters were stunning. Candace, the youngest, was the more talkative of the two. She'd come straight from work and was dressed in a lemon-yellow suit and wore her hair even shorter than mine. Rachel, the oldest, was dressed in a T-shirt and jeans, her long hair in a braid down her back. She was as friendly as her sister but in that condescending way that some attractive people have of relating to their less-than-fortunate peers. Both women had beautiful skin the color of a new penny.

We made small talk for a while and I found out that Candace was twenty-three and a sales rep for a medical-supply company and Rachel was twenty-five and in law school.

"Thanks for sitting with Mom earlier. She's really torn up over this. If Joy doesn't make it, it will just kill her," Candace said. Rachel nodded in agreement. I couldn't help but notice that neither one of them looked too distraught over the thought of losing Joy. It must have been hard for them to have a sullen, hostile Joy come to live with them. It must have also been hard for Joy to live with these two beautiful girls. It would have been enough to give anyone a complex.

"Are you very close to your cousin?"

Both young women shifted uncomfortably.

"Not really," Rachel said. "Joy's not an easy person to be close to. Even when you think you're getting close to her, she'll do something to push you away. It's all Aunt Rita's fault. If she hadn't been running around with all those men, Joy wouldn't be the way she is."

"Which way is that?" I asked, suddenly annoyed. Rachel was twirling her braid around her finger and looking down her nose at me. Her sister gave her a slight and not-very-subtle nudge under the table.

"What she means is," Candace said, glaring at her sister, "Joy had it rough growing up. She had a wall built around her. We tried to do the close-family thing. You know, treat her like another sister. But Joy was never interested, and after a while we sort of gave up. Besides, Joy was always so obsessed."

"With what, her painting?"

"No, with the man who murdered her mother."

"I thought her mother committed suicide."

"She did, but the man she was engaged to at the time left her at the altar. He also ran off with most of her money. After that, Aunt Rita got real depressed. She lost her coffee shop. About three months later, she took an overdose of sleeping pills. As far as Joy's concerned, it was murder all the same."

"Was he ever seen again?"

"No," they both said simultaneously.

Rachel got up from the table, suddenly bored with the topic of Joy, and asked us if we wanted anything from the vending area. We said no and she left the lounge.

"You'll have to excuse my sister. She and Joy have never even been remotely close. Joy and I always got along better but that's only because we stay out of each other's way."

"So, no one ever saw the fiancé again?"

"To be perfectly honest, Joy thought she saw him all the time. She'd get so worked up over it that it scared me. All she talked about was making him pay for what he did to her mother."

"Do you think she really saw him?"

"Who knows? They were living in Cincinnati when all this happened. I can't imagine what he'd be doing here in Willow."

"Did you ever meet him?"

"No. We went to Cincinnati for the wedding. That was going to be the first time we were going to meet him. He never showed up."

Clara Mills arrived looking a little rested. We told

her there was no change in Joy's condition. I started to leave when I overheard Mrs. Mills ask her daughter Rachel if she would go to Joy's apartment to feed her fish.

"Ma, you know what a horrible neighborhood she lives in. I'm afraid to go over there," Rachel said in a whiny voice that set my teeth on edge.

"Don't look at me, either," said Candace Mills. "Last time I was over there my rims got stolen."

"I'd be happy to do it, Mrs. Mills," I said, and couldn't help but notice the relief on the faces of all three Mills women. Clara Mills thanked me and gave me the key.

Joy's apartment was in a rundown complex ambitiously called Green Meadow Estates located about four blocks from Kingford College in an area that can best be described as the armpit of Willow. It was a brick four-story building with six small units on each floor. Joy lived on the second floor. Rap music was blaring out of one unit. There was a couple practically having sex in the stairway who looked very annoyed at being interrupted as I excused myself and sidestepped them. Joy's unit was B6. I let myself in and was surprised at how neat it was. One whole end of the tiny apartment had been turned into a studio, which explained the slight odor of paint and turpentine. The other end had a living room area with a couch that turned into a rollaway bed. Off the living room was a kitchenette.

Joy's strange and colorful artwork adorned every wall. There were paintings of headless men, strange birds with women's heads, and lots of paintings of mouths, some screaming, some bound with tape or gags, none of them smiling. Joy was one weird, angry chick.

I quickly found the small aquarium and shook some fish food into it. I watched Joy's tropical fish greedily flock to the top of the tank. The water in the tank looked murky, and I wondered if I should clean it while I was there. The apartment needed some fresh air. I walked over to the biggest window in the place, which was at the end with Joy's studio. She must have taken advantage of the light from that window. I noticed that there was a painting on the easel covered by a sheet, as well as a pile of paintings on the floor by the window. I resisted the urge to look under the sheet and opened the window a few inches to let some fresh air in. Then I went into the bathroom off the kitchen.

The bathroom was tiny with a sink, a mirrored cabinet over it, a toilet, and a shower stall. The Mickey Mouse shower curtain was pulled shut. There were snapshots taped all over the walls. There were pictures of a young smiling Joy with a woman. Judging from the woman's resemblance, I figured it was Joy's mother. One picture in particular caught my eye and I froze. It was taped to the bathroom mirror. In it was a teenaged

Joy, no longer smiling; her mother, who was beaming; and a man who was also smiling his familiar shark's tooth grin. It was Jordan Wallace.

I took a closer look at the picture. It looked as if someone had taken an ink pen and drawn an X across Jordan's face. I wondered if Joy or her mother had done it. I didn't have time to wonder for very long.

I saw in the mirror that the shower curtain behind me shook slightly. I whirled around just as a man jumped out of the shower. He was an older man, possibly in his mid-fifties. He looked wild. His graying hair was in thick, long dreds hanging almost to his shoulders. He was thin, wiry, and dressed in black sweats and raggedy tennis shoes. He reeked of liquor. For one tense moment we stared at each other. Then suddenly he grabbed me, shoving me hard through the bathroom door. I landed on my back on the kitchen floor. The impact of my landing knocked the breath out of me before I could scream. The intruder sprinted toward the door for his getaway and in his haste stepped on my fingers. I cried out, clutching my hand to my chest. I rolled over on my stomach and saw the intruder collide with a young woman as he ran out the door. She dropped the book bag she was carrying and fell sideways against the doorjamb. I stood nursing my injured fingers. The girl was holding her arm. We stared at each other a moment before she asked me who the hell I was and what was I doing in her apartment.

She thought the intruder was with me. I explained otherwise.

It turned out the young woman's name was Cory and she was Joy's girlfriend. Now I knew what Rachel had meant by the "way" Joy was. Joy was a lesbian. Talk about a news flash. I had no idea. Cory was light skinned, tall, thin, and small boned, birdlike in her features. She wore her reddish hair in braids and wore granny glasses over eyes red from crying. She was pretty in an unadorned natural way. She had just come from the hospital. She hadn't been able to see Joy. Joy's aunt and cousins didn't approve of their relationship. They didn't know Cory and Joy were living together because they hadn't visited in months.

Cory gave me some ice for my hand. I could flex my fingers, so I figured nothing was broken. However, my back was killing me. Except for having been scared half to death, I was okay. Cory decided nothing was missing. I wondered how the man had gotten in and what he was looking for.

"Oh, it's easy to break in here," Cory said matter-of-factly.

"Joy's locked herself out a lot and used a bobby pin to pick the lock. I used a credit card once to get in when Joy and I had a fight and she locked me out. There are a lot of crack heads and winos around here. Some of them get desperate and break into apartments looking for money and anything they can sell for drugs and liquor."

I sat on the couch while Cory made us some tea. I used the time alone to think. Jordan had been Joy's mother's fiancé. He'd run off with her money, leaving Rita Owens broke and depressed. She lost her business and later killed herself. Joy was the obvious candidate for vandalizing Jordan's car. She was probably responsible for the notes as well. She was seen arguing with him, and I caught her snooping around Bernie's house after the funeral. Did she kill him too?

Where was Joy the morning Jordan was killed? The note I found would be proof she was there, but there would be no proof she wrote it or how long it had been there. Joy was tiny and rode a ten-speed bike. She could easily have been mistaken for a child. I got up from the couch and walked over to the window. On a whim I uncovered the picture on the easel. The scene was a familiar one. The painting vividly depicted a man sprawled out on a floor and facing the wall next to him. His arms were stretched out in front of him. The man's head was a mass of blood, brains, and bone. Blood stained the collar of the man's shirt and splashed the wall next to him. I turned to Cory who'd come in from the kitchen.

"I think Joy's in big trouble," I told her.

After much ranting, raving, crying, and pleading, Cory finally convinced me not to go to the police until Joy could talk to them herself and tell her side of the story. She swore that Joy had never mentioned Jordan Wallace to her, and as for the snapshot with the X, Joy hated all her mother's boyfriends. Cory claimed she had no idea that the man in the picture was the same one who had been murdered a week ago. She also claimed that on the morning of the murder, Joy was taking a final exam, and although she could be nasty and hateful, Joy could never murder anyone.

I didn't quite believe her but didn't know what else to do. Neither one of us stated the obvious—that Joy might never regain consciousness. Cory refused to acknowledge that possibility, and I felt it cruel at this point to force it on her. Instead, not trusting her, I went into the bathroom and took the snapshot and started to take the painting.

"What the hell do you think you're doing?" demanded Cory, who was standing in front of the door blocking my way out.

"I think these things will be safer with me until Joy wakes up."

"You can't just come in here, accuse Joy of murder, and then run out of here with her shit. Put it back, now!"

Cory was pissed and I guess I couldn't blame her. However, the evidence I was holding in my hands was proof that Joy was involved in some way with Jordan's murder, which could only mean good news for Bernie and me. I didn't want to antagonize Cory further, but I wasn't leaving empty-handed. I looked over my shoulder at the easel that I'd just taken the painting from and noticed the window next to it that I'd opened when I first got to the apartment. I walked slowly over to the easel, trying to figure out how to get the painting out of the window without Cory seeing me.

"That's right, put it back," said Cory watching me closely.

Thankfully, the phone rang and as Cory turned to answer it, I quickly slid the painting out the open window and watched as it fell into the bushes below. I then grabbed another painting from the pile on the floor next to the window, put it on the easel, and covered it up with the sheet. Cory turned toward me, still on the phone, and nodded her approval. Then she held out her hand for the snapshot, which I'd already put in my purse.

I pulled out an item from my purse and dropped it purposefully on the floor before Cory could grasp it. It sailed under the coffee table. She shot me a dirty look, then bent down to retrieve it. I shoved past her and ran out the door and down the hallway like the devil was on my heels. Cory was about to discover that what I dropped was actually my library card. I rounded the corner at full tilt and downed the stairs two at a time.

Then disaster struck. I tripped and went flying like a human cannonball, straight into the amorous couple that

I'd encountered when I first arrived. We all tumbled down the remaining half dozen steps and landed in an awkward heap at the bottom of the narrow stairway. There wasn't much room to move. My efforts to free myself resulted in me accidentally poking the female half of the duo in the eye, eliciting a yelp of pain and a string of curse words that would make a gangsta rapper blush. In an attempt to get my feet under me, I ended up straddling the male half of the couple. He quickly recovered from his shock and grinned up at me with a mouthful of gold teeth. It was then that I noticed that my T-shirt had ridden up, exposing my bra and ample cleavage. I rolled off of Goldie, who looked a little disappointed that our slapstick threesome was over, and narrowly avoided a vicious kick to the kidneys from his outraged and now half-blind girlfriend. I ran out of the building wondering how I had managed to piss off so many people in such a short amount of time. I was praying the painting was still in the bushes and hadn't been taken by a crack head looking for something to sell. Lucky for me it was still there; I grabbed it, ran back to my car, and took off—but not before I heard Cory screaming my name, and a few other choice words, from the apartment window. It was hours before I noticed all my hubcaps were gone.

I drove around for a while trying to figure out what to do. If Joy had killed Jordan, why did she leave a note? How did she get into the house? Did Jordan let her in? Why was he killed in the house where Vanessa was staying? Had Joy followed him over to Archer Street? How would she have known Vanessa wasn't at home? For that matter, did Jordan know that Vanessa wasn't home? I knew that Joy had a class on Friday mornings from nine to eleven. Even if she was taking the final for that class the morning Jordan was killed, she could have finished early and still had time to kill him. At the very least, she had to have been at the scene or how else would she have been able to paint that picture? I was certain Joy must have been following Jordan. She must have been the one to send Bernie the letter telling her about Jordan and Vanessa. She must have done everything she could think of to make Jordan's life miserable. Killing him would be so final. If I knew Joy at all, making Jordan's life a living hell and being an eternal burr in his behind would be more her style. I also had to wonder how Jordan took Joy's assault on his life. Why had he come to Willow in the first place? Why had he stayed once he knew Joy was here, especially when he knew she held him responsible for her mother's death?

I finally went home and on my door was a note. It read: *I was in town on business and stopped by to take you to lunch.*

Sorry I missed you. Call me. Carl.

Damn!

TEN

The next day I called about Joy. There was no change. She'd made it through the night, however, which was a good sign. I'd also called Carl and agreed to have dinner with him on Saturday. I decided to go see Bernie. I figured if I called her she'd say she was busy, so I'd just show up unannounced. I wanted to know if there'd been any break in Jordan's murder, leaving Joy off the hook. It seemed ironic that Joy could pull through only to spend the rest of her life in a jail cell.

It had gotten hot outside, so I put on white shorts and a red tank top. Mrs. Carson was sitting on her porch around ten when I left the house. Mahalia was draped lazily across her lap, making a sound like a busted carburetor as Mrs. Carson stroked her back.

"Beautiful day, isn't it, Kendra?"

"It sure is, Mrs. Carson."

"Your boyfriend came by lookin' for you yesterday.

Sure is good-lookin'. He’s still married, ain't he?"

"He's not my boyfriend, and his divorce will be final any day now," I said patiently.

"You mean that's what he's tellin' you. You got to be careful when it comes to these married men. They can be devils. Say anything to get what they want. Why, my niece Tammy got mixed up with a married man. He could tell her anything. Could tell her shit was mud and rain was blood and she'd believe it. Of course, even he wasn't mixed up in some murder."

"I'll see you later, Mrs. Carson. You have a nice day."

"Okay, you ole foolish gal, don't listen to me. You'll be the one cryin'."

There were police cars at Bernie's house. Bernie was standing on the lawn with Diane and another man I didn't recognize. I saw Detectives Harmon and Mercer come out of the house. Both were wearing white latex gloves. Some of Bernie's neighbors were standing on the sidewalk watching and no doubt whispering about falling property values. I walked over to a woman and asked what was going on.

"I'm not quite sure," she said in a stage whisper. "But I think the police have a warrant and are searching the house. Why it's just like *Law & Order.* It's so exciting."

Great. If I was wondering how things could get any worse, I'd just gotten my answer. I felt immediately guilty that I had something in my trunk that could put an end to all this. I just wasn't one hundred percent sure about Joy. I walked across the lawn to Bernie. She looked relieved to see me, which was a surprise.

"Are you okay? What's going on?"

"They're searching my house. They have a warrant but they won't tell me what they're looking for." I could hear the anxiety in her voice, and it jacked my guilt up another notch.

"Are you sure they can do this?" Diane asked the harassed-looking blonde man next to her. Bernie whispered to me that he was Diane's lawyer. She'd called Diane when the police had shown up at her door and Diane had called her lawyer, Emmett Palmer.

"It's a legitimate warrant signed by Judge Corning," he said wearily as if he'd already said it a thousand times.

"I don't know why I called her. She's only making things worse," Bernie whispered. "When they showed up at my door I panicked and couldn't think of who else to call."

"How long have they been in there?" I asked.

"Almost an hour. I couldn't stand to watch them tearing my house apart, so I came outside."

I saw a police officer with white gloves on carrying a trash bag. He carried the bag over to Detective Mercer. Mercer looked inside the bag, then nodded for the officer to take it away. I felt sick.

After another twenty minutes, the police were finished. I caught up with Detective Harmon and asked her what was going on. She would barely acknowledge me, let alone tell me anything.

"I happen to know that Vanessa Brumfield had been stalked by a man named Russ Webster. He could have killed Jordan Wallace, mistaking him for Vanessa." I was grasping at straws.

"You mean Russell Webster alias Russell Wells aka Roger Williams. Extradited back to New Jersey six months ago and is in jail without bail awaiting trial for felonious assault on an abortion clinic doctor. Miss Clayton, we know what we're doing. Do you? Because if I were you, I'd follow your friend Ms. Gibson's lead and get yourself a lawyer to advise you. You'll definitely need one when we decide to bring you in to give us a new statement concerning what really happened the night you took Ms. Gibson to her house on Archer Street." She got into her car and drove away leaving me standing openmouthed on the curb.

I went inside to help Bernie put the house back together. A half-assed attempt had been made by the officers to put things back where they were. But the overall effect was that of a tornado. Drawers had been pulled out, their contents stuffed hastily back inside. Cabinets had been emptied and a planter housing a rubber plant had been overturned. Even the trash had been gone through. Diane had predictably left claiming to have a lunch date, even though it was only ten thirty. The neighbors, the show being over, reluctantly went about their business.

Bernie and I cleaned in silence. Both of us were wondering what the police had carried out in that trash bag. I was haunted by Harmon's last statement to me. Who'd have thought a little lie could potentially get me into so much trouble? Now I had even more that I was holding back from the police. After an hour, Bernie came and told me she'd made coffee, and we sat down in the kitchen to drink it.

"They know that I knew about Jordan and Vanessa," she said to me as I stirred sugar and cream into my coffee.

"How? And thanks for letting me know."

"Well, I didn't tell them. I don't know how they found out," she said defensively.

"Did you honestly think you could hide the fact that you knew from the police? I'll tell you another thing too. I don't think Vanessa told either. She's involved with a doctor at Willow Memorial. She wants to bury any involvement she had with Jordan. I doubt she would have told them anything."

"That's all the more reason for her to kill him in my book. Damn! I wish I knew what they took out of here."

"Could it have been anything of Jordan's?"

"No, they came and got all of his stuff right after it happened. They even impounded his car from Frank

Z's. They think I did it. I can just feel it. Can you believe I've been down to that station twice more since I made my first statement? I don't know how many more times I can answer the same questions."

I felt sorry for her and at the same time relieved that I hadn't been called back down to the station—at least not yet. What would I say if I were?

"Bernie, do you know anything at all about Jordan's past?"

"Not really. He was born in Cleveland. I know his parents died in a car accident when he was little. He was an only child, and he went to live with his grandmother in Columbus, his father's mother. From what I gather, she had a lot of money, which is where Jordan got his expensive tastes. She must have spoiled the hell out of him. That's all I know. Jordan didn't like to talk about his past, or the future for that matter. He was a real here-and-now type person. I don't think he thought much beyond what he wanted at any given time. I don't think he thought about the future consequences of anything he did."

"Which was what got him killed," I said bluntly. Bernie looked at me strangely.

"Sorry, but you saw him just like I did. Whoever killed him was pissed as hell. What could he have done to make anybody that mad at him?"

Contributing to the suicide of a loved one would fit under that category. Did Joy, being as tiny as she is, have the physical strength to batter Jordan to death? Six years of pent-up anger and hatred could give someone considerable strength.

"Did Jordan have a key to the house on Archer?"

"He did when he lived there. He gave it back to me, but I couldn't find it anywhere. I just figured I lost it here in the house somewhere."

"Were any keys found on him?"

"Just my car keys and his key to this house. I can't figure out how he got in over there. Vanessa had to have let him in and then killed him. She must have snuck back into town from wherever she was, killed him, and then snuck back out. It's the only thing that makes any sense."

"Could he have gotten a duplicate key made? I mean, he was seeing her behind your back. It's possible, you know," I reasoned.

"Well, of course it's possible. But why would he? If the only reason he would go over there was to see her, why would he need a key if she was letting him in? And if he had a key, why wasn't it found on him?"

"You've got a point. So, now what?"

"Girl, I don't know. Diane's lawyer left me his card. I'm going to call him and see what my plan of action should be. I'm not going to just sit here and let them come and get me. I can't believe this is happening. I thought this would be over by now."

She poured me some more coffee and I told her

about Joy's accident.

"That's awful. What was she doing out on Commerce Road late at night?"

"I don't know." I was sipping my coffee when another thought suddenly hit me. If Joy had been following Jordan around, did she follow him the morning he was killed? Did she witness his murder, and could the killer have seen her and lured her out to Commerce Road to run her down on purpose? The thought made me nauseous. As much as I didn't want to and despite the promise I'd made to Cory, I had to go to the police.

"You okay, Kendra?" Bernie asked, placing a comforting hand on my arm.

"I'm fine, Bernie. I'm just thinking about what a mess this all is. So, is Diane still bugging you about selling the business?"

"Yes, Lord. She's been bugging the hell out of me."

"I'm surprised she doesn't want to run it herself. She's always struck me as being the type who loves being in charge."

"Diane work? Now that's a laugh. Working entails showing up and putting forth an effort. The only thing Diane puts any effort into is her appearance. Besides, she used to work at Gibson Realty when she first came to town. She was a part-time receptionist. As soon as she snagged Ben, she quit and hasn't looked back."

"Oh, I didn't realize she wasn't from here. Where's

she from?"

"Somewhere down South. Let me think. Macon. That's it, Macon, Georgia."

"How'd your mother feel about Diane?"

"Couldn't stand her. She would have tried to put a stop to the relationship but she had her hands full with me and Raymond Hodge," she said, wincing.

"She used to hate it when Ben and Diane would come over for dinner. Mother loved to cook, and Diane was always on some diet or so she claimed. She'd load her plate up with food and then never eat it. Would just pick at it and run her mouth about stuff no one wanted to hear about. Then later on I'd catch her in the kitchen stuffing her face when she thought no one was around. It was really weird, like she was too embarrassed to eat in front of us. She's still that way."

"Maybe she's bulimic. You ever catch her throwing up?"

"No, I just think she's weird, not to mention self-centered, arrogant, and a snob. It's all about appearances with Diane. Do you know she never buys anything on sale because she wants to brag about how much she pays for everything?"

The cheapskate in my soul winced at that foreign concept. Finding bargains was half the fun of shopping, as far as I was concerned. If it's not on sale, clearance, at a garage sale, or received as a gift, then I wasn't meant to have it. I haven't gone the freebie route like

Mama, but who knows.

"So, what does she do all day?"

"She goes to the country club, she shops; she belongs to the Willow Women's League, and they do charity work for the homeless and the various AIDS foundations."

"Diane cares about the homeless?" I laughed and tried to envision Diane handing out designer blankets and baskets of gourmet food.

"Are you kidding? Diane's rich friends at the country club belong to the Willow Women's League, that's why she joined. When I was still living over on Archer Street, Diane came over to see me one day. I was out working in the backyard. While she was there, old Crazy Frieda came down the alley looking for cans. Diane saw her and went off. Started yelling and screaming at the poor woman, telling her to get out of my trash and go get a job. It was really embarrassing. I felt so bad I started leaving a bagful of cans out for her every week. So in answer to your question, no, Diane doesn't care about the homeless."

I felt compelled to tell Bernie the truth about Elfrieda Barlow and her homeless status. Just like almost everyone else, she had no idea.

I was confused and more than a little worried. I knew I needed to go to Detectives Harmon and Mercer with everything I knew. But what I knew pointed straight to

Joy. She had no way of telling them anything different at this point. I was fairly certain Bernie was innocent. I owed it to her to tell the police. I headed back to the hospital. I wanted to see if there was any change in Joy's condition before I went to the station.

I ran into Joy's aunt Clara in the parking lot. She was elated. Joy had regained consciousness. She could hardly stand still to talk to me.

"I'd just walked into the house from seeing Joy and the phone rang and it was the hospital telling me she was waking up!"

She practically ran ahead of me into the hospital. I followed close behind her. When we reached the intensive care unit, Clara Mills went straight into her niece's room. Not being a family member, I wasn't allowed in. I watched through the window to Joy's room, which had until now been closed off by mini-blinds. Joy looked very tiny in the big bed. Her face was swollen almost beyond recognition. Both eyes were black and opened to slits. Her head was wrapped in bandages and her leg was in a cast. Her aunt sat next to her, held her hand, stroked her cheek, and talked softly to her. I had the feeling Joy knew everything that was going on, even though she just stared straight ahead the whole time.

I sat in the waiting room for about twenty minutes while Mrs. Mills talked to Joy's doctor. When she came out, she told me the doctor thought there might be some brain damage but Mrs. Mills, however, was hearing none of it. There was nothing anyone could say that would convince her that Joy wasn't going to be just fine in due time.

"Mrs. Mills," I said before she turned to go back into Joy's room, "does anyone have any idea why Joy was out so late on Commerce Road?"

"No, I have no idea. I asked that friend of hers, Cory. She claims she doesn't know either. It's probably something we'll never know. The doctor said that Joy may not have any memory of even getting up that morning, let alone why she went out that night." She went back into Joy's room, happy in the knowledge that her niece was on the road to recovery, while I was on my way to do something that was going to cause her more grief. I felt like crap.

I left the hospital and went straight to the police station. I was told that Detectives Mercer and Harmon weren't there. I left a message for one of them to contact me. I went through the drive-through at Wendy's and got a burger and fries. I parked and ate in my car. Willow Federal Bank was across the street, and I watched the people who had business at the bank come and go. I was finishing up my burger when I noticed a man and a woman come out of the bank. I was shocked when I saw who the two people were. It was Carl and Vanessa.

I watched them walk over to Carl's car. They were

deep in conversation. I was too far away to see the expressions on their faces. Then Vanessa reached into her purse and pulled out what appeared from where I was sitting to be a white envelope. The kind you get from the bank. I watched as she handed it to Carl. He folded it in half and put it in his suit pocket. Then they embraced for what seemed like an eternity but was probably only a minute. Carl bent down and gave Vanessa a kiss on the lips. Then they both got into their separate cars and drove away—in opposite directions I was pleased to notice. The whole encounter took less than five minutes, but it was enough to make me almost physically ill.

What were they doing together? I could only assume she was giving him money, hence the visit to the bank. I'd only been out on one date with Carl Brumfield. I don't know why I should be so upset over seeing him with his ex-wife. I didn't know what was more upsetting to me, the thought that Carl was still in love with Vanessa or the thought that what I'd just witnessed had something to do with Jordan's murder. Why did Vanessa give Carl money? Was she paying him off for something, like killing Jordan for instance, or paying him to keep quiet about knowing that she did it? I couldn't ask Lynette what they were doing in there. She and Greg had both played hooky from work and had gone to a Reds game. I don't know how long I sat in stunned silence before I drove home.

ELEVEN

When I got home, I pulled out a legal pad and wrote down what I knew so far. I put down five names on the page: Bernie, Vanessa, Carl, Joy, and Jordan. First I listed everything I knew about Jordan: he was from Cleveland, was an only child, parents killed when he was twelve, went to live with his grandmother in Columbus. His grandmother was rich and spoiled him. He used women mainly for money, and he may have attended Morehouse. He was engaged to Joy Owens's mother, stood her up at the altar, and ran off with her money. He came to Willow more than a year ago. Why? Moved in with Bernie, was involved with Vanessa Brumfield, and was killed in Vanessa's rented house. How did he get in?

Next was Bernie: She was in love with Jordan. She found out about Jordan and Vanessa by anonymous letter. She threatened to end the relationship if he didn't break it off with Vanessa. She was in the vicinity of the crime scene at the time of the murder. Something mysterious happened to a man Bernie was involved with in the past. What really happened to Raymond Hodge, and how well did I really know Bernie?

Then came Vanessa Brumfield: She was separated from her husband and was involved with at least two other men, Jordan and Dr. Ted Adamson. She was pregnant. But whose baby was it? She was out of town the day Jordan was killed. Her father is dying, so why risk leaving town? She may have been away having an abortion. Was Jordan blackmailing her? Could she have had an accomplice? Why was she giving Carl money?

Joy Owens was angry and deeply disturbed over her mother's suicide. Rita Owens killed herself over the loss of her business, money, and being left at the altar by Jordan Wallace. Joy was stalking Jordan, sending anonymous letters to Bernie. Who else got one? Joy vandalized Jordan's car. She painted a picture of Jordan's murder scene. She had to have been there. Did she see who killed him? Who ran her down, and could it have anything to do with Jordan's murder? I suddenly remembered how happy she looked when she came into the restaurant the day after Jordan was killed. Could she have been an accomplice who had to be silenced?

Carl Brumfield. What did I really know about Carl? His wife, Vanessa, left him. Why? He and Vanessa had been seen arguing loudly by one of her neighbors. What was it about? Did he know about her and Jordan? He and Vanessa had been planning to start a family when she left him. Had he found out she was pregnant by another man and killed that man—Jordan? Why was Vanessa giving him money?

I was more confused than ever. I sat around my apartment wondering if I should take Mama's advice about Carl and break our date for Saturday. Then I started thinking about his smile, the way he smelled, and our goodnight kiss. I felt more comfortable with this man than I had a right to feel, given the circumstances. I was saying a silent prayer that he wasn't involved as I drifted off to sleep on my couch.

The phone woke me up around five thirty. I answered and got an earful of Mama babbling something about Bernie and to turn my TV on. It took her three attempts before I grasped what she was saying and groggily turned on my set to the Channel 4 news. I sat stunned as I watched bouffant-haired news reporter Tracy Ripkey reporting live from Bernie's house. My stomach knotted up as I watched a stony-faced Bernie being led away in handcuffs after having been arrested for the murder of Jordan Wallace.

I listened as Tracy Ripkey went on to say that the arrest was based on evidence found in the suspect's home and by a sworn statement given by a former employee of the suspect's late mother. Footage was then shown of a trim black man in his early fifties coming out of the police station. He was dressed in a cream suit and a light blue shirt and was identified as one Raymond Hodge of Atlanta.

The reporter had gone on to say that Raymond Hodge had fled Willow in fear of his life after an affair with Bernice Gibson had gone sour and she had allegedly attacked him with a paperweight, seriously injuring him. As I watched Raymond Hodge dodge the reporters and microphones being stuck in his face, he turned and stared directly into the camera and said, "No comment." I got a good look at him and almost fell off the couch. Even though he was cleaned up, had gotten a haircut, and was in a suit, I was looking at the same man who had broken into Joy's apartment.

I heard squawking on the phone and realized Mama was still on the line.

"I just don't believe it!" she kept saying over and over. Neither could I.

"Why on earth are they arresting her over what some foolish man said happened more than twenty years ago. Althea told me about Bernie and that man. I'd have knocked him in his head too!"

"Did you know about Bernie hitting him in the head with that paperweight?" I asked in amazement.

"Yes, I knew all about that. Althea said Bernie knocked him out cold. He had a cut on his scalp that bled like crazy. She took him to the emergency room. They stitched him up. She gave him five thousand dollars not to press charges and a job referral with a real estate company in Atlanta and told him to get out of town. He took the money and ran."

"Did you know Bernie thought all these years that she may have killed that man? How could Althea do that to her?"

Mama sighed wearily.

"Children don't come with an owner's manual, you know. You do the best you can and hope and pray your kids will turn out okay. I agree that Althea didn't handle that situation very well. She could have at least told Bernie what she'd done. But it's hard to watch someone you love making a big mistake. She thought she was doing the right thing. I think she was afraid Bernie would run off to Atlanta if she knew where he was."

Well it had all come full circle now, I thought. I wondered how Raymond Hodge even knew about Jordan's murder if he'd been in Atlanta all this time. The raggedy, long-haired drunk I had encountered in Joy's apartment bore little resemblance to the polished, sharply dressed man I'd just seen on television. But I knew it was him. He had that same wild trapped look in his eyes that I'd seen in Joy's apartment.

"They need to be arresting that Vanessa Brumfield. If they knew what they was doing, they'd be looking at her real close," Mama said indignantly.

"All right, what do you know that I don't?"

"Well, I was in Denny's today with my ladies senior

circle from church. You know we go out to lunch every month. It was Mattie Lyons's turn to pick the restaurant this month. We were shocked because she usually picks Ponderosa. The chicken wings were almost raw the last time we went there. Anyway, our waitress was this tired, pitiful—and I mean pitiful—looking white woman. Kept getting everybody's order wrong. Looked like she was going to cry at any moment. She finally did cry when Donna Ivory yelled at her for putting tomato on her sandwich when she definitely said no tomato. Donna's allergic to tomatoes, you know. Her lips swell up as big as her behind if she eats any, and she gets these big ugly red hives all over her body—"

"Mama please," I begged. It took her forever to tell a story, and the last mental image I needed was of Donna Ivory's butt-sized lips.

"All right, missy, don't rush me! As I was saying, our waitress ran off crying to the restroom. Another waitress came over and corrected all our orders. I asked if the poor woman was okay, and she pulled up a chair and started telling us all the woman's business. It seems our waitress had been none other than Edna Cox, Denton Cox's wife and Vanessa Brumfield's stepmother, and she has plenty to cry about. Not only is her husband dying but she just found out that Vanessa is the sole beneficiary of a two-hundred-and-fifty-thousand-dollar life insurance policy. All poor Edna's going to get is the small house they live in and all her husband's debts. Vanessa has made it clear she's not sharing."

"You've got to be kidding!" Now I knew why Vanessa had left Carl. Her father must have promised to make her his sole heir if she left him, not knowing how soon that would be. Two hundred and fifty thousand dollars would make a sizable down payment on a house in Pine Knoll. It would also entice a man like Jordan Wallace. Vanessa would be a single professional woman with her own money, just like Bernie and just like Rita Owens had been. I wondered if Jordan had known about Vanessa's inheritance and found out the hard way that she wasn't sharing.

"We're not looking at any other suspects at this time, Miss Clayton," said Detective Trish Harmon with what I swore was a smirk. I'd gone to see her the next morning and was waiting for her when she arrived at the station.

I had laid out everything I knew, or rather almost everything, to Detective Harmon, and she wasn't biting. As far as she was concerned, Joy Owens could have painted that picture based on the newspaper's description of the crime scene and a little imagination. She also pointed out that even if Joy had been stalking Jordan, there was absolutely no proof. The one note that was found had only one set of prints, mine.

As for Vanessa, she had an alibi that had been

verified and, as far as the detective knew, there was no crime in being left two hundred and fifty thousand dollars by your dying father.

I glared at her across her desk, which was as neat, orderly, and anal as she was. Today she was dressed in a dark brown pantsuit and a white high-button blouse. There was a picture of her with a dark- haired bespectacled man who had his arm around her waist. I almost didn't recognize her. Her hair was long and dark brown and she was actually smiling. She noticed me looking at the picture.

"That's my husband, Paul, and me. He died ten years ago. Car accident."

When Paul Harmon died he must have taken a piece of his wife with him. She barely resembled the happy woman in the picture. I momentarily felt a stab of pity for Trish Harmon. It quickly disappeared with her next statement. "We have strong evidence that Bernice Gibson killed Jordan Wallace. She knew he was cheating on her with her tenant Vanessa Brumfield. She lured him over to her rented house on Archer with a note. We now know she borrowed a car from a coworker, left work, let herself into the house, and killed Mr. Wallace. The rest you know. We have a witness who can testify that Ms. Gibson is a violent person."

"Now wait a minute," I said. "What are you talking about? What note?" I hope she didn't notice that I hadn't asked whose car Bernie had borrowed.

“Do you honestly think I’d share that information with you?” Harmon’s phone rang and she turned to answer it.

I looked past her and noticed a slip of paper enclosed in a baggie sitting in a plastic tray on the table behind her desk. I got up, quickly reached past her, grabbed the baggie, and looked at the note. It was a half sheet of lined notebook paper that looked like it had been in the trash. It had what looked like coffee stains on it. There was some writing on it in a strange, pale-pink shiny ink. The note read:

be at my place at eight and don't be late!

It was signed "love, v." The handwriting was a childish looping scrawl.

Harmon ended her call and turned to see me with the baggie in my hand. She jumped out of her chair and tried to snatch it out of my hand but I took a step backwards.

“Are you out of your mind?” she hissed and looked around the room to make sure no one had witnessed her letting evidence get away from her.

"Are *you* trying to tell me Bernie wrote this note? This isn't even her handwriting, and what kind of ink is this?"

"Actually, it's lipstick,” she said, sighing and

snatching the baggie from my hand, “and of course Ms. Gibson would have disguised her handwriting to make Mr. Wallace believe the note was from Vanessa Brumfield. We've already obtained a handwriting sample from her. I'm sure the results will be conclusive."

I remembered a week or so ago when Bernie first told me about Raymond Hodge on Diane's patio. She told me that if the police really wanted her to be guilty, they would find a way for her to have done it. Her theory was coming true.

"So this is the smoking gun that made you arrest Bernie? A note that isn't even in her handwriting, doesn't have Jordan's name on it, and could have been written by anybody! Where did you find this?"

"In Ms. Gibson's purse. We also found Mr. Wallace's missing keys and half of a broken, bloodstained baseball bat, which we believe to be the murder weapon, in her gardening shed. Is that enough of a smoking gun for you, Miss Clayton?"

"You do realize that there must have been at least a hundred people in and out of Bernie's house after Jordan's funeral? Anybody could have planted that evidence. Why would Bernie hide this stuff on her property? And as for her purse, it's always a mess. Someone could have slipped that note inside and she would have never known it was there!" I said vehemently.

"Be that as it may, Bernice Gibson has the strongest motive. We've yet to come up with any person who has a stronger one."

"I just gave you two!" I was practically vibrating with anger. "And why did you decide to search Bernie's house anyway?"

"I can't tell you that," Harmon said, glaring at me. "Now, unless you have something you'd like to confess, I don't want to hear anymore. Stay out of police business, Miss Clayton."

"Was it an anonymous tip, maybe a letter typed like the one I found?" She looked up abruptly, letting me know I was right.

"I don't have time for this. Evidence is what we need, not speculation. And we have plenty of evidence against Ms. Gibson. Now, if you'll excuse me, I have a lot of work to do." She bent over her paperwork without another word. Having been dismissed, I promptly got up to leave and almost ran into Charles Mercer carrying a box of doughnuts. He said something to me that I didn't catch. I was so pissed that I didn't stop to find out what it was.

I arrived at the Willow County courthouse later that morning for Bernie's appearance in front of the judge. It took all of five minutes. She was led into the courtroom dressed in an orange jumpsuit. Her usually immaculate French roll was coming undone. She looked tired and more than a little scared. She was led over to sit next to her lawyer Emmett Palmer. The courtroom was packed. I was able to find a seat at the back. Diane was sitting in the row behind Bernie and her lawyer. Next to Diane I was surprised to see Trevor, who was looking more than a little bored. I scanned the room to see if Raymond Hodge would make an appearance. I didn't see him. I did see Vanessa Brumfield, hiding behind a pair of dark sunglasses, slip into the back row, two seats down from me. She hadn't noticed me yet.

When the judge asked Bernie how she pled and she answered with a clear "not guilty," I quickly looked over at Vanessa and saw a look of smug disbelief on her face. After a few minutes of arguing over whether or not to grant bail, the judge set Bernie's at five hundred thousand dollars. I knew Bernie would be able to pay. I turned to leave just in time to see Vanessa quickly slip out the door. I followed her out to the parking lot and caught up with her.

"I'm real surprised to see you here, Vanessa. Did you come to gloat?"

She gave me a look that could have frozen water.

"Look, I'm just as curious about this whole thing as anybody else, more so since it happened where I lived and I was questioned by the police. It's obvious to me that someone was trying to set me up, and it was more than likely your friend."

"If anyone was set up, it was Bernie. I have to wonder if maybe it should be you sitting in Bernie's place. Two hundred and fifty thousand dollars is a hell of a motive for murder in my book. What happened? Did Jordan want a piece of it to keep your affair secret from Daddy, or was there something else he knew about that would have blown your inheritance?" I looked pointedly at her stomach. She backed away from me, openly shocked at my blatant innuendo.

"You nosy bitch," she practically spat at me. "Mind your own damn business!" She turned to walk away and I started to follow her; then she had a change of heart and turned back to me, smiling slyly.

"Okay, you want to know the truth. Yeah, I fucked Jordan Wallace. I fucked him every chance I got. So what! He wasn't married, and I was on my way to being single again."

"What about Dr. Adamson? Aren't the two of you an item?"

"Ted's a nice man but he's no red-hot lover, and I'm not married to him either. I can do whatever I want with whomever I want. I let good sex cloud my judgment, and I mistakenly confided in Jordan about my inheritance and how I had to leave Carl to get it. Jordan thought he could blackmail me into giving him half my inheritance by threatening to tell my father about us. He was wrong, dead wrong!"

"Why all this honesty now? Is it because an innocent woman is in jail for something you did? Or maybe you had an accomplice."

She rolled her eyes. "I didn't kill him, and if she didn't do it, then she has nothing to worry about, does she? I can afford to be honest with you because I have nothing to lose now. Besides, it's just your word against mine."

This time when she walked away, I let her.

I worked at Estelle's that afternoon. Things were better between Gwen and Alex. With Joy being in the hospital, the tension between them had melted, making it more pleasant for everybody. Alex had been to the hospital to drop off some flowers that we'd all chipped in for and reported that Joy had been moved from ICU to a regular room. I needed to talk to Joy about Jordan. I just hoped I got a chance to do it when her aunt wasn't around.

I headed over to the hospital when I got off at six. Visiting hours were over at eight o'clock. As I was entering the hospital, I ran into Joy's aunt. She didn't look pleased.

"There's nothing wrong, is there?" I asked warily.

"Nope, everything's right as rain. Joy's getting better, though her memory isn't the greatest right now. But she's awake and on the mend."

"Oh, well is it okay if I go up and say hi?" She still looked grim despite what she'd just said.

"Of course. You go right on up. Joy's not alone though. Her little friend Cory is up there with her." She shook her head in disgust. "Try as I might, I just can't understand it. Anyway, will you tell Joy I'll be back in an hour?"

"Sure, Mrs. Mills." I watched her walk off still shaking her head. She was going to have to accept Joy and Cory's relationship if she wanted to remain in Joy's life.

I found Joy's new room and knocked a couple of times before I walked in. Joy was sitting up in bed. The swelling had gone down in her face, but her head was still wrapped in bandages. Cory was sitting on the edge of the bed, and I got the impression I'd just interrupted something. Cory instantly tensed upon seeing me. Joy just looked surprised and a little confused.

"You certainly look a lot better than when I was here last time," I said softly as I approached the bed. "Do you remember me, Joy?"

Joy stared at me for a moment. "I work with you, don't I?" She sounded unsure and looked over at Cory, who shot me an evil look. I ignored her.

"That's right. How are you feeling?"

"Better. What's your name again?"

"Kendra. Does that sound familiar to you?"

"I remember now," she said, still sounding a little unsure. I never thought I'd see Joy Owens looking so vulnerable.

I started to ask her another question when Cory interrupted me. "Can I talk to you outside please?"

I reluctantly followed her out into the hall. She spun around to face me. Her face was contorted in rage. "You really think you're slick, don't you?"

"I'm just visiting Joy. What's the problem?"

"No, you just want to grill her about that man her mom was engaged to. Can't you see she barely remembers your name? How is she going to be able to remember anything about that man? And didn't they arrest somebody for his murder? It was all over the news yesterday."

"They have the wrong person."

"And you think Joy's the right person?" Her hands were clenched at her sides ready for battle.

A nurse walked by and gave us a curious look.

"That painting proves she was at least in the house and saw the body. Maybe she saw something that she doesn't realize could help the case."

"Maybe she did but she's in no shape to answer any questions now."

"Has it occurred to you that maybe Joy's accident was no accident and might have something to do with this? That Joy may have witnessed something that caused someone to want to kill her and that they might try again?"

"It was an accident, an accident! She was out on a dark country road late at night. It was a hit-and-run, pure and simple. Now go away and leave us alone!" She spun on her heel and went into Joy's room, leaving me staring after her in shock.

I drove around for a while to calm myself down. I put a Sade tape in my cassette deck and let the mellow, mournful sound of her voice lull me into a calmer mood. Calmer not happier. I was pissed. How could Cory claim to care so much about Joy and not at least consider what I said?

I didn't feel like going home. I stopped at Frisch's Big Boy instead and got some hot-fudge cake to make myself feel better. Chocolate has a very therapeutic effect on me. While I ate, I started wondering where Raymond Hodge was. There are only a few places in Willow to stay. There was of course the Holiday Inn. I really couldn't see him being there. The media would easily find him. There were a couple of bed-and-breakfasts that mainly catered to the rich parents of Kingford College students and visiting professors. Then there was the Heritage Arms. It was a swanky name for what was actually a roach motel at the edge of town.

I lost my virginity at the Heritage Arms the summer before I went away to college. It was the perfect place for illicit activity and for people trying to stay on the down low. I had a secret summer romance with the son of one of my mother's friends. His name was Ricky Sanders, and it was a secret because he was older, engaged, and could have been arrested. I was too young and naive to have the good grace to feel guilty about helping him cheat on his fiancée. In the end, I went off to Ohio State and he got married. Ricky's now on his third marriage and has six kids. I guess he's going to keep doing it until he gets it right. Considering that Raymond and Bernie had an illicit affair of their own twenty years ago, I was betting Raymond Hodge knew the Heritage Arms well.

I headed over there. I hadn't decided if I was going to try and talk to Raymond Hodge. I still remembered our last encounter. To be on the safe side, I tossed a can of pepper spray in my purse that Mama had given me a while back. She'd gotten it free for filling out a magazine survey on home security. It seemed a little too convenient that he had shown up in town to give a statement against Bernie. I wanted to find out why he'd come back to Willow and how he even knew about Jordan's murder.

I pulled into the gravel parking lot and headed to the office. The motel itself consisted of two separate one-story buildings. It hadn't changed much at all since I'd been there. The last time I was there, the buildings were painted a dingy white with blue trim. Now they were painted a dingy gray with black trim. The office was located in the first building, the one that faced the road. The second building was at an angle behind the first making an L-formation. Country music was blaring out of a radio on a shelf behind the front desk, which was manned by a scrawny teenaged girl with braces. She was chewing gum and bobbing her head to Shania Twain.

"Yeah, you want a room?" she asked after giving me the onceover.

"No, I just wanted to ask you a question," I said loudly over the loud music.

"What?"

I glared at the radio until with great reluctance she finally turned it down.

"Can you tell me if a man named Raymond Hodge is staying here? He's a tall, slim, black man in his fifties."

"Nope," she said with a loud pop of her gum.

"Nope he's not here, or nope you can't tell me."

"Can't tell. It's against the rules." I wasn't surprised. A year ago, a woman caught her husband and his secretary at the Heritage Arms and shot and killed them both. Her husband had registered with his real name. The desk clerk on duty had told the man's wife he was staying there. Hence, the new anonymity rule.

"It's very important that I find him."

"You a cop?" Her eyes narrowed just a bit.

"No, I'm not."

"Sorry, can't help you." She turned the radio up and turned her back on me. That was the last straw. I wasn't about to let this monosyllabic, gum-popping child be the fourth person in one day to tell me to beat it. I was going to get an answer to my question, and she was going to give it to me. Unfortunately, the only way I could think to do it was to burst into tears, loud, heart-wrenching sobs that got the clerk's attention right away. Her eyes were as big as saucers as she quickly turned off the radio.

"Lady, are you okay?"

"No, I'm not." Angela Bassett had nothing on me at that moment. "The man I'm looking for is my daddy and he's an alcoholic. Every now and then he takes off and checks into a cheap motel and drinks until he blacks out. It used to only happen once or twice a year, but he's getting worse. This is the second time this month he's done this. I just want to make sure he's okay. Can't you please tell me if he's here?" I even wrung my hands for a more melodramatic effect.

The clerk looked torn. She was clearly moved by my story, as her eyes were glistening just a bit. Maybe she, too, had a relative overly fond of alcohol. Most of us do. However, I could tell she was still reluctant to break the rules, so I made it easy for her.

"Just nod yes or no. Is a man that fits the description I gave you staying here?"

The clerk hesitated just a bit, then nodded yes. Bingo.

"Is he staying here alone?" Another yes.

"What room is he staying in?" A vigorous no.

"Okay, okay, is he staying in this building?" A slight no nod. I felt a little like I was playing charades.

This was going to take forever.

"The next building..."

I finally found out that my drunk daddy was in room 10B. He had checked in on Sunday. He'd had at least one visitor since he arrived. The clerk didn't know if it was a man or a woman, just that she'd noticed two shadows behind his curtained window as she left to go home. The clerk hadn't seen him all day and hadn't seen anyone go in or out of his room. Information gathering was hard. I didn't envy private investigators one bit. I decided to have a chat with dear old dad since I was here. I felt around the bottom of my purse for the pepper spray.

Room 10B was the very last one on the end of the second building. I approached it warily. The curtains were drawn and I could see the dim glow of the TV. I thought I saw a figure go past the window. I knocked softly, fully expecting a shocked Raymond Hodge to be the fifth person that day to tell me to get lost. There was no answer.

"Mr. Hodge, are you in there?" Silence.

"Look, I know you're in there. Open up. I need to talk to you. I'm a friend of Bernice Gibson, and I'm not going away until I talk to you."

The door opened a crack.

"You alone?" croaked a raspy, disembodied voice from inside.

I said I was. It opened a bit more, and like a fool

whose mother never taught her any better, I walked in. The fleeting images I remembered were of a darkened room that smelled like a distillery. I also caught a glimpse of a trashcan heaped with liquor bottles. The only light in the room came from the TV, which had been turned down and was casting eerie flickering shadows on the walls. The door slammed shut behind me. I turned my head just in time to see a shadowy figure moving quickly toward me. Before I could turn completely around, I heard glass breaking and simultaneously felt an explosion of pain in my head. I sank to my knees and fell forward into darkness. So much for the pepper spray.

When I finally woke up in the hospital the next day, I had a concussion and a cut on my scalp that took ten stitches to close. I'd been hit over the head with a bottle, probably one from the pile that I'd seen in the trash. Mama was sitting by my bed when I woke up. Her usual rich coloring looked washed-out. She looked old and tired and that scared me more than what had happened to me.

She helped me sit up in bed. My head felt huge and my tongue felt thick. I tasted blood and discovered that I must have bitten my tongue when I hit the floor. I had a bandage on the back of my head. Mama sat down on the edge of the bed and laid a cool, comforting hand on my forehead. The tenderness of her touch overwhelmed me, and hot tears spilled down my cheeks. Mama's the only one I can be a complete baby around. I hated for anyone else to see me cry. Mama sat by silently, letting me get it all out of my system. When I was finished, she gently wiped my face. I gave her a weak smile. Then she let me have it.

"Girl, are you trying to give me a heart attack? What in the world were you thinking?"

I was thankful that she was speaking quietly in deference to my wounded head. I shook my head miserably and winced.

"I wasn't thinking. That was the problem. I just wanted to talk to Raymond Hodge. I didn't know he'd attack me." But was I really surprised given our last encounter? The memory of his wild eyes in Joy's apartment should have kept me away. I felt incredibly stupid.

Mama proceeded to tell me how the desk clerk had found me after seeing someone running from the room. When the ambulance and police arrived, the clerk had been babbling about how I'd been attacked by my drunken father. It took Mama forever to explain that my father was in fact living in Florida and didn't drink at all. She looked at me expectantly. One good thing about a head injury was that I could always pretend that I didn't know what she was talking about. She'd never believe me though. She knew all of my tricks.

"Well, I hope they caught him and put him in jail," I

said quickly, changing the subject and taking on my role as victim-in-search-of- justice.

Mama was momentarily speechless. I groaned. "Don't tell me, let me guess. Raymond Hodge is still on the loose."

"No, baby, Raymond Hodge is dead. They found him in the bathroom of that hotel room after they loaded you into the ambulance. He was stabbed to death in the bathtub. Whoever attacked you must have killed him."

Now I was scared.

Detectives Mercer and Harmon stopped by that morning to get a statement from me. They told me much the same thing as Mama had about Raymond Hodge. The knife used to kill him was found in the bushes outside the hotel room. There weren't any prints on it. I was lucky not to have been stabbed myself. I had been admonished by everyone who stepped into my room about interfering in police work. Not to mention being threatened with a charge of obstructing justice by a tight-lipped Harmon. But they needn't have worried; I had learned my lesson. I was going back to minding my own business. I was released later that morning, even though I still felt like crap. These days you have to be practically on death's door to warrant any kind of a hospital stay.

Mama had wanted me to come and stay at her

house, but I wanted to be in my own apartment in my own bed. I felt sure that whoever had attacked me did so because they panicked and I was in the way of a clean getaway. Still, I was very wary. I went around and locked every window and dead-bolted my door. I even wedged a chair under it for good measure. My phone rang and I almost jumped out of my skin. It was Bernie.

"Are you okay? I heard about you being attacked!"

I explained to her what happened.

"Kendra, I appreciate everything that you're trying to do for me, but you gotta promise me no more Nancy Drew. There's a lunatic running around. First Jordan, now Raymond. I just don't understand what's going on."

"Well at least now the police have to realize that you didn't kill Jordan, right?"

"Wrong, I was just questioned again. Seems now they think that I killed Raymond Hodge in retaliation for telling what I did to him twenty years ago and to keep him from testifying against me in the trial. Only this time they have no proof. I was out on bail but I had been with Emmett Palmer all afternoon discussing my case. Raymond Hodge. I just can't believe it. Where did he come from and where in the world has he been all this time?"

I told her that according to the news, he'd been in Atlanta. I also told her what Althea had done. She was silent so long I thought she'd hung up.

"You know, I can't even be mad at her anymore. I'm sure she was just trying to protect me. I just wish she'd have told me that I hadn't killed him. Damn, I could really use Mother now. She'd know what to do, plus she'd tell that Detective Harmon where to go and how to get there."

"Bernie, do you have any idea who could have planted that stuff in your house?"

"I didn't even know half of those folks who came to the house after Jordan's funeral. It could have been anybody."

It could have also been Joy for that matter. I did find her snooping around Bernie's house. Was she trying to find a place to plant some stuff? As long as Cory and Joy's aunt were around, I'd never get a chance to talk to Joy alone. Neither Vanessa nor Carl had been at the house, but they could have paid someone to plant evidence there. Was I really still suspicious of Carl? We did still have a date for Saturday night. I couldn't believe I was still thinking like this. Hadn't I vowed I was going to mind my own business? This was going to be a lot easier said than done.

I ran myself a hot bath and sprinkled in some of my favorite aromatherapy bath salts. I'd left all my good tapes in my car, which Alex had been nice enough to bring home for me, and I wasn't about to leave my apartment to go out to get them. Just then I remembered that I still had Jordan's CD case sitting on my kitchen counter. I'd brought it in and meant to take it to Bernie and forgot in the excitement of the past few days. It was a brown leather case the size of an attaché case. I opened it and was surprised to see that Jordan had had very eclectic taste in music. There must have been about a hundred CDs by everyone from B.B. King to Evelyn Champagne King, Kenny G to Warren G. I perused the tapes and finally decided on Phyllis Hyman.

In my rush to get to the bathroom to check on my water, I knocked the case off the counter. Cursing, I bent to pick up the CDs that had skittered across the kitchen floor. When I went to put them back in the case, I noticed the lining was worn away and revealed something yellow. I pulled and it came out. Underneath was a large manila envelope.

I turned off my bathwater and sat down at the kitchen table to examine my find. There were several things inside the envelope. The first thing I pulled out was Jordan's driver's license. But I was surprised to see that the name on the license was Wallace Jordan Graham. The next thing I pulled out was the title to his car. Jordan had acquired the car in December 1976. The previous owner was listed as an Ina Graham with an address in Columbus. Next came a picture.

It was an old, faded color snapshot showing a much younger, slimmer Jordan sporting an afro and wearing a blue shirt opened almost to the waist with a large gold medallion around his neck. I'd be willing to guess that it was his zodiac sign. He was sitting next to an elderly woman whose floral-print dress was clashing with the flowered print of the couch they were sitting on. Her hair was gray and curled into tight poodle curls all over her head. She was decked out in pearl jewelry. Jordan's arm was around her shoulder, and they both had the same toothy grin, though the woman's looked like hers was due to dentures. This had to be Jordan's grandmother.

Standing behind them was another younger woman. She wasn't smiling. She was grossly overweight and had her hands on her large hips. She was wearing a tight red shirt, and her crocheted white vest was pulled tightly across the front of a shelf-like bosom. Her hair was pulled into one big Afro puff on the top of her head with yellow barrettes on either side of it. She had quite a funky look on her face. In fact, she looked pissed about life in general. I flipped the picture over. There were no names written on the back, just the month and the year, July 1976. No wonder she looked so mad. Seventies fashions weren't exactly kind to the larger person. The clothes had looked ridiculous on non-overweight people. I wondered who she was.

The last things I pulled from the envelope were what really shocked me. It was a marriage license and certificate issued to a Wallace J. Graham, aged twenty-two, occupation: self-employed and to a Delores D.

Briggs, aged twenty-three, occupation: nurse's aide. Both had been issued on December 1, 1976, in Las Vegas, Nevada.

So Jordan had been married. Was he still married? I looked in the envelope but there were no divorce papers or wedding pictures. Was this why he was going by an assumed name? Was he hiding from his wife or possibly other women he screwed over? My guess was both. I should have turned this stuff over to the police. Instead, I called Carl and told him I'd meet him in Columbus for our date. I planned on visiting the address listed on the title to Jordan's car. Ina Graham had to have been the grandmother's name. Was I being stupid? Yes. But my life was already at risk from involving myself in this crazy mess. I figured I must not have been hit on the head hard enough with that bottle to knock any good sense into me. I certainly wanted to find out who had done it before they killed me next time.

TWELVE

Saturday morning it rained. By midmorning the rain had stopped, leaving behind a muggy heat that seemed to rise from the pavement, making the air feel like a sauna. I had all the fans in my apartment on full blast, but I only succeeded in moving hot air around. Today would be the first time in two days I'd ventured out of my apartment. My head felt fine, although I still had stitches. Luckily, they didn't have to shave very much of my hair to treat my cut. It had grown about a half an inch in the past few weeks and was just long enough to hide the stitches. At worst I'd look like a Little Orphan Annie. I took a silk scarf and tied it around my head to keep sweat from running in my face. It actually didn't look half bad. It was kind of retro, like I could have danced down the Soul Train line back in the day.

I had plans to meet Carl in Columbus at his condo for dinner later that evening. I couldn't wait to sample his skills, culinary of course—yeah, right. I had a whole day to kill before then. I wrote down Ina Graham's address, 2012 Chesterline Drive, and called the library to find out where in Columbus it was. After finding out it was on the east side, I put my white silk halter dress and some dressy sandals in a garment bag, I tossed my make-up bag in my purse, and I took along Ina Graham's address and the snapshot of Jordan and the two women. I prayed the iffy air conditioning in my car would bless me with some relief on the way.

I stopped at the drugstore before hitting the road to get a candy bar or two for the trip. I hadn't yet eaten and didn't want anything heavy with all the heat. As usual, once I got in the store I thought of a few other things I needed and picked them up as well. I was on my way to the checkout line when a thought hit me. I backtracked to the aisle where the condoms were and stood there staring. Should I? It was only our second date, but I couldn't get that kiss out of my mind and it had been so long—too long since I'd been with a man. Would he think I was sleazy if I pulled out a box of condoms? And what would I say if it got to that point? "Here, baby, hope these fit. I took a chance 'cause I didn't know your size." While I stood there pondering the chances of getting my groove on that night, a velvety voice with the hint of a Southern drawl spoke to me.

"Hi there, sugar."

I turned and saw the woman from the funeral home,

Winette Barlow, Crazy Frieda's sister-in-law. She was smiling her bright-red-lipsticked smile and was dressed in a red silk pantsuit and three-inch black pumps. Somehow she managed to look fresh and cool despite the heat.

"It's Kendra, right?" she asked, eyeing the display of condoms in front of me with amusement. I had turned red with embarrassment.

"Yes. How have you been, Mrs. Barlow?"

"Child, call me Winnie, everybody does. I was hoping I'd see you around somewhere to thank you for stopping by during Elfrieda's visitation hours. You forgot to sign the guestbook."

I wondered if she'd forgotten that I was there for someone else's funeral.

"I would have stayed longer, but I didn't want to interrupt your visit with the Ivorys."

The smile immediately fled and she rolled her eyes so hard I thought they'd turn inside out. "Oh, trust me, honey, you weren't interrupting a thing. The Ivorys were friends of my late husband Henry and his first wife, Francis. When Francis died and Henry married me, they didn't come around very much, which was fine by me. I was fifteen years younger than Henry. I like gambling, love to dance, and I don't think having a drink now and again is going to cause me to burn in hell for all eternity. And, as you can see, I love the color red. Donna Ivory thinks I'm a scarlet hussy. But that's okay because I think she's a hard-faced, holy-rollin', hypocritical heifer!"

Can you say that three times fast? I thought. This was a woman after my own heart.

I laughed. "Well you certainly call it like you see it."

"I'm usually not so blunt. I'm just still mad at that simple woman for what she said about Elfrieda and all that nonsense about her knowing her time was near and acting strange. I don't know who or what that woman saw, but it wasn't Elfrieda."

"Why do you say that?" My curiosity was piqued.

"Because when I arrived home from my brother's, I found her dead in her bed. That was on Thursday, May seventeenth. The doctor said she died in her sleep the night before. So she couldn't have been in any alley behind Donna Ivory's house the morning of Friday, May eighteenth, unless it was her ghost."

The morning of May 18 was when Jordan had been killed. Whoever Donna Ivory saw must have been the killer. But the Ivorys said they hadn't seen anything out of the ordinary. And they hadn't. Crazy Frieda rummaging around for cans wasn't anything out of the ordinary. So what if she got her days mixed up. Only it hadn't been her. Had it been the killer in disguise?

"You okay, honey?" Winette Barlow was looking at me strangely.

"Oh yes. I'm fine."

"Good. I've got to run now. I'm off to Atlantic City with my singles group. You take care, sweetie."

She reached past me, grabbed an economy-sized box of Trojan Magnums, flashed me a big smile, and headed off down the aisle. Well, there was obviously no shame in her game. Following her lead, I snatched up a box of condoms and headed to the checkout counter.

My air conditioner blessed me with relatively cool air on my thirty-minute drive to Columbus. I munched my Snickers bar and sang along with Lisa Stansfield, still amazed that a white girl from Great Britain could sound so soulful.

Traffic on 70 was backed up because of construction. I vaguely remembered Carl warning about this on the phone the other night. I had meant to take Route 40 but forgot in light of what Winette Barlow had told me. What did it mean? For starters, it meant that whoever killed Jordan, or whatever his name was, had planned it far in advance. The killer had known that it wasn't unusual for Crazy Frieda—man, I had to stop calling her that—to be in the alley. No one would think anything of seeing someone dressed in raggedy clothes lurking in the alley. Everyone would assume it had been Frieda. Who would know about this? Everyone who lived on either side of the alley, which included Vanessa and Bernie.

Could I really see Vanessa dressing up and lurking in the alley behind her own home waiting for Jordan to show up? Actually, yes I could. Bernie also knew about Frieda and her cans. I remembered her telling me about leaving cans out for Frieda when she lived in the house. I wondered how she could have found the time to borrow Iris's car, put on a disguise, wait in the house, kill Jordan, change clothes, pick up the programs at the printer, and be back at the center without a hair out of place. It seemed unlikely but I guess not impossible.

What about Joy? If she'd been following Jordan, she'd have followed him over to Vanessa's and could have seen Frieda in the alley. Did it give her an idea? Could she have seen something she wasn't supposed to and been run down on her bicycle as a result? I did have a hard time envisioning Carl dressed as an oversized bag lady lurking in the alley. Or was it just lust clouding my judgment? Probably. I planned on finding out why Vanessa was giving him money. Were they accomplices? Did they pretend to split up, knowing Vanessa's father was dying, after which they would collect the insurance money and reunite? Did Jordan get in the way? Where was Jordan's wife? I didn't see any divorce papers in the envelope. Were they still married? And just how did Raymond Hodge fit into all of this?

Chesterline Drive was a nice, quiet, tree-lined street of mainly two-story homes. I parked in front of 2012, a white stucco bi-level, and looked around before getting out. Whoever lived here now was taking good care of it.

The lawn was immaculate and edged neatly. The front of the house was framed by high bushes that hid the front door from the street. There didn't appear to be anyone home as far as I could tell. There was no car in the driveway and no signs of life coming from inside. I got out of my car and noticed an older woman across the street in front of a big brick two-story, sweeping grass from her sidewalk. I walked across the street.

"Excuse me, ma'am. Do you know if anybody's home across the street?"

She looked up at me and appeared slightly annoyed at having been interrupted from her task.

"You try knocking on the door?" she asked sourly. She had on dirty gardening gloves, blue sweatpants, and a yellow T-shirt with a picture of a cat on it. Her white tennis shoes had grass stains on them and a hole in the left toe. I could see her black sock peeking through. Her face was heavily lined and I guessed her age to be anywhere from fifty-five to a hundred and five. I couldn't tell.

"It doesn't look like anybody's home. Do you know who lives there?"

She gave me a suspicious look.

"Of course I know who lives there. What kind of person doesn't know her neighbors? Are you selling something? Because if you are, I'm not interested and neither are the Taylors. They got enough problems. He just got laid off from his job, and they don't have money to spend on foolishness."

"No, ma'am, I'm not. Actually, I'm wondering if you also knew the previous owners of that house, the Grahams? I knew Mrs. Graham's grandson, Wallace."

She stopped sweeping and stared at me. "If you're a friend of Wally's then you know he hasn't lived across the street in over twenty years."

Wally? "I just met him last year. He was involved with a friend of mine."

She laughed and her wrinkles arranged themselves into a smile. "Oh, really. Wally always was quite the ladies' man. You sure you're not the friend?"

"No, Ms. ah?"

"Lambert, Tangy Lambert," she offered grudgingly.

"No, Ms. Lambert. To be perfectly honest with you, I knew Wallace Graham as Jordan Wallace. He was murdered a few weeks ago. A good friend of mine was involved with him and has been charged with his murder. I just need some questions answered. Can you help me?" She dropped her broom in the grass and invited me inside her house.

Tangy Lambert's place was clean but cluttered. Almost every surface was covered with knickknacks and piles of newspapers and magazines. The whole place smelled strongly of cat, coffee, and cigarettes. She offered me a seat on a hard recliner, one of the few clear spaces for sitting, and disappeared into the kitchen. A large yellow cat pounced into my lap from out of nowhere, scaring the life out of me. It sat heavily in my lap rubbing its head against my chest and purring. The thing must have weighed at least thirty pounds. What was she feeding this monster? She came back a few minutes later with two tall glasses of lemonade. I drank a third of it before I noticed a cat hair in it.

"Caesar likes you. He likes very few people." She said it like I should be grateful.

I smiled to show how honored I felt and even stroked Caesar's head for good measure. Caesar decided he liked where he was and proceeded to fall asleep. I felt my legs start to go numb.

"So what's this about Wally being murdered?"

I told her all about what happened, including Bernie's arrest and Jordan's involvement with Vanessa.

"That's too bad, really it is, but it hardly surprises me. Wally always did have a way with women, starting with his grandmother. She spoiled him rotten. After her husband died in an accident at work, she came into a chunk of insurance money and moved across the street. It must have been thirty-odd years ago. She was the first colored lady in the neighborhood. When her son and daughter-in-law were killed in a smash-up on 1-70 up in Cleveland, Wally came to live with her. He must have been about twelve and a cutie even then. Ina never got to see him much before then 'cause she didn't like her daughter-in-law, so they hardly ever came to visit."

"Is this his grandmother?" I asked, pulling the snapshot out of my purse and handing it to her.

"Yes, this is Ina all decked out in her pearls. She loved her pearls. Where'd you get this picture?"

"I found it in his things after he died." At least it wasn't a complete lie.

"Who's this other woman?"

She looked hard at the picture a minute.

"She lived with them for several months before Ina died. Oh, damn, I can't remember her name. It'll come to me in time. She was a nurse's aide. At least that's what I was told. Took care of Ina when she was sick. Ina had Alzheimer's."

The marriage license I found listed Jordan's wife as being a nurse's aide. Surely the sullen, obese woman in the picture wasn't Jordan's wife. She didn't exactly look like his type. Maybe she had some money. There would have to have been something she had that Jordan had wanted or needed. What had it been?

"Dee Dee, that's what they called her. She was from somewhere in the South I believe. She had an accent as thick as molasses. Can't remember her last name though."

"She doesn't look too happy in this picture."

"I felt sorry for the poor thing. She of course had it bad for Wally. In fact, I think she was someone he met while he was in college at Morehouse, and she followed him here after graduation. I was real surprised that

Wally even graduated. Wasn't exactly the academic type; more into extracurricular activities, if you know what I mean."

"So, she just showed up here, and they let her stay?"

"Yeah, I was always surprised by that. But Ina had Alzheimer's and even though she wasn't real bad then, she still needed someone to stay with her all the time. Wally was too busy running the streets, and he wasn't the type to stay at home and take care of his sick grandmother anyway."

"I'm surprised he didn't try and put her in a nursing home."

"Well, he might have looked into it and found out the same thing I did when I was thinking of putting my father into a nursing home years ago. The state would have taken everything, including his house, and left him with fifteen hundred dollars. I wasn't going to let that happen. I can't imagine Wally letting it happen either. His grandmother was his meal ticket."

"What was Dee Dee like?"

"Quiet, but not shy. Was real self-conscious about her weight. Ina treated the girl like crap, always making fun of her. Used to call her names. Dee Dee took it all in stride on the surface, but I saw real hatred in her eyes at times. It scared me. And smart, the girl was smart as a whip. She wouldn't let many people see that side of her. Told me once men didn't want smart women. I told her she was crazy. I think she may have had that eating disorder. The one where you stuff yourself and then throw it all up later."

"You think she was bulimic? Why?"

"I went over there for dinner once while Dee Dee was there. She hardly ate a thing. Later, I went into the kitchen to see if she needed any help cleaning up, and I saw her stuffing food in her mouth like she was starving. It was weird."

It dawned on me that I'd recently had an almost identical conversation as the one I was having now. Who had it been about? I couldn't remember.

"How did Jordan—I mean Wally—treat her?"

"He was kind of indifferent. The more she worshipped him, the more indifferent he became. I believe Ina used to try and pit the two of them against each other. She would be real nice to Dee Dee in front of Wally, making him think that Dee Dee was her new favorite and that she was going to leave all her money to her. Ina wanted Wally to stay home more and he would for a week or two to get back into Ina's good graces, then it would be back to the way it was."

"It sounds like Ina Graham wasn't a very nice woman."

"Oh, she had her good qualities. She could be very kind when she wanted. She was just very insecure and lonely."

"What happened to them?"

"Ina died. It was right after Thanksgiving. She must

have left everything to Wally 'cause he sold the house and everything in it about two weeks later. I haven't seen him since. Dee Dee showed up here around that time. She'd gone back home after Ina died. She came back here looking for Wally. I told her he had sold up and left. She was heartbroken. I asked her how she'd been doing and she told me she'd gotten married but it hadn't worked out. I didn't even know she was seeing anyone. She only had eyes for Wally."

"Would you know how to reach her?"

"The funny thing is, her sister came looking for her. Must have been about five years ago. Seems Dee Dee never went back home after she came up here looking for Wally. Just disappeared. Her sister needed to find her because their mother was dying and her last wish was to see Dee Dee again. I don't know if she ever found her. She left me her card. Let me see if I can find it."

She got up and left the room, and I took the opportunity to gently nudge Caesar out of my lap. He shot me a reproachful look and went to finish his nap on the couch, wedged between a pile of *Life* magazines and a stack of newspapers. I stretched my legs out to get the circulation going again and wondered for a split second if the cat still liked me.

"Here it is," she said, gleefully waving a small square of paper. "It pays to be a pack rat."

I took the card and looked at it. Carol Briggs-

Mason, CPA. It listed an address and phone number in Atlanta, Georgia.

"Can I have this?"

"Yeah, keep it if you want. But it's five-year-old information. It might not be the same anymore."

I'd just have to take a chance.

"Who can I say is calling?" asked the woman who answered the phone.

Luckily, Carol Briggs-Mason was still at the number listed on the card and was working on Saturday to my great surprise. I was at a pay phone at the Eastland Mall and was hoping I had enough time left on my phone card to complete the call.

"My name is Kendra Clayton. I'm calling from Ohio. Tell her it's about her sister Dee Dee."

"One moment, please."

I listened to a Muzak version of a Celine Dion song for a few minutes before she finally came on the line.

"Yes, Miss Clayton, how can I help you?" She sounded very professional with a husky Southern drawl. Suddenly I was tongue-tied.

I explained who I was in one breathless rush. There was no sound from the other end of the line, and for a minute I thought she'd hung up on me.

"I guess I don't know how I can help you," she said finally with a tired sigh. "I haven't seen or heard from Dee Dee in more than twenty years. She could be dead for all I know."

"I was just wondering what you could tell me about her. It might help me to understand Wallace Jordan's past and why he was killed."

"You mean you want to know if she could have killed him?"

"Yes." There was no reason to beat around the bush.

"I don't have the time to talk about this right now. I just came in to finish up some work before they close the building at noon. You can give me your number, but I'm afraid I won't be able to call you until tomorrow."

I was disappointed but gave her my number and Mama's number, thanked her for her time, and hung up.

THIRTEEN

Seven thirty found me sitting in Carl Brumfield's condo in Worthington. The condo was a two-bedroom unit with white walls and beige carpeting throughout. Not much personality, and it had probably cost him an arm and a leg. Carl had livened it up with a few Jonathan Green prints, an aquarium of tropical fish, and a few plants courtesy of his mother. The furniture was the typical bachelor sparse with a caramel-colored leather sofa as soft as butter and a great entertainment center, complete with a Sony PlayStation and an assortment of video games.

After spending the rest of my day window-shopping, which is the only kind of shopping I could ever do in a mall, and changing in the restroom (not one of my better ideas), I was grateful to be sitting on Carl's living room floor, going through his CDs listening to

Earth Wind & Fire's "That's the Way of the World" and sipping a glass of wine. I'd kicked off my sandals and made myself right at home while Carl was busy getting dinner together. I got up from the floor and took a look at his family pictures on the mantel above his fireplace.

"These are my parents," he said, coming up behind me and gesturing toward a picture of an attractive older couple.

I felt his breath against my ear and a chill went down my spine. He put his hand on my waist and gently pulled me back against him.

"You look just like your father. Are these your sisters?" I asked, gesturing toward a family picture.

"Yeah, that's Anita with the braids. She's a flight attendant and lives in Newark, New Jersey. The other one is Monica. She and her husband own a car dealership up in Cleveland."

He was still standing close behind me and had started kneading my shoulders ever so slightly.

"They're very pretty," I said, pulling away just a bit. "Your parents must be very proud of all of you."

"I think so. We haven't given them too much grief, and we've all done pretty well. Of course, I'm the only divorced one. That doesn't sit too well with my mom."

"Did your family like Vanessa?"

"My family, in their hearts, wanted to see me with a black woman. They didn't know Nessa very well and they didn't try to. But they weren't unkind to her, just sort of indifferent."

"You know, I could have sworn I saw you earlier this week. I was at Wendy's on State Street in the drive-through. I thought I saw you at the bank."

He nodded and gave me a sheepish "I'm busted" grin.

"Yeah, that was me. Vanessa and I were closing our joint accounts. I'd been wanting to do it for weeks but with her father being sick and the other stuff going on, she didn't have time—"

"Carl, it's okay," I said, cutting him off. "You don't owe me any explanation. I just wondered if it was you." I breathed a silent sigh of relief and prayed he was telling the truth.

"I hope you like lasagna. It's one of the few things I know how to make. I'm glad you called and said you wanted to come here for dinner tonight. I've been eating out all week because I've been busy moving and putting stuff away. That's another reason why I was in Willow. I really needed to get my share of our savings account. I closed on this place Thursday and closing costs were more than I expected. Vanessa had been putting me off for weeks. I was beginning to wonder if she'd spent the money buying fancy clothes trying to impress her new boyfriend."

"She has a new man in her life?" I asked innocently, peering over the top of my wineglass.

"Oh yeah, some doctor at Willow Memorial. I'm

sure her father's pleased as hell."

"How do you feel about it?"

"Me?" he said, a little surprised by my question. "I'm fine. As far as I'm concerned, she's a free woman and can do what she wants with whomever she wants. Just like I'm a free man. I wondered how I'd feel once I got my half of our savings. Getting that money meant it was really over. But it was cool. Wasn't bad at all. And in case you're wondering, I also knew about her and that dude who was murdered. Saw them through the window when I went over there one night to talk about the divorce," he said, looking away from me.

"Did you ever think she may have been involved in his murder?" I asked carefully.

"Nah, Nessa's harmless. She has her faults, and she's greedy, but murder... I don't think so." We were silent for an awkward minute. Then Carl broke out one of his brilliant smiles.

"Man, how'd we get on this subject? Come on, dinner's getting cold." He took my hand, pulling me toward the dining room where dinner was on the table and smelling good.

I wondered if I should tell Carl about my attack. If he'd noticed my bald spot he hadn't mentioned it. I was also relieved that he didn't seem to care who Vanessa had been sleeping with and that he had an alibi for Thursday night when I was attacked.

The lasagna was great, as were the salad and

homemade bread. Carl had acquired the bread maker in his divorce settlement. We were having a great time. I drank a little too much wine and was feeling no pain.

"You know, if you drink much more of that stuff I'll have to insist you stay the night."

"I can think of worse places to spend the night."

"Such as?"

"My lonely apartment." I gave him a look that should have dispelled any questions he may have had as to my meaning.

Carl's eyes widened in surprise, then he smiled.

"Would you like to dance?"

I nodded my agreement and we headed into the living room. Five minutes later, the lights were low; Peabo Bryson's "Feel the Fire" was playing on the CD player. And dammit, I was feeling that fire, too, as we danced slowly. He smelled great and I buried my face in his neck. I heard him groan softly as I started nibbling his earlobe and kissing along his jawline. When I reached his mouth, we stopped dancing and stood there kissing hungrily. He pulled me tightly to him and I felt the hardness of him pressing against me. His hands blazed trails of fire up my bare back to the tiny buttons at my neck that fastened my halter dress. He quickly unbuttoned them, letting the top of my dress fall to my waist. Gently cupping my breasts, he bent down and took one hardened nipple into his mouth, bathing it with his tongue. I moaned and felt like I would melt into a puddle at his feet.

That's when the rock came crashing through the window.

We jumped apart like two little kids caught with our hot little hands in the cookie jar.

"What the hell!" Carl shouted as he raced to the front door. He flung it open just in time to see a car speeding off into the night. I quickly fastened my dress and stared at the broken glass and the ruins of our evening. Shit!

I helped Carl clean up the glass and tape plastic over the hole in his living room window. We worked in silence. Carl was looking grim and angry but had refused to call the police.

"You know who did this, don't you?" I finally asked when we'd finished. "Does it have anything to do with a case you're prosecuting? Are you going to answer me?" I asked when he didn't speak right away.

"I'm sorry, Kendra." He sat on the couch and gestured for me to sit down next to him. "I do know who did this. And it doesn't have anything to do with my job. I thought I had put all this shit behind me when I moved back here to Columbus."

I poured us some more wine because suddenly I was quite sober. I waited for him to pull himself together and tell me what the hell was going on. Finally he did.

"When Nessa left me, I was a mess. It was

completely out of the blue. I was hurt, confused, angry. It didn't help matters when I found out that she had been lured away from our marriage by promises of big money from her father. Anyway, I was lonely and got involved with someone I had no business getting involved with. She was the widow of a fraternity brother of mine. We were both Kappas involved with the graduate chapter out of Dayton. He died of a heart attack last year, and his widow and I started kicking it a few months after Nessa left me.

"I'd never really been attracted to her before then. She was a little too flashy for me and was about twelve years older. But one thing led to another and before I knew it, I was in deep. I wasn't even divorced yet and she was planning our wedding. She called me at all hours of the day and night. Kept showing up at my job. Bought me expensive gifts. She really freaked me out. Finally, I broke it off and she started stalking me. It was like that movie *Fatal Attraction,* only with no rabbit boiling in my pot." He gave me a weak smile.

"You better keep an eye on those fish," I said.

He laughed shakily.

"She hasn't bothered me since I moved here. Now this."

"I know you don't want to go to the police, but you may have no choice. You can't live like this. Has she ever threatened to hurt you physically?"

"No, just hang-up phone calls, love letters. I came

out of work one day and my tires were punctured. I don't have proof, but I'm sure she did it. She's hinted at committing suicide. But I don't think she'd ever do it."

"She must be following me if she knows where I'm living now. When I first moved back here, I was living with my parents, waiting for the financing on this place to go through. She hasn't bothered me in about two weeks. I thought I was home free, now this. I just hope she doesn't start bothering you. Damn, this is such a mess."

I did end up spending the night at Carl's place. Having been hit over the head with a bottle left me very wary about driving home late at night with a rock-wielding crazy woman on the loose. I decided not to tell Carl about my attack. He had problems of his own. Carl let me have his bed while he slept on the couch. We spent the rest of the evening playing with his PlayStation. Somehow this wasn't what I had in mind.

FOURTEEN

I drove home the next morning after Carl cooked breakfast. He made a mean omelet and again I wondered about his other skills. While reaching for my car keys in my purse, my fingers brushed against the box of condoms I'd brought with me. I guess I could have tried to seduce him between games of Ms. Pac-Man, but after the rock incident, my heart wasn't in it. The mood, along with the window, had been shattered. I made him promise me he'd think about getting a restraining order. And he made me promise I'd let him make it up to me for our ruined evening. He didn't have to twist my arm.

When I got home, I had a visitor waiting for me. It was Mama. She was sitting on Mrs. Carson's porch drinking iced tea. They had been laughing and talking until they saw me. Then Mama's face changed into a thundercloud and I almost ran. I would have rather faced Carl's love-struck stalker.

"Where have you been? I've been calling all over the place looking for you since yesterday. I was so upset I missed church! Girl, you may be damn near thirty but Annie Ruth here had to keep me from cutting a switch and taking it to your behind! After what happened to you last week, I can't believe you're out running the streets." She leaned back into her chair dramatically like I was just going to be the death of her. The urge to roll my eyes was killing me. I didn't give in to it because I didn't want to see my seventy-two-year-old grandmother fly off the porch and beat the crap out of me. I could have kicked myself for not calling her.

Mrs. Carson was looking everywhere but at me, and I could have sworn I heard her raggedy cat Mahalia, who was lounging in her lap, hissing with laughter. Two little girls who were riding their bikes down the street had stopped to stare and rode off snickering at seeing a grown-up getting scolded. I just sighed and walked up onto the porch. I wrapped my arms around her and buried my face in her neck. She smelled like roses.

"I'm sorry, Mama. I got tied up in Columbus and forgot to call you. I didn't mean to scare you."

"Well, I won't ask what you were doing in Columbus, who tied you up, or why you're lookin' like something the cat dragged in. All I ask is that you show me a little consideration. It would just kill me to have to call your parents and tell them something bad had happened to you. Do you understand?"

"Yes, ma'am." Now that I'd been properly chastised, I was given a glass of iced tea and sat and listened to the two of them gossip. I didn't dare tell them about what I'd found in Jordan's tape case, about my visit to his old neighborhood, or about Carl's stalker. Mama would have killed me. I just smiled and sipped my tea, all the while listening for my phone to ring. I was very interested in what Dee Dee's sister had to say.

"As I was saying, Estelle, I could have just killed her. I was all set to pull into that handicapped spot at Kroger and she just whipped right in and snatched it from me. She ain't handicapped, unless those tight skirts of hers have restricted the supply of blood to her brain and she's mentally handicapped. And me with my bad knee had to park halfway across the parking lot. I was sore the rest of the day."

"Did you say anything to her? 'Cause I would have. You know me. If a person needs tellin' what's what, I tell 'em." Mama shot me a glare. I wasn't completely forgiven.

"Naw, I didn't want to cause no scene. I just picked up my prescriptions and left. I did see her in the store with her little miniskirt on. She's too old to be dressin' like that. She looked like a middle-aged hooker in that getup she had on."

"Who are you talking about?" I asked finally.

"Diane Gibson," they both said simultaneously. Mama took a sip from her glass and continued.

"See, she forgets that there are people in this town who remember when she wasn't so skinny or so rich. When she first came here she was a chunky heifer. And talked like she had a mouthful of mush, her Southern accent was so thick. It wasn't until she set her eyes on Ben Gibson that she lost weight and gained an attitude. Althea couldn't stand her. Thought she was strange from the start and that it was weird how she never talked about her family or her past. Ben couldn't see it though. He was too much in love."

As I sat there and listened to them talk, a familiar burning sensation started in the pit of my stomach. My heart started beating so loud that I could hear it pounding in my ears. Diane! Twenty years ago, Diane had been Dee Dee Briggs. Why hadn't I seen it before? Diane who came from Macon, Georgia. Diane who had everything and everything to lose if anyone found out she never divorced her first husband. She was married to Bernie's brother and could have known about Raymond Hodge. Did she track him down so he would come to town and implicate Bernie, and then killed him when he was no longer useful? She knew about Frieda Barlow rummaging for cans in the alley behind Archer Street. Diane didn't work, so there was no way to track her movements on any given day. Bernie had told me that Diane had some strange eating habits just as Tangy

Lambert had. Dee Dee would be a suitable nickname for a Delores D. Did the D stand for Diane? She had enough access to Bernie's house to plant any evidence she wanted.

Could I be right? If this were true, how could she have gotten into the house on Archer? Did she steal Bernie's keys? I had always wondered why Jordan had chosen Willow for his new home. Had he come here to blackmail his now-rich wife? How had he managed to track her down? Was she responsible for Joy's accident and if so, why? A lot of things still didn't add up. I had to be sure, which is why I needed to speak to Carol Briggs-Mason. I just prayed that she would call me back soon; then I would take what I found and everything I knew to the police.

I was eating dinner at Mama's at five o'clock. Usually I'm able to do her cooking justice, but I still hadn't gotten my phone call and was nervous and on edge. Alex and Gwen were also at Mama's for dinner. They told me that Joy would be released from the hospital soon into the care of Cory, much to the dismay of her aunt Clara. That information, coupled with the fact that Gwen and Alex were making goo-goo eyes at each other, led me to the conclusion that Gwen now knew that Joy was a lesbian and was no threat to her and Alex's relationship. I'd seen this honeymoon phase with them before. It wouldn't last long.

After dinner, Gwen and Alex volunteered to do the

dishes. I made a quick call to Bernie. There was no answer, so I left a message telling her to call as soon as possible. No sooner had I hung up the phone, it rang again. It was Carol Briggs-Mason, finally.

"Sorry it took me so long to get back to you. I had to wait until I was home alone and had some privacy. I haven't caught you at a bad time, have I?"

"No, not at all. I won't keep you. I just wanted to know about Dee Dee and when you last saw her."

"Let's see, it must have been 1976 around Christmastime. She came home unexpectedly. We were surprised to see her. She had gotten a job taking care of an elderly lady who had Alzheimer's in Columbus, Ohio."

"How'd she end up in Columbus?" I heard Carol make a disgusted sound.

"I'm sure she followed that slick pretty boy, Wallace Graham. She met him when she was at Spelman. He went to Morehouse and was from Columbus. When I think about that whole situation it just makes me sick."

"What happened?"

"He used her, that's what happened. Dee Dee was never much to look at. Always struggled with her weight. She got picked on and teased so much she developed a real complex about eating in front of people. Anyway, she was very smart and got a scholarship to Spelman. That's where she met Wallace. He was gorgeous all right, but soulless. He'd use anyone to get what he wanted. He started paying Dee Dee a lot of attention, you know, really building her up. It started out that he would get her to type his papers; then she was actually writing his papers. She also did all of his projects and was helping him cheat on exams. Making up crib sheets for him. Morehouse prides itself on turning out men who help build up the black community. I don't know what the hell happened to this guy."

That wasn't actually saying much for Dee Dee either, but I knew better than to say so.

"So what happened with Dee Dee's education?" As if I had to ask.

"It went straight down the toilet. She was so busy doing Wallace's work, she flunked out of Spelman. She tried to hide it from us, but our mother found out. She was so hurt. Dee Dee was too ashamed to come home. She ended up going through a nurse's aide program and got a job at a nursing home. It was just such a waste. Hell, she could have been a doctor, not just some damn nurse's aide. And of course, Wallace graduated from Morehouse. Whatever his degree is in, it should have my sister's name on it."

"Did you know that Dee Dee married Wallace in December 1976?"

"What are you talking about? Dee Dee never said anything to me about marrying Wallace. As much as she loved that fool, she would have shouted it from the highest mountaintop if he'd wanted to marry her."

I told her about the marriage license I found.

"I can't believe it! When she came home that year, she seemed happy, but I just thought she was just happy to be home. She never said a word to me about Wallace. Probably because she knew how I felt about him. She said the lady she was taking care of died and she was taking time off before finding another job. We were hoping she'd go back to school."

"The lady she was taking care of was Wallace's grandmother, Ina Graham. I understand you were looking for her at Ina Graham's address several years ago. You didn't know it was Wallace's grandmother?"

"No, I had no idea. I just had an address from a birthday card she sent me when she worked there. I was hoping maybe the woman had relatives still living in the house that might know where Dee Dee was. I talked to a woman who lived across the street, but she hadn't seen her in years. Dee Dee left right before Christmas, and we never saw her again. Then my mother became ill about five years ago and wanted to see Dee Dee before she died. I never found her."

"Just out of curiosity, what was Dee Dee's middle name?"

"Diantha, after our grandmother. Why?"

"Just wondering. Listen, I know this has been hard for you. I won't take any more of your time. Thank you for calling."

"Wait! Do you really think my sister killed Wallace? Do you know where she is?" She sounded close to tears.

"I'm sorry, I can't say. I really didn't mean to bring up any bad memories."

"If you do know where she is, give her a message for me. Tell her she broke our mother's heart." I heard her choke back a sob. Boy, I really knew how to rake up some shit. I listened to her blow her nose. When she came back on the line, she had pulled herself together. "No, don't tell her that. If she has any kind of a conscience, she knows that already."

Dee Dee may have known. Diane Gibson, however, was another matter.

It was late when I got home. Gwen, Alex, and I had played cards for a while until Mama shooed us home so she could go to bed. When you get up at the crack of dawn, you tend to go to bed early. I was planning on working a double at Estelle's the next day to make up for the hours I'd missed the week before when I'd been attacked. I was going to see Detectives Harmon and Mercer first thing in the morning, but I needed some sleep too.

Before I got out of the car, I pulled the picture of Wallace and Dee Dee, aka Jordan and Diane, out of my glove box for another look. I had a small penlight attached to my key chain and I held the picture under the light. Try as I might, I couldn't see Diane Gibson anywhere in Dee Dee Briggs's sullen face. "Well I'll be damned," I said out loud. I did see something I'd missed before. Ina Graham was decked out in pearl jewelry. The pearl choker she had on was identical to the one Diane had worn to Jordan's funeral. The fact that she could wear her victim's grandmother's jewelry to his funeral answered any questions her sister and I had had about her conscience.

My phone rang as soon as I walked in the door. It was Bernie.

"I just wanted to touch base and see how things were going," I said.

"Emmett is hoping we can get a trial date in a few weeks. Kendra, I'm so scared. I can't believe any of this is happening." She sounded so defeated. I was beginning to think it would be better to take everything I'd found and see the detectives that night.

"Bernie, this is going to sound strange, but when did Diane first move to Willow?"

"Diane? Why do you want to know?"

"Just humor me, please."

"Ah, I think it must have been early 1977. I remember because our regular receptionist left right after Christmas. Her husband was in the military and got transferred to Japan. I had to take her place until someone permanent was hired. Mother hired Diane as her replacement. Why?"

"Do you know anything about her family?"

"She told us her parents were dead and she was an only child. What's this all about, Kendra?"

I gave her a brief account of what I'd found out. She was stunned. We both agreed it would explain a lot. Bernie got off the phone. She was feeling overwhelmed by all of the implications of what I'd just told her. But not before she told me that Ben's will left everything to Diane since she was his wife. That will would be null and void if they weren't legally married.

I kicked off my shoes and headed to the bathroom to run myself a bubble bath. I flipped on the bathroom light and froze. Diane Gibson was sitting on the side of my bathtub with a gun pointed right at my heart.

FIFTEEN

"How'd you get in here, Diane?" I couldn't take my eyes off the gun in her hand.

"Did you forget that Mrs. Carson lists all of her rental properties with Gibson Realty? We have copies of all the keys."

"What do you want?" My legs were shaking, and I leaned against the doorjamb for support, still not taking my eyes off the gun. Diane was dressed in jeans and a black sweatshirt. She had a Bengals baseball cap turned backward on her head. She looked like a teenager. She also looked crazy. Her eyes had a strange glaze to them, and I wondered if she was on something.

"You're looking a little shaky there, Kendra. Why don't you come on in here and have a seat? I've been waiting for you all night." She motioned with the gun for me to sit on the toilet seat. I did what any intelligent person in my situation would do. I sat.

"What do you want?" I repeated, my voice barely a whisper.

"Oh, come on, girlfriend, you know what this is all about, don't you?" She was eerily calm, and it was freaking me out.

"Jordan. I know you killed him and Raymond Hodge. You really need to turn yourself in, Diane." Her head jerked back a little in shock.

"You surprise me, Kendra. Why would you care who killed Jordan? I know you couldn't stand him. And you never even knew Raymond Hodge. What difference could it possibly make to you that they're dead?"

"It makes a big difference when Bernie could go to prison for it."

"Emmett's not a bad lawyer. He might even be able to get her off, though I doubt it. Then I'll finally be able to sell Gibson Realty. Jordan was a real bastard, and it cost me a lot of money to keep his mouth shut. I really need some money."

"Were you paying Raymond Hodge too?"

"Ben told me about Raymond Hodge and Bernie years ago. Althea paid Raymond to get out of town after Bernie attacked him. He ended up working for a real estate company in Atlanta. But his dumb ass was screwing his boss's wife for years. The man found out and made sure Raymond never worked in real estate again. I tracked him down and brought him to town. He wasn't hard to find on skid row. He'd do anything for a drink. He was useless most of the time. I got him all cleaned up to make his big statement against Bernie. After that, he got all big time on me and started blackmailing me. He had to go. Besides, he had one foot in the grave anyway, cirrhosis of the liver. I just helped him along a little faster." She said it like she was talking about taking out the trash.

"So you were the one who attacked me?"

"It wasn't personal. I had to get away, and you had no business being there in the first place." She emphasized each word by tapping my knee with the barrel of the gun. I was so scared I had to concentrate on the towel rack to keep from peeing my pants. As long as I could keep her talking, I might be able to think of some way to get out of this alive.

"How did Jordan find you after all this time?"

"There was an article about Gibson Realty that ran in both the newspaper here and in Dayton about a year and a half ago. There was a picture of Ben and me with the article. Jordan saw it because he was living in Dayton at the time. I still can't believe he recognized me. Next thing I know, he was screwing Bernie and threatening to tell Ben we were still legally married unless I paid him."

"So he had to go too?"

"Oh yes! He had to go. After everything I did for

him, he stabbed me in the back. He used me, then threw me away. After I'd found happiness, he tried to take it from me—not once but twice." She was staring off into space as if she were reliving some distant past. If I positioned my foot just right, I might be able to kick the gun out of her hand. But suddenly she came back to Earth and tightened her grip on the gun.

"You must have hated him very much. I saw what you did to him, Diane."

"Trust me, he had it coming. I was Mrs. Ben Gibson; slim, rich, beautiful. But he came to town and made me feel like fat ugly Dee Dee all over again. Sure I was good enough when he wanted me to do all his damn schoolwork for him or when he wanted a blowjob. Or even when he wanted me to make sure his grandmother didn't wake up from her nap one day." She noticed my shocked expression.

"Why do you think he married me? It wasn't because he loved me. It was all part of the plan. He was afraid she'd change her will and leave him out. She wasn't in her right mind, and he thought she might actually do it. So, one day when she lay down to take a nap, I smothered her with a pillow. He got his grandmother's house and money, and I got him. Only I didn't know that he never planned to keep his end of the bargain."

"And no one suspected?" I was feeling more and more panicked with each passing second.

"Ina Graham was an old black biddy who had Alzheimer's. She was in her eighties. As far as anyone was concerned, it was natural causes. There was no autopsy. We flew out to Las Vegas the next week and got married. He even cheated me out of my honeymoon. He spent all of his time in the casinos. I spent all my time crying in the hotel room.

"Then he told me to go home to Macon and he would come get me. He never came. I went back to Columbus looking for him. The house had been sold and he was long gone. But there was one thing he forgot about. Ina had all of her jewelry in a safe-deposit box at the bank. I had the key because she would have me go down to the bank and put certain pieces in and take others out. I went down to the bank and took everything out. I sold most of it. I was broke. I kept a few pieces. I couldn't bear to go back to Macon, so I hopped a bus and ended up here. I got a job as a receptionist at Gibson Realty where I met Ben Gibson, the only man who ever really loved me. But you already know that, don't you?"

"So you killed Jordan and set up Bernie, killing two birds with one stone? That must have taken some planning."

"It was easy actually. I got the idea when I found a note to Trevor from his skanky girlfriend in our mailbox. I used it to lure Jordan over to Vanessa's. I knew she'd be at work. Everyone knew he was screwing her; everyone except Bernie, that is. I sent Bernie an anonymous letter telling her about it. Then I dressed up as that crazy bag lady who's always roaming all over town looking for cans. I'd stolen Bernie's extra set of keys and had them copied and put them back in her purse before she even knew they were gone. All I had to do was sneak in the back way and wait for him to show up. He surprised me, though. I thought I'd have to unlock the door for him, but he had his own key and let himself right in. I was on him as soon as he walked into the dining room. He never saw it coming."

"Did Joy Owens see you? Is that why you ran her down?"

She snapped out of her trance and looked genuinely confused. "Oh, her. I saw Jordan talking to her a couple of times and wondered if she was in the plot too. I called her up pretending to be interested in buying some of her artwork and arranged a phony meeting to get her out of her apartment. I sent Raymond's drunk worthless ass over there to look for that marriage license Jordan was holding over my head. I thought she might have it. Raymond ended up falling asleep in the apartment and almost got caught. She got run down, did she? I don't know anything about that." I watched her reach over and turn on the hot water in the bathtub. Then she pushed in the stopper and sprinkled in some bath salts, all the while keeping the gun trained on me.

"I can see the suspense is killing you," she said,

smiling serenely. She then reached down beside her and picked up the bottle of Darvocet that I'd gotten from Lynette for my back. I watched her read the label.

"It's such a shame when people take medicine prescribed for someone else, mix it with alcohol, pass out, and drown in the bathtub, don't you think?"

I couldn't say anything—my mouth was too dry. It was obvious what she was planning to do. I just had to figure out how to distract her.

"Look, Diane, if you're afraid I'll tell on you, it would be your word against mine. Come on, this is crazy." I was aware that I was becoming hysterical. "Besides, if you kill me, you'll never know where the evidence is that implicates you."

"It can't be too hard to find. I'll have plenty of time to look for it while you're in the tub. Now, here, take these." She was holding out a handful of pills and motioned for me to wash them down with a half a bottle of wine I recognized from my fridge. "Don't be afraid, Kendra. It'll be quick."

I did as I was told, figuring I'd have a better chance against pills than a gun. Even with wine, I gagged on the pills and ended up spitting up most of them down the front of my blouse. But not before I swallowed a good many of them. Diane did not look pleased. She held the gun to my head until I finished the rest of the wine.

"Diane, how can you do this? Haven't you killed

enough people? Don't you know you broke your mother's heart?" Her face twisted in rage, and she slapped me so hard I felt my teeth rattle. She got right in my face and pressed the gun hard against my temple. Spittle flew in my face.

"You want to know about broken hearts, bitch? My mother used food to manipulate me all my life. When I was bad, she withheld it; when I was good, she rewarded me with it. I couldn't go out to play until I cleaned my plate. She loved to see me eat. She encouraged me. So when I hit puberty with a weight problem, whose fault was it? Hers? Hell no, it was mine. When I couldn't get a boyfriend and had no social life, it was, 'Dee Dee, why you so fat? If you weren't so fat you'd have a boyfriend. Dee Dee, why can't you be slim like your sister Carol?' For years she teased and berated me in front of family and the few friends I had. I'd try to diet and what would she do? Bake a cake or my favorite cookies. Then yell at me when I ate it. I hated that woman! That's why it was so easy for me to kill Ina Graham. She reminded me of my mother. Now, enough is enough. Take off your clothes and get into that tub!"

I was crying now as I unbuttoned my blouse.

"No one is going to believe I mixed pills and alcohol, Diane. I already told Bernie about you."

"I don't give a damn what you told Bernie. Without proof, it's just a guess. Yeah, I'll be at your funeral alongside Bernie and your stuck-up grandmother, shaking my head and saying what a shame it is. Don't worry. I'll take good care of Carl."

Any other time I'd be really pissed about anyone talking badly about Mama. However, in my current situation, with a gun practically up my nose and pills and alcohol in my system, she could have said my grandma wears combat boots and I would have heartily agreed, plus supplied the size and color. But what was that she said about Carl? The bathroom was becoming steamy from the scalding- hot bathwater. At this point, drowning was the least of my worries. I'd boil like a lobster if I got into the tub.

"What did you mean about Carl?" The pills were starting to take effect and my words came out in a slur.

"I mean when I'm rid of you, I'll have my man back. How do you think I felt when I went over there last night with a housewarming gift and saw the two of you through the window? You had your hands all over my damn man. Mine! See, that was Jordan's fatal mistake. After Ben died and I fell in love with Carl, Jordan found out and threatened to tell him we were still married. He tried to take away my second chance at happiness. Well, he found out the hard way that I wasn't going to let him take anything else away from me. And if I'd known you were trying to steal my man, I wouldn't have bothered with that bottle; I'd have stuck that knife in you just like I did Raymond. Now get in that tub!"

So this had been about Carl all along!

In her anger, she backed into the stand against my bathroom wall and knocked over a glass jar of cotton balls, sending it crashing to the floor. She glanced at the broken glass, and I took that instant and gathered what little strength and nerve I had left to shove her with all my might against the wall. As she hit it with a thud, her hand flew up and the gun went off in an explosive blast. I felt the bullet graze my right ear and heard more shattering glass as the bullet hit the bathroom mirror behind me.

I managed to knock the gun out of her hand and watched it skitter across the bathroom floor. Diane dove after it, and I dove after Diane, grabbing her legs in a vain attempt to pull her out of reach. I felt the burning sting of broken glass as it bit into my knees. I could hear a voice calling my name from down below and a pounding noise. I was in a fog but realized it was Mrs. Carson pounding on her ceiling with her cane and calling me. Diane half turned onto her back. I still had one of her legs. She kicked out with her free leg and caught me hard, right in the head. She grabbed the gun and aimed it at me. Mrs. Carson's loud voice called from down below, "Kendra! What's goin' on up there? Answer me! Are you all right? I'm comin' up there!"
Diane gave me one last dark look and then sprinted off down my hallway and out the door. I laid my head on

the bathroom floor, and before I lost consciousness I heard three sounds that I'll never forget—a woman's scream, the yowl of an angry cat, and the crack of splitting wood.

EPILOGUE

It's been almost a month since this all happened, and I still can't believe it. Diane's dead. In her haste to get away, she'd tripped over Mahalia, who was lying across my top step. She fell headlong down my steep steps, and as she tried to catch herself by grabbing the wooden railing, it gave way, sending her crashing to the ground below. The railing had been weakened when I'd fallen against it the month before. Diane had broken her neck and died instantly.

I was taken to the hospital and had my stomach pumped, a disgusting experience, and was again kept overnight with another concussion. I decided to stay with Mama for a while after I was released. I just couldn't bring myself to go back to my apartment. I know I'll go back eventually, but I can't say when that will be. Maybe after the nightmares are over. I'll never know why Diane didn't shoot me when she had the chance. But it's not anything I'm questioning too hard. I've been offering up extra prayers of thanks every night before I go to sleep.

The charges against Bernie were dropped. Now she's agonizing over whether to have her brother and mother's bodies exhumed to see if they, too, were victims of Diane.

Trevor is of course in denial and is telling anyone who'll listen that his mother was innocent. He had even contemplated suing Mrs. Carson and me over the steps his mother fell down. I hear Vonnie talked him out of it. She's pregnant and doesn't want the father of her unborn child caught up in litigation.

Vanessa's father died two days after my near-fatal encounter with Diane. Vanessa had promptly taken the insurance money and bought a luxury condo in Pine Knoll. Her doctor boyfriend dumped her soon afterward. From what I heard, he found Vanessa's credit card statement with a charge to an abortion clinic on it. Being a staunch pro-life advocate and not knowing if it had been his child Vanessa had aborted, he broke off his relationship with her. Vanessa didn't let any grass grow under her feet though. Lynette and I went to the Red Dragon for lunch one day, and who did we see cuddling in a booth together? Vanessa and my blind date, Drew Carver. Some people deserve each other.

As for Carl and me, well, what can I say? We've been seeing each other on weekends and talking almost daily on the phone. He's been very supportive and understanding when I need my space, and I've been able to convince him that what Diane did as a result of her obsession with him was not his fault. So far, so good.

Things are slowly getting back to normal. The summer session is in full swing at the literacy center. But there was still one thing that was bothering me, which is why I found myself knocking on the door of Joy Owens's apartment. Cory answered the door. She looked tired and wary upon seeing me.

"Joy's asleep," she said by way of greeting. "I'll tell her you stopped by." She started to close the door when I stopped her. "How's she doing?" She closed the door behind her and leaned wearily against it.

"She has her good and bad days. She gets the cast off her leg next week. She's not her old self yet. Her memory is still bad. It'll take some time for her to be one hundred percent again."

"Cory, you're the one who ran Joy down that night, aren't you?" I asked as gently as possible.

Cory looked as if she was about to cuss me out; then she buried her face in her hands and slid into a heap on the floor.

"I didn't mean to, I swear. It was an accident," she said, sobbing.

"What happened?"

"I followed her that night. I didn't believe that story

about meeting a buyer for her paintings. She's cheated on me before, and I wanted to see who she was meeting. She spotted me following her, and we got into a big fight right in the middle of the road. She said some terrible, nasty things to me. I was so mad I got into my car and instead of putting it into drive, I accidentally threw it into reverse and backed right over her. I didn't mean to. I love Joy." She was crying so hard her thin shoulders were heaving.

"So you left her in the middle of the road?"

"I knew I'd hit something. I thought it was her bike. I never even looked back. I just went home. I didn't know what I'd done until the next day. God, if I have to take care of her the rest of her life, I will."

I didn't know if I believed her. Before I could say any more, Joy called out from inside the apartment. "Cory, where are you?" Cory gave me a pleading look.

"Go pull yourself together. I'll go sit with Joy. I promise I won't say anything."

She reluctantly left and I went inside. Joy was propped up on the couch. The huge cast on her leg was the only testament to her accident.

"Cory went to get some fresh air. How are you doing, Joy?"

"Fine. I heard you almost got your ass killed. Didn't you hear that curiosity killed the cat?" I looked at her closely. She sure sounded like the old Joy. She laughed spitefully.

"That's right. There's nothing wrong with me. I remember everything and have for a long time now. I just want to teach Cory a lesson. I'm going to work her ass into the ground. Running over me and leaving me for dead isn't anything I'm likely to forget anytime soon. In a few weeks, I'll miraculously get my memory back. I can't keep this idiot act up much longer. Then she'll really have hell to pay."

"She said it was an accident, Joy. She loves you."

She rolled her eyes. "Whatever." She was definitely back.

"Well, since you remember everything, were you the one sending Jordan the notes calling him a murderer, and did you vandalize his car?"

"Hell yes. I wanted to make that bastard's life as miserable as possible. I didn't think any of those other wimpy bitches he screwed over would ever do anything to him. I was wrong though, huh? Who'd have thought Diane Gibson had the balls."

"Why were you snooping around Bernie's house after Jordan's funeral?"

"I wanted to make sure that motherfucker was really gone. I saw his body in that house that night. I used to go over there and peek through the window while he was screwing that Vanessa chick. Sometimes he'd see me and chase me down the alley. That night I went over there and the back door was standing open, so I walked in and there he was, dead on the floor in his own blood.

It was over. All those years of hating him for what he did to my mother, and it was over. I looked through that big mansion. I wanted to make sure I couldn't find a trace of his ass anywhere."

"You were the one Bernie heard in the house the night she found his body. Why didn't you come forward? It could have saved us all a lot of trouble."

For a second, she looked as close to being sorry as I was ever going to see her look. In an instant, however, the look was gone.

"Damn! I was scared, okay. I ain't never seen no dead body before. I didn't want the police thinking I killed him! It all turned out right in the end, didn't it?" she said defiantly. And it had, just barely though.

"And for the record, you were the one who told the police about what happened between me and Jordan in the parking lot that night, weren't you?"

"You need to unknot those panties, girlfriend, 'cause you'd have told on *my* ass if it had been the other way 'round, and you know it. I had to do my civic duty, didn't I?" She smiled sweetly.

I shook my head in disgust and wondered how much bad karma I'd incur if I bitch-slapped an invalid. Cory slipped back into the apartment and gave Joy a loving look. Joy's face instantly became slack and her eyes glazed over as she fell back into her act. I desperately wanted to tell Joy that she was playing a dangerous game. I wanted to tell her about the pitfalls of playing with people's emotions and stretching the limits of their love and devotion. I'd witnessed the outcome firsthand. But I knew she'd never listen to me. It was a lesson she'd have to learn, needed to learn, on her own. I got up, said my good-byes, and without a backward glance, I left.

ABOUT THE AUTHOR

Angela Henry was once told that her past life careers included spy, researcher, and investigator. She stuck with what she knew because today she's a mystery writing library reference specialist, who loves to people watch, and eavesdrop on conversations. When she's not working, writing, or practicing her stealth, she loves to travel, is connoisseur of B horror movies, and an admitted anime addict. She lives in Ohio and is currently hard at work trying to meet her next deadline.

www.angelahenry.com

Also by Angela Henry

The Company You Keep
Tangled Roots
Diva's Last Curtain Call
Schooled In Lies
Sly, Slick & Wicked

The Paris Secret

CPSIA information can be obtained
at www.ICGtesting.com
Printed in the USA
LVOW03s1418191117
556905LV00002B/438/P